MISCREANTS, MURDERERS, & THIEVES

a collection of short stories
about devious behavior

with contributions by

Don Bapst
David Beeler
Shawn D. Brink
Gabriel DiDomenico
Dori Ann Dupré
Dane G. Kroll
Ethel Lung
Casey Mensing
Suzanne Crain Miller
Samuel W. Reed
Katherine Tomlinson
Will Wallace
Nicholas Zeman
& Jared Sloger

Miscreants, Murderers, & Thieves
a collection of short stories about devious behavior

Reed Press

ISBN: 978-0-9990677-3-4

Cover design © 2019 by David Beeler & Samuel W. Reed

Printed by KDP Press

For all of the authors that inspired the participants of this book,

For my mom and dad, without whom I would have never willed the courage to find myself,

And for my wife, Emily, who has always stood by my side,

Thank you.

FOREWARD

What you behold is something truly unique; a stunning compilation of mischief, larceny, and death as told by thirteen emergent authors, hand-picked to showcase their distinct perspectives and diverse writing styles, as they reinterpret and reimagine the central theme of crime.

Inside, you'll find a doctor with a taste for the macabre… Cat burglars who would rather give than take… And a world so saturated with superheroes it takes a special kind of villain to stand out…

In short, there's a little something tasty for everyone. Go ahead, grab a spoon and dig in…

The entire goal of this series is to introduce readers to undiscovered independent authors who deserve to be recognized for their hard work and talents in an otherwise oversaturated market. I strongly encourage you to like and follow all of the contributing writers on social media. If you find a story you especially enjoy, I hope you will seek out further reading from these fine wordsmiths, and even share your findings in a post or a review online.

Without the support of our families, our friends, and our fans, none of us this would be possible, so thank you all very much.

And thank you for picking up a copy of *Miscreants, Murderers, & Thieves*. I hope you enjoy.

~Samuel W. Reed
Editor/Author

CHAPTERS

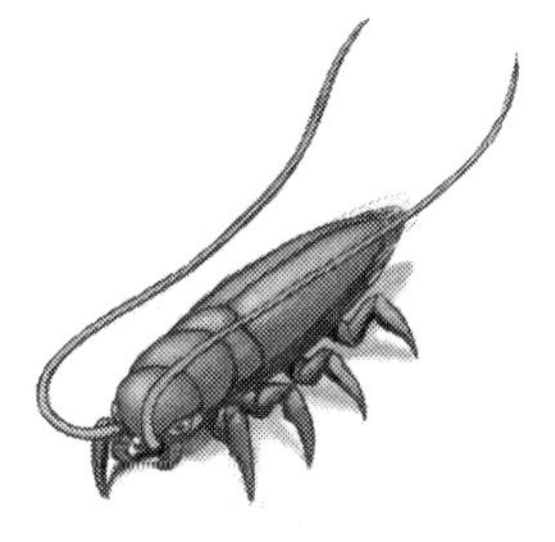

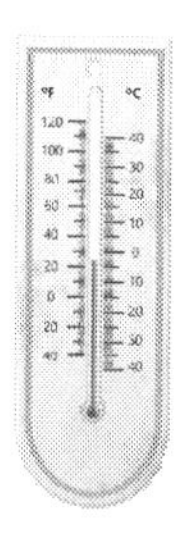

THE TEMPERATURE AT WHICH LOVE FREEZES

by Katherine Tomlinson

The front door shut with a soft but emphatic click as Jonathan slipped out of the house. Even though he knew Kaye wouldn't have heard it—she slept like a hibernating bear—he still found himself looking over his shoulder to make sure she hadn't wakened, that she wasn't following him with her dead brown eyes.

But Kaye had merely grunted and turned over, burrowing deeper into the 600-thread count sheets and goose-down comforter.

There was only one person who would send Jonathan a text in the middle of the night; only one person whose text he would *read* in the middle of the night.

When the phone had buzzed, Jonathan had grabbed for it, fumbled for his glasses on the bedside table and read the message without turning on the light.

Come outside. I have a surprise for you. <3

Lila had attached his favorite picture of her, the one he'd taken after surprising her in the shower.

With barely a glance at his sleeping wife, Jonathan had slid out from beneath the covers, squeezed his bare feet into the fleece-lined slippers Kaye had ordered online without checking his size, and padded silently across the carpeted floor.

He tied his plaid bathrobe tightly before venturing out into the cold, well aware that all he had on underneath the flannel was a pair of thin cotton boxer shorts.

Outside, Jonathan breathed deeply. Purged of the vague daytime petroleum scent that always lingered in the wake of rush-hour commuters using his street as a short-cut to the freeway, the night smelled like fresh pine needles.

There was an icy mist in the air that threatened to turn to sleet, but the chill felt good against his warm skin, over-heated by the furnace bulk of his wife lying next to him on a bed that had been too small to share for at least a year.

He stepped past the circle of brightness cast by the porch light, squinting toward the dark street expectantly. There was no sign of Lila's car.

Still, he didn't expect to be waiting long. He and Lila had engaged in these after-midnight rendezvous before. She'd pick him up and they'd drive somewhere and they'd have sex like teenagers, only better because they knew what they were doing. Then she'd drive him back home and he'd get back into bed with Kaye none the wiser. She seemed to be permanently stuffed up with allergies, so she'd never smell the sex on him, and he would rise before her in the morning and wash all the guilt off of him before breakfast.

It was very quiet out. And still no Lila.

Jonathan ventured out onto the sidewalk in front of the house, narrowing his eyes against the streetlights in hopes of sharpening his night vision.

Jonathan looked up and down the street, and across it too, but there was no sign of Lila's silver-blue BMW. She loved that car, which he had leased for her, writing off the expense as "marketing costs."

It was money well spent. Lila had been grateful.

A shred of plastic grocery bag drifted past on the street, pushed by the cold wind like urban tumbleweed. Nothing else was moving in either direction.

Jonathan wondered if he'd misread Lila's text or misunderstood it.

He wondered if the text had been lost in the ether for hours and was only just now coming through and if he'd missed her earlier in the day.

It was clear there'd been some kind of mix-up.

With a last look around, Jonathan exhaled a sigh and trudged back up the walkway to the front door.

He was mildly surprised to find it wouldn't open.

One of the first things he'd done when he and Kaye had moved into the house was change the lock so it would shut but not latch unless turned with a key.

Probably it's just frozen in the cold, Jonathan decided. *It's an old house*. But after he jiggled the handle and pulled and tugged, it became clear that the door was, in fact, locked.

Jonathan was irritated, but not yet concerned. They kept a spare key to the front door beneath a fake rock hidden in the rose bushes that bracketed the front porch like a pair of parentheses.

It took him a while to find the fake rock and he scratched himself on the thorny branches of the winterized rose bushes in the process. When he reached down to pick up the phony stone one of the thick, hard thorns embedded itself in his forearm, drawing a single tear of blood, which he ignored as he stared below at the cold, bare dirt.

He was puzzled at first, but that soon gave way to a feeling that he identified as … panic.

He patted the pockets of his robe, unconsciously searching for a phantom key but finding only a random cough drop wrapped in sticky paper.

"Fuck," he said out loud, closing his robe a little tighter.

He considered lobbing the fake rock at his bedroom window but knew Kaye would never hear it. She was a heavy sleeper and she'd been snoring when he left their bedroom.

Jonathan climbed the steps back onto the porch and considered his options. The house was at the end of a cul-de-sac small enough that he and Kaye knew all their neighbors but the housing crisis had taken its toll on the neighborhood and only two of the houses were occupied. Their nearest neighbors had gone to visit their children for the holidays and the man who lived in the house across the street worked the night shift.

Jonathan sighed. The windows on the first floor of his house were all covered by iron security grates. Even if he managed to break the glass, it wouldn't do him any good; the openings were too small to wriggle through.

He walked around the house toward the garage, wondering if he could pry the roll-down door open wide enough to crawl under it.

He knelt on the damp, cold concrete to get some traction on the door handle but couldn't budge it more than an inch.

Fuck, he thought again, and then, *it's getting cold.*

In fact, it wasn't actually getting colder, but the wind had picked up significantly, making it feel like it had.

Jonathan stamped his feet to warm them up, and then tried jumping jacks to get the blood flowing in the rest of his body.

The exercise didn't help.

He began to shiver, at first imperceptibly and then so violently that his teeth began to rattle.

He started next door with the vague notion of breaking into the neighbor's house, but halfway across the lawn he tripped on one of the pop-up sprinklers that kept their grass green in summer.

He fell heavily and by the time he'd gathered himself, he'd forgotten his plan and returned to the house.

He was beginning to have a hard time thinking straight.

A few minutes later, it seemed like a good idea to shuck his robe and kick off the slippers, which were now loose on his cold-shrunken feet.

By the time he stepped out of his boxers, he was feeling light-headed and calm. He didn't even see the shadow lingering in the window.

Inside the house, which she kept heated to 78 degrees against the Minnesota winter, Kaye watched as her husband peeled off his boxers in what she had learned was known as "paradoxical undressing." It was a sign that the body and mind were starting to shut down in the cold, a symptom of extreme systemic distress. Jonathan would have been very distressed if he had been aware of just what a pitiful sight his shriveled penis and testicles presented. He had been vain about his cock, and rightfully so, especially when it was fully aroused. Not that she'd seen it fully aroused in some time. Now it seemed to her just like the rest of him; pathetic.

It was 23 degrees outside and the forecast called for sleet and possibly snow before the night was over. The wind was from the north, sweeping down from Canada and dropping the perceived temperature to somewhere around minus 15. That was cold, but not spectacularly cold.

Kaye had read that in parts of Siberia empty plastic bags would freeze within minutes in the frigid temperatures; freeze and then crack like glass.

She'd seen movies where people were flash-frozen by liquid nitrogen and then shattered like fine china. She'd have liked to have seen Jonathan break into a million frozen shards. But that might have looked suspicious to the police. Better to keep it simple. A lot of people simply freeze to death every winter. She'd looked it up.

There'd be no reason for the police to question her story that she'd found him dead on the front lawn after he'd inexplicably wandered out into the cold. They'd find the 25-year-old scotch in his belly in the autopsy and nod knowingly. Most cold-related deaths involved alcohol Kaye had read. Jonathan always had a drink or two before bed. She knew it was the only way he could stomach lying so close to her night after night.

The police probably wouldn't check his cell phone but if they did, it would be a bonus. The text had come from a burner phone Kaye had picked up the day after their last anniversary, the anniversary where he'd gotten her a $50 gift certificate to Bed, Bath, and Beyond. It had been easy enough to schedule the text to arrive in the middle of the night.

The number wouldn't track back to Lila of course, but Kaye had attached one of the nude pictures she'd found in Jonathan's computer. Lila's skanky face had been clearly visible. It wouldn't take the police long to find her and to ask her why she'd enticed her lover out of the house on such a cold night.

Kaye had watched a lot of *Forensics Files*. The police wouldn't find the photo on Jonathan's computer. Kaye had replaced his hard drive after duplicating everything on the system except for the pictures and the incriminating emails. It had taken her close to a month, but she was nothing if not patient.

Kaye really didn't bear her rival any ill will, but if Lila was implicated in Jonathan's death, well, it'd be gravy.

At the thought of gravy, Kaye's stomach growled.

Maybe I'll make some ham and red-eye gravy, she thought. *Once all the commotion dies down. Maybe some biscuits, too. Something that'll stick to my ribs on such a cold morning.*

Kaye smiled as she turned back to her cozy cotton bed. She had always loved the cold.

About Katherine Tomlinson

Katherine Tomlinson was born in Washington DC and has lived in three countries and seven states. She writes crime and horror under her own name, as well as fantasy and sci-fi under the pseudonym "Kat Parrish." She currently lives in the Pacific Northwest near a haunted cemetery.

For more info visit
http://kattomic-energy.blogspot.com/

EQUITY

by Don Bapst

The hole was no bigger than the circumference of a pencil. A perfect black circle punched out of the wood paneling just over their new bed - the one they'd picked out together after moving into their new house. That was almost a month ago now, and Sebastian was sure there'd been no such flaw in the wood before, not when they were setting up the contemporary frame and sliding the mattress on top.

At a glance, it would be easy to mistake the tiny black hole for a knot in the wood, integral to its character. He pressed the tip of his pinky into the space. It was definitely a hole, but how deep he couldn't tell, as he couldn't get his finger into it to explore.

Carlos was the one who'd insisted on the paneling, which Sebastian found too dark for their bedroom, but he never said a word. He'd learned to focus on what mattered. Sebastian had always heard that was the key to keeping a marriage together ... knowing when to concede. As far as he was concerned, the bedroom décor was Carlos' thing. What mattered more to Sebastian were things like a functional kitchen, a space for entertaining, a spacious shower, and a roomy tub. They had all that and more in their new place, which he loved almost as much as he loved Carlos, and the idea that they were finally able to live together as a married couple - officially recognized at last - if not here in Ecuador, then at least back in Argentina where they'd met.

Maybe the workers had been drilling or something. Only there was no dust on the floor under the hole. No sign of light coming through from the outside. Just a perfect circle, no less than an inch deep.

The doorbell made Sebastian jump. The contractors had returned to tighten the cabinet hinges. Every day since they'd moved into their new home it seemed there was someone else at the door. Something else that had to be fixed. At first, it was all finishing touches and quick touch-ups, but it felt like now it was happening more and more. It had only been three months since they'd left Buenos Aires where Sebastian had run a boutique marketing agency for more than a decade. But Sebastian was ready to settle down, and he knew Carlos missed his mother who lived outside Guayaquil. Sebastian, whose parents were deceased, had insisted it would be good for Carlos to be near her. Plus, he thought the slower pace and lower costs in Ecuador would do them good. They'd planned to move into the center of town, but then they fell in love with the layouts, and maybe even more importantly, the prices of the Catanga Villas out in the new walled communities on the fringe of the humid, coastal metropolis. Not to mention, Carlos' mother absolutely insisted.

The flawless pitch from Guillermo, a chiseled young salesman with perfectly coifed hair hadn't hurt, especially since he kept batting his long eyelashes and telling them what a nice couple they made. Plus, buying new construction meant they wouldn't have to fix anything for a long time. Little did Sebastian know how many workers it would take to touch up the initial work.

"Hola, I'm here to fix the cabinets."

"Yes, come in, uh, but can you take off your shoes? New carpeting."

The guy - a kid, really, in worn jeans and a t-shirt bearing the Catanga logo - might have rolled his eyes for a moment, but he dutifully unlaced his boots and set them aside. In just a few years, same-sex couples had gone from being either invisible, or worse, pariahs, to earning enough acceptance to be treated, at least by workers and customer service reps, as true clients. Still, Sebastian had trouble finding a way to ask them to take off their shoes that didn't make him sound like a fussy old housewife.

The worker didn't even blink after walking past their wedding pictures in the living room. He looked right past the images of the grooms embracing in their tuxedos, fixating instead on the cabinets in the distance. "So it's the hinges, is it?"

"Yes, you can see how this door is a little slanted…" In demonstrating the problem, Sebastian felt stupid, like he should be capable of dealing with it himself. But they hadn't unpacked everything yet, and he still had no idea of the whereabouts of his tools. The kid whipped a screwdriver from his handy-dandy belt and before Sebastian could finish explaining he had the whole thing tightened up. Sebastian watched in dismay.

"Wow. That was quick."

"It's what I'm here for."

"Well, while you're here, you mind checking out something else?"

The contractor said he'd never seen anything like it. He put it on the punch list then ambled back over to the entryway where he pulled on his boots. When Sebastian closed the door behind him, there was a squeak. Crap, he thought, more loose hinges? He tried swinging the door back and forth a couple more times, but he couldn't reproduce it. He closed the door and went back to the bedroom to inspect the pencil-thin hole.

"Weird," observed Carlos as he turned down the bed. "Maybe it was a flaw in the wood we didn't notice."

"Maybe," mumbled Sebastian as he brushed his teeth. He looked over his shoulder to watch Carlos settle into bed. The change of pace was doing his husband good.

"I made a sale to a new couple from Quito today."

"That's great, honey!"

"It's a good thing we bought when we did, 'cause these places are going like crazy." It was Carlos' new job as a realtor that had put them in touch with their builder in the first place, and now the new units going up all around them formed over half of his sales. "I just wish they could get them built faster."

"Settle down, mister," Sebastian teased as he crawled into bed. "Don't forget we moved here to give ourselves some room to breathe … Spend some time with your family …"

"The faster we get rich, the faster I can relax."

Sebastian smirked, but Carlos wasn't joking. Sebastian smiled at his young partner, giving him the validation he knew was necessary. It seemed like only months had passed since Sebastian found Carlos, barefoot on the beach, wandering aimlessly through life and Buenos Aires. But now Carlos had gotten a taste of success, and a burning desire for more. If only he could make Carlos understand that he didn't have to worry so much. They had a decent savings from his agency back in Argentina and a great new house. This was supposed to be a place to settle into a new routine, one focused on family, and building a home … and instead, it was like they switched roles. But Sebastian knew if Carlos was trying to prove anything to anyone, it was to himself. So, if he wanted to go out and bust his ass and earn his keep for a couple years, why not let him get that out of his system...

Squeak!

"What was that?" asked Carlos.

"Oh, good. It's not just me. I was getting worried." Sebastian had heard it numerous times over the course of the afternoon, but he was never able to locate it. By the time Carlos got home, it had stopped, and he had determined it was all in his head. But now it was closer than ever, like it was coming from inside the room.

Carlos jumped out of bed, moving quickly towards the window. "It's coming from over here." He yanked up the blinds, and the squeaking, which was really more of a shrill squeal than a squeak, repeated itself, accompanied by an odd rustling sound.

"It's a bug!" Carlos exclaimed after seeing a thin, metallic beetle with inch-long striped antennae exploring the air. As Sebastian moved forward to study the primordial creature, its wings fluttered open.

"God damn!"

"You scream like a girl."

"Look at that fucking thing!"

About three centimeters long, the beast was about the circumference of a pencil, with a bark-like shell beneath its shiny cockroach wings.

"You think that's what made the hole in the wall?"

"Obviously."

Sebastian raised a can of shaving cream over the creature.

"Don't!"

"Why not?"

"We should save it."

Sebastian gave Carlos a questioning look before fastening the cap back on the shaving cream.

The pest control inspector arrived late the next afternoon. Carlos was out walking his third client of the day through a model home, which left Sebastian to take care of the bug. Carlos had told Sebastian it was probably just a milled beetle that had come in from the lumber, no big deal, before he pecked him on the cheek on his way out the door.

"So it came out of the wall, you say?" pondered the inspector in his bootie-clad work shoes in the kitchen as Sebastian got the specimen out of the freezer. The insect's metallic wings reflected blue and green through the frosted sides of the container in which he and Carlos had managed to capture it. The inspector took off the cover and peered over the specimen. "It's a beauty. Probably an Asian longhorn boring beetle of some kind. Terrible for trees, but harmless in homes. They hatch out of the wood in search of live trees and die when all they have to eat is dried out wood and concrete. Problem solved."

So Carlos had been right. Seemed he was learning a lot in his first months of selling homes to people.

"You're kind of lucky. You don't get to see one of these every day."

"It moved!"

"No, I don't think so. Maybe a reflex?"

"Ugh." Sebastian shivered with disgust.

The inspector couldn't take his eye off the crustaceous beast.

"You mind if I take her with me? She's a rare beauty."

The only thing Sebastian wanted less than some kind of Asian longhorn boring beetle was a zombie Asian longhorn boring beetle coming back to life and haunting his dreams with the constant squeal and hum from the incessant burrowing of the decrepit bug.

"Be my guest," Sebastian offered, as he handed the inspector the Tupperware.

Within a week there were more holes. In the baseboard trim. In the insides of the bathroom and kitchen cabinets. And again in the paneling over their bed. And Sebastian continued to hear that infernal squeaking or squealing or whatever the hell it was those hateful things made after boring their way out of the wood and into their home, fluttering from the darkness on those shimmering little wings in search of food, but he never could find another trace of them. And the sound seemed to permeate his every waking thought. He could hear it emanating faintly from some distant crevice or vent or so he thought. He feared the worst. And in his mind, even worse than having an infestation of wood-burrowing bugs, was that the sound was only his imagination, and he really wasn't hearing anything at all.

Unlike that first bug in the bedroom, Carlos never seemed to hear a thing. Nor did he see the latest excavations in the wainscoting. Of course, he was never home now as he stayed late most nights chasing another sale.

"We've been over this. They're harmless. They'll die off. Let it go."

Sebastian could never impress on his husband that the bugs were a problem. It didn't matter how many holes he found or how none of their little cadavers ever seemed to surface. And discussing Carlos' new propensity for work was not an option.

"What if you came home early for a change and we …"

"I'm on a roll here! And you were the one who wanted to leave your agency …"

Sometimes Sebastian wondered if Carlos was right. Maybe deep down inside he missed being absorbed by all the challenges that came with running his own business. What if Carlos actually enjoyed being consumed by the kinds of stressors that had once driven him crazy at his job? What if, deep down, Sebastian missed being so immersed in his own work that he didn't have time to worry about the little details? Perhaps the only reason he could hear that creature so clearly was because he'd finally cleared all the other sounds of commerce and conflict from his brain.

Maybe the shrill screams of that insect were the only signs of life in this empty new house to take their place.

Sebastian thought Carlos' Mom might have an idea of how to get through to him. She lived near the top of the historic Las Peñas district where brightly painted old homes dotted the hillside along steep staircases rising all the way up to the sky-blue lighthouse on top. These were the crumbled and twisting paths once ruled by drug lords. Now they were patrolled by armed policemen in an attempt to make the neighborhood palatable for tourists out for a photo op. Sebastian had initially wanted to find something here, but Carlos had insisted on the villa. He'd grown accustomed to more contemporary amenities in the trendy Recoleta District where they'd lived in Buenos Aires … not to mention maintaining a healthy distance from his mother.

"Ojos Azules!" she said, answering the door. *Blue eyes*. She always called him that, which made him feel like he was something special to her. From another culture and time, having never learned the correct words for speaking of her son's "husband," she had found her own way to accept them, Sebastian thought, and he was happy to make the effort to meet her on her terms.

"Not so blue," he giggled, giving her a peck on the cheek. She seemed to get tinier every time he saw her. But though her body was frail, her dark black eyes stared right through him. It was as if she were always checking to make sure he was up to the standards she held for her only son. He still didn't know whether to call her by her first name or Mrs. Rodriguez, and "Mom" would take some further negotiation. For now, he got by with "It's so great to see you!"

As they sipped homemade *colada morada* from glass jars, he described the joy of settling into the new home, the pride Carlos was taking in his new work, and eventually the challenge of their creature invasion.

"You'll want to get that taken care of," she said, pouring him another class of the spicy, purple drink.

"That's what I've been telling Carlos." He was thrilled she was seeing things his way. Maybe she'd be able to talk to him, and…

"Now that Carlos is the breadwinner you'll need to take on the house yourself. Maybe you're not used to handling things on your own."

This wasn't how he'd hoped things would go.

"Carlos is finally getting his wings," she went on. "Let him do his thing the way you did back in Buenos Aires." She said the name of his native city with a slight roll of her eyes, as if mocking the place's reputation for sophistication. "And bugs were here long before people. You can learn a thing or two about resilience by watching them." She left him with a folktale about a pale demon who tried to rob the rainforest of its treasures, and he guessed it wouldn't be on this visit that she'd let him call her "Mom."

Walking along the waterfront towards the city center, he called Carlos but it went straight to voicemail.

"Hey, love, I saw your mother today. We should have her over some time. We don't see her near enough." Can a voicemail record sarcasm, Sebastian wondered? "Hope you're having a good day. Love you."

Resilience. Humph. He'd teach these bugs a thing or two.

He did a quick web search for a local pest control company and called to set up an appointment. "It's like a beetle," he explained. "But narrow. With giant antennae." The receptionist repeated his description like a criminal psychologist repeating the delusions of a psychotic prisoner. He shouldn't have given up his specimen to the last inspector.

He wandered the streets of Guayaquil as he talked. He was so focused on getting rid of these monsters devouring their home that he switched into auto-pilot, unknowingly roaming down less-ventured alleys between narrow residential streets. When he ended his phone call he looked up to find himself on Padre Aguirre, the street where Carlos had first taken him to show off the gay scene in Ecuador's largest city. A cluster of venues clogged the *Zona Rosa*, but Sebastian considered them teenage dance clubs more than the hub of the "gay district" they proclaimed to be. It was getting late in the afternoon. The sun had already dipped below the horizon, yet none of the metal shuttered doors had been lifted to prepare for the impending festivities of a humid Friday night. Rounding a corner to find a bus station, his soles stuck to the pavement. It was inevitable; although the blurred memories eventually faded, the physical remains of past parties could never be fully washed away. A rat scurried across his path and into the gutter. He gasped, looking up to find someone standing in a doorway across the street staring at him.

"They don't usually bite." The guy was short and stocky with rough, worker's hands.

Sebastian half shrugged, half nodded. He pretended to remember where he was going and tried to advance with purpose, but his steps were hesitant.

"Not like those bugs of yours …"

Sebastian stopped. How did he know about the bugs? Had he heard him on the phone?

"Excuse me?"

"You're a bit far from home, aren't you? Catanga Village?"

"How did you know?"

The man in the doorway disappeared into the dark hallway beyond, leaving the door wide open. Sebastian looked both ways, only he wasn't worried about getting run over by a car, just that no one saw him run into the dilapidated old apartment after the stranger inside. The abandoned building was pitch black except for a shard of fading sunlight streaking through a crack in the paint covered window; just enough light to see the muscular silhouette of the man as he grabbed Sebastian by the crotch and spun him around.

"I made a mistake," Sebastian pleaded.

The man got right in Sebastian's face and shoved his tongue down his throat. It was soft and warm and it had been too long since Sebastian had longed for intimacy with a stranger, but now was not the time. He shoved the persistent man away crying. "Please, stop. I'm married."

The man yanked him back and put his stubbled chin right in Sebastian's face. Sebastian thought the man was going to kiss him when he leaned forward and whispered in his ear.

"Get out while you can." And then he disappeared out a back door, leaving Sebastian alone in the dark.

* * * * *

The lights were on when Sebastian got home. He had never been good at keeping a poker face.

"Why weren't you here to sign for the package?" snapped Carlos as he entered. "I told you the new light for the dining room was coming today. And what makes you think we can afford to keep taking cabs?"

They slept in separate beds that night. Sebastian woke to the doorbell at nine. It was the new bug guy, a nervous-looking older man with a big tool belt and a sweaty brow. His eyes darted around as if he were awaiting a siege. Maybe he'd seen the pictures of their wedding. Maybe there was something about this job he didn't like.

Sebastian showed him the holes on the backs of the cabinets and along the baseboards. He attempted to describe the bug he'd surrendered to the previous inspector. He tried to confine his descriptions to objective details and nothing but the facts. The guy seemed to be getting more and more fidgety by the minute. He tapped on a few walls and then put his ear to one. Sebastian wondered what would happen if one of the creatures hatched through at that very moment and burrowed into the worker's brain.

"There's a species of long-horned beetle from a remote region of the rainforest that's been decimating trees throughout the whole area," the guy said, packing up his equipment. "They're harmless to humans, as far as I know, but they can eat through just about anything. I think that's what we're dealing with here. I'll send you a treatment plan and an estimate."

"How long will it take?"

"Could take months. You might have to live off-site for a while."

Carlos was not impressed. "You said yourself the guy was freaked out by our wedding picture. He's probably trying to scam us."

"No, I thought that at first, but then I think he was freaked out by the holes, recognizing them as a sign of infestation."

"You're paranoid. We're going to take care of this."

The knock on the door made Sebastian jump.

"I got it," Carlos insisted. Every look and gesture from Carlos made Sebastian sink with guilt. Even though it was just a kiss, he had liked it. He had wanted more. After moving to a new city where he didn't know anyone, only to be left alone all day with those things screeching around him, he hadn't realized how closed off he had become from everything until that moment. But he worried about what the man knew. Had he been following Sebastian, and for how long? What was he warning him about?

"It was the guy from the pest control place." Carlos held up a letter. "See, he confirmed what we already knew. They'll die off, just like the builder told us."

"But why did he come over? He could have emailed that."

"He wanted to tell us to our face that we were living in sin and to seek salvation from Jesus Christ. So I told him where he could shove it," Carlos glowered. And in his mind, Sebastian couldn't help but wonder if the look was really intended for him.

Trapped in the strong arms of the man in the blackness, Sebastian struggles to escape. "Please let me go. I'm married." But the man holds him tighter and tighter, pressing their faces together. He can taste the acrid sweat on the man's scratchy cheek, which scrapes his lips as he's drawn into a deep kiss from which he can't break free. And now there's a tickling at the back of his throat where a pair of antennae brush against his uvula. He wretches to try to break free of the kiss and catch his own breath, but the creature fills his throat, growing inside as it chokes him …

Sebastian woke up with a start, covered in sweat. The sheets were rank with body odor. Sebastian was relieved to find it was nothing more than a dream.

He threw the covers off and rushed out of bed, pulling on his robe as he ran to the bathroom.

"Carlos!" Sebastian exclaimed as he searched for his husband when he listened and heard laughter and voices coming from downstairs. "Carlos?"

Sebastian descended the stairs cautiously. There was a worker in a Catanga shirt talking. "They don't build 'em like this anymore!" Sebastian realized it was the guy who installed their garage door opener back when they'd first moved in.

Carlos' mother made her way through the visitors cluttering the living room, serving snacks and drinks to everyone from a tray. With each step Sebastian took, he recognized another group of familiar faces. All the Catanga workers were there: the ones who put in the plumbing and the appliances, the ones who'd installed the carpeting and touched up the trim. They were all there in their crisp uniforms, facing the picture window, which was blocked by a presentation screen.

Guillermo, forever the salesman in his crisp business suit, stood in front of everyone with the Catanga logo projected onto the screen. A halo formed around his head. As Sebastian looked at him, he noticed for the first time that the logo was actually an abstracted drawing of a beetle framed by a pyramid.

"At the rate we're going," Guillermo said to Carlos, who stood by his side grinning ear to ear, "We'll have this entire district inhabited in three years." Guillermo squeezed Carlos' hand and raised it high into the air, in a collective triumphant salute.

"Go Catanga!" Guillermo pronounced.

"Go Catanga!" Carlos chimed in.

"Go Catanga!" chanted the disciples.

"Carlos?" Sebastian spoke out from the crowd.

Everyone turned to Sebastian. Twenty smiling faces gleamed back at him.

"Sebastian! You're finally up!" Carlos dropped Guillermo's hand, but not before Guillermo gave it a good squeeze.

"What is all this?" Sebastian questioned.

"Our future!"

"You're wasting your time on that idiot," a voice called out from the sidelines.

"Give him a chance, mom."

Guillermo stepped in to make sense of it all. "Carlos has been trying to tell you, but you've been so … impatient, shall we say?" Guillermo gave Carlos' shoulders a playful squeeze, never taking his penetrating stare off Sebastian.

"But …" Sebastian was dumbfounded, unable to speak.

"You really shouldn't have called a pest control company," Carlos shared.

A collective hiss rose from the assembly.

"The bugs are eating our house! They're parasites!"

"Honey, don't you think that's a bit harsh?"

"I told you not to marry that one, but you never listen to your mother."

"The Catanga Beetle is cherished for its healing properties," explained Guillermo, his eyes never leaving Sebastian's as he massaged Carlos, "which is why we decided to engineer the species to enhance its purifying properties and give our development project its unique foundation. Not to mention our name."

Sebastian tried to get through the crowd to his husband, but the Catanga workers formed a series of concentric walls around him with their bodies, pinning his arms to his sides.

"Originally from Asia," Guillermo continued, "the Catanga spread around the globe during the last housing boom through milled lumber, the kind used in cheap new construction back then, but it was here in the rainforest that the creature truly blossomed. With a bit of genetic modification, we've made the Catanga an irreplaceable asset in the sustainable recycling of building materials. They literally consume the building over time, but in the process, they create new jobs! After all, the Catanga leave some, uh, patchwork that needs some tending to from time to time. But it's a small price to pay when you consider the tangible benefits."

"We're selling so many of these properties," added Carlos, beaming. "It won't be long before we can get out of this shithole and move somewhere like Los Angeles. We already have contacts there who want us to sell Catanga-treated woods across North America and Europe. We're going to be rich!"

Guillermo shook his head. "And that's just the beginning. You see, some people believe Catanga beetles are capable of purifying the toxins out of our planet. Some people believe they are the great recyclers of the world because they eat the waste around them. Some people believe that by introducing the Catanga to the human body, you can eradicate diseased human cells, too. The version of the insect in your house is merely a prototype. Once we've perfected the species illness will be a thing of the past. Cancer a footnote in the history of medical science. In fact, the Catanga will soon stop living off the wood. Instead, they'll live in *partnership* with their human hosts, in perpetual symbiosis."

Sebastian looked horrified as Carlos nodded along in agreement like a maniac. It was like he was on drugs. Or drank the kool-aid. Either way, his sanity had been lobotomized. Carlos looked wildly at Sebastian, shouting over the room, "I've never had so much energy!"

"Carlos?"

"Leave him alone!" Carlos' Mom screamed. "Can't you see that he's finally found his way?"

Sebastian tried to protest, but a hand smelling of drywall dust and fresh paint covered his mouth. Another worker's paint-splattered hand held one of the beetles in front of his face. Another hand locked his head in place, forcing him to stare at the thing.

"It's my son's turn to be king of the castle now."

The insect's crusty black and grey shell was tougher than an oyster. Its barbed black legs writhed in the air as if trying to find ground on which to run. The metallic ebony pincers snapped shut, barely missing the tip of his nose.

"By this time next year," said Carlos' mother. "We'll all be multi-millionaires."

"I'm sure you'll find that you'll be much happier once you've tried living with it for a while," Guillermo offered, ever-the-salesman. "You know what they say: 'Be sure to give a new property at least two years.' That's how you begin to build true equity in your home. Look at me. I started with nothing. And now I'm living in first world luxury."

As Sebastian watched Guillermo, he swore a pair of antennae raised from the salesman's head and reached down to scratch him, only to realize it was a different bug, crawling on his own face, searching for an entry point. It pinched a little as it burrowed its way into his left nostril and up his nasal passage, like the dried remnants of a cold you try to blow out in the shower. But as it dug deeper into the soft tissue between his eyes, there was a flicker, and as it crept deeper into his brain, Sebastian suddenly remembered the worker he met in Guayaquil and wished he'd heeded his warning. He wished he had listened to his gut so many times in the past. Like when he left his shop back in Argentina, the place he loved. A home he adored. And like a flick of a switch, it was forgotten.

Sebastian sat up, passively. The struggle was over. Carlos kneeled beside him as the crowd watched Sebastian for a reaction. Sebastian searched Carlos' brown eyes for meaning, but found only the soft glow of happiness. Sebastian smiled at his beloved husband and they embraced tighter than they'd ever embraced before.

"Welcome home."

About Don Bapst

Don Bapst is a screenwriter, playwright, novelist, and award-winning filmmaker. His English translation of Gabrielle Wittkop's landmark French novel *The Necrophiliac* was called a "masterpiece" by *The Guardian*, and his psychological thriller *Calculating Euphoria* is in pre-production with Leomark Studios in Los Angeles. Don is also an experienced world traveller and has visited six of the seven continents, and lived on three.

For more info visit donbapst.com

MURDER AT THE MAGIC CASTLE

by Gabriel DiDomenico

This wouldn't be his last case. His last case would be his first case, gone cold like the uncanny L.A. winter. The chill crept in every night like a revolving scythe, sending citizens to kneel before their gas heaters which blew old dust into the room like forgotten gods awakening from a deep slumber. Quinn's first case swept in on cold memories nearly every night, forcing him to kneel before the aging crime scene photos like his own dusty alter.

The thirteen-year-old victim had a collection of Tiffany jewelry. She had died violated and strangled in a rage. She felt everything before her execution. A silver chain was twisted around her throat so tight that it cut into her neck. Her head wobbled like a Dodgers bobblehead when the coroners lifted her body. Alice's parents couldn't account for the jewelry, let alone afford it. Her closest relatives from father to uncles had alibis. Quinn felt sick every time she crept into his thoughts. The twenty-five-year-old vampire he secretly invited into his home every night, as he continued to uncover what he thought were connections to similar murders stretching back even further. All of them unsolved.

Alice had been thirteen. Now Quinn was sixty-five. Twenty-five years. He could hardly believe it was ending. Alice was his first case back when he earned his detective's badge in the LAPD. Luck of the draw. He had closed every case to come his way except for that one. Even did a big spread on him in a local rag back a few months ago because of it. But Quinn still promised himself before the mirror every night that he would catch Alice's killer. He had made the same promise to his ex-wife for over ten years. And now she was long gone, and his own daughter completely grown. Quinn often felt like he had given up a bit of his humanity to help other people keep theirs. That's what he told the reporter, anyway.

He had fearful dreams of searching but never finding whatever he was after. He was ready for a simpler time, when he could play games with grandchildren, and not with bad guys, or the dead they left behind. He was tired in his old age and was trying to catch up for the time he missed. With his daughter. With his few friends. But the dreams never went away.

A thirteen-year-old with $30,000 worth of designer gear. It was the only clue worth investigating, everything else about Alice was precious and innocent. Quinn made a fist and pounded his knuckles into the wall between the bathroom mirrors. A ridiculous fart noise squeezed out of the hidden speakers in the tiny restroom. The Magic Castle was full of such gags and hidden gems. It was supposed to be a night of wonder and awe with his daughter, who had invited him the night before out of the blue. But now there's a dead body and Quinn had the place locked up tight. No one could leave or enter, so the guests, magicians, and waitstaff were all acting out a real-life murder mystery, leaving Quinn to play law and order in a den of illusion and magic.

If Alice wasn't my first case maybe I would've found her killer.

Quinn cleared his throat aggressively and tucked his tie inside his button-down. He walked out into the bar and for a split second he was confused as to where in the castle he was located. The Magic Castle was actually a mansion in Hollywood off of Franklin Avenue, right next to the motel where Janis Joplin died. The mansion had been transformed into a maze, full of hidden doors and Easter eggs. From moment to moment Quinn wasn't necessarily confused, but as he thought about the next room, or hall, or the whole building's interior, and how it all fit together, and how it all worked, he found that he couldn't understand it at all. In a lot of ways it reminded him of Los Angeles.

The magician's body was on the floor surrounded by blood. It looked like an exhibit from Madame Tussauds Wax Museum just up the street. Everything was cold, the blood turned black, rigor mortis already setting in. Quinn had tried to save the man's life, but Precio, the dead magician, was already a goner. The next course of action had been to close off all the exits, hopefully trapping the killer inside. The only people allowed in were uniformed cops to guard the exits and one medical examiner, Jeff.

"Knife wounds to the jugular and carotid arteries. No defensive wounds," Jeff declared as Quinn circled the body, studying the blood spray. He stepped into a clean space, orbiting closer and closer to the corpse, crip walking in slow motion through the crime scene's negative space to avoid the bloody arcs.

If he still had hair it probably would have popped into a full afro from all the electricity thumping through his veins. People forgot he had degrees in sociology, psychology, criminology, and art history. They just saw another black man, always underestimating what he was capable of. It used to bother him, but over time he grew accustomed to the fact, proud even, that he always proved them wrong.

Jeff's eyes opened wide, finally seeing what Quinn had seen; a skilled killer who moved in the slim spaces where the blood was absent. No bloody footprints, either, no discarded knife. It was as if Precio fell through evaporating razors.

"Suicide?" Quinn offered, though not convinced himself.

"There's no way these wounds were self-inflicted." Jeff scoffed. He nodded up to the cameras embedded in the molding around the ceiling, tucked into the corners. "Did you check the tapes?"

The security footage gave him nothing. Quinn saw it for the thousandth time in his head, visualizing both the security video and his own memory side by side - the same thing, but different angles. Precio stepped off the stage, or collapsed, and he was immediately surrounded by audience members, clamoring to help. And then, just when he seemed okay, and the guests returned to their seats, he grabbed his throat, blood spurting everywhere. Then Quinn shoved his way through guests and bouncers, just in time to see the dead man's eyes cloud over.

"Nothing was caught on camera." Quinn relayed. There were cameras all over the mansion. The murder happened on tape in a room full of people drunk on illusion. And nobody saw anything. The camera angle was askew, and the crowd was so distracted they didn't catch anything but the aftermath as people scrambled to get away from the spraying blood.

This isn't just a killer Quinn realized as he took a step back from the scene. *They're a magician...*

Given the laws of nature, there are an endless range of combinations formed from only a handful of tricks. This is true of both crime and magic. Unfortunately, magic tricks reminded Quinn that he could only deduce the solution after he was tricked, just as he could only solve a crime after it had been committed.

Quinn wasn't much into magic, usually. He dealt in facts. There were enough lies and misdirection and deceit in his trade, he didn't have time for it. But this time was different. His daughter asked him to be there. And when his daughter asked him for anything, he did it.

She was feisty, his daughter. Most times there was no way out of it. She was smart, successful, and emotionally more mature than most people her age. He must've done something right as a single parent, he liked to think. He checked in on her frequently over the hour that passed as the police searched inside and out to help him narrow down who killed Precio, the world-famous magician he had never heard of in his life.

"Let the guests walk. This was an inside job." Quinn told a uniformed officer, and she relayed the order into a radio. This would narrow down the suspects significantly, and keep anyone from live-streaming the gore. But, if he was wrong, the killer would go free. Quinn raced up to the second-floor dining room where his daughter waited for him. A surge of men in fine suits and glamorous-looking women sheathed in luxury shuffled out the fire exit. Everyone but his daughter, Gwen.

"Alright kid, you don't need to go home, but you can't stay here." Quinn chuckled as she glared back defiantly. He knew what was coming. It was the same argument Gwen had taken up with him since she could rebel against bedtime. He noticed that the bottle of bourbon he bought for her, rare aged Bib & Tucker, was still sealed. Disappointment seeped into his gut.

"I promise I'll be quiet" she begged. She was stone-cold sober, he could tell. Even he'd had a couple of drinks. A place like this practically forced it down your throat. She was radiant in a way he hadn't noticed before, like she was glowing from within. And yet Quinn stood exhausted, shoulders burdened with guilt.

When he first arrived, hours ago, Gwen gave him a bear hug, the only hug she knew how to give. Something she learned from him. All upper body strength and a mix of *I love you* and *I'll kill you.* He could tell this was more than just a casual get together at the nuthouse. He wondered if she had somehow gotten news of his plans, but he couldn't figure how. Of course, she had a way of surprising him dating way back.

After Gwen made him a father, his ex-wife foresaw their lives stretching out into predictable mediocrity. She refused to condition Gwen to a lifestyle that was *just enough* and *safe.* Quinn's wife became reckless in her rebellion while Quinn stuck to fatherhood and the job. Eventually, Quinn arrested his wife for a number of substance violations and for the endangerment and corruption of a minor. Gwen remembered bits and pieces, but thankfully she was too young to process the details. He made sure she was always safe after that.

And since she never asked, he never told.

Quinn was granted custody for his stalwart adherence to the status quo. Gwen was saved from a toxic environment, and ultimately it saved everyone involved. Everyone but Quinn. Quinn went back to work, where he was able to focus and rise through the ranks to become a detective with an unprecedented record, except for his very first case. Gwen was raised in a loving and supportive home. And after a few years of hardship, his ex-wife cleaned up and found a great job at UCLA. Then, when Gwen was old enough, she decided she wanted to move to her mother's and go to college where she earned degrees in business and finance for free. It took grit for her to do that, to move in with her mother, renew that relationship, and work to create her own life. It was a great risk to become independent in a culture that teaches people to be worthless.

Quinn was proud of her accomplishments. He remembered worrying as his job continued to take its toll that his closeness with his daughter would somehow ruin her. So when she stepped out, he backed away. It seemed his ex-wife felt the same way; she wasn't here tonight, and she never talked to Quinn. Now he was the bad influence, according to her.

"Are you really kicking me out?" accused Gwen.

"Gwen..."

He could tell she had something on her mind, something she wanted to share, the whole reason for bringing him here to begin with, but she never said it. Quinn didn't have time for the back and forth, and he knew she wouldn't give in. He had other things on his mind, too.

"Okay, stay here. I'll be back."

Quinn returned downstairs, back to the scene of the crime. He ran down the suspect list as he waited for his first interrogation. There was the cowboy comic that opened for Precio. He had on a leather fringe jacket, bolo tie, and spotless white cowboy boots. Southern preacher turned illusionist. A real goofball, but charming as hell. It was all part of the act. Then there were the bartenders and waiters, the busboys, not to mention the other headliners, none of whom Quinn really suspected all that much. He had his sights on someone else. An unlikely culprit, but in Quinn's mind, the most likely candidate by far: Precio's assistant, a fifteen-year-old girl. He couldn't quite place it, but something about her made him uneasy. He'd had that queasy feeling before, too. And nearly every time, the person that made him queasy was found guilty.

At the top of Precio's act, she stood center stage in a tuxedo with a ghost-light shining on half of her skeletal body. Her hair was pulled back tight and stuck in place with spikes that fanned out in a halo. Renegade wisps of hair framed her face. Quinn had already checked the spikes and none of them were sharp enough to puncture the skin. He thought of Alice when he looked at her, only this girl wasn't the victim, she was the number one suspect.

"Ladies and Gentlemen, may I introduce the master of illusion, Precio D'avila!" The girl stepped aside into the darkness, but no one was there. Her hands remained in the light and then the stage lights faded up. Her hands did not move, fingers outstretched with palms up, but in the time it took for the lights to fade up her hands became an old man's, and where she should have been standing now stood the old magician, Precio. It was a good trick. Quinn clapped as he tried to enjoy himself. He had no idea in a few minutes he'd be puzzling out Precio's murder instead of the tricks he pulled onstage. But in retrospect, Precio's face looked dead under the stage lights, like if he sweated too much it might slip off to reveal a clean white skull. He looked around, curiously, puzzling over where his assistant had gone.

"Uhmmm..." he had muttered, nervously looking into the crowd.

Suddenly, his assistant stuck her head out from the curtain. "Go on, Pop-pop."

The crowd laughed. Precio searched their faces, scared. Like he was being forced into something he didn't want to do. He mumbled something, nearly tripping over himself in his ridiculous costume as he stepped over to a table that had been hiding in the shadows. He unwrapped a new pack of cards and began to shuffle with terrible skill, muttering to himself, and searching the crowd the entire time. And then he did something amazing. He threw the cards into the air in frustration, and in the scattering of hearts and diamonds, the spades and clubs seemed to freeze for a split-second, suspend in the shape of a person, and when they fell the girl was there again, in the midst of the fallen cards.

Everyone erupted with applause. Even Precio seemed surprised. The girl smiled, shared a look with Precio, and bowed, before disappearing back off stage. And then Precio made eye contact with Quinn. His eyes widened with recognition and urgency. Only Quinn had never seen the man before, or so he thought, as he was crawling with *deja vu*.

Quinn wondered about the girl's motive: *was Precio holding her career hostage?* He felt for certain the few tricks they had witnessed were illusions of the girl's invention. Maybe the only way to perform them was to give them to a famous magician.

But that didn't account for why he walked off stage. He was heading right toward Quinn when he collapsed on the ground. Everyone swarmed him. The audience, waitstaff, magicians from prior and future acts. And then, he was fine. Or at least it seemed he was fine. Up on two feet, a look on his face like he didn't know what hit him. And then in that instant, in the moment when everyone returned to their seats, took their eyes off the subject, and went back to their place, it happened. And everyone in the room missed it.

Now Quinn waited with Gwen as she sipped her club soda. They had seen Precio's final show. He was a dud, too. But who knows? Maybe that was part of the act. An act he never had a chance to finish. His grand finale ended with people screaming while he died on the floor with blood spurting from his neck. But still, there was something in that moment … the moment he came off stage, when he looked into Quinn's eyes. The urgency. The fear.

"So... A magician's quarrel?" Gwen always liked to put together the pieces of Quinn's puzzles.

"I don't know. Probably." He searched her eyes, looking for the easiest way to let her down. He knew there wasn't one. "It's gonna be a long night. Why don't you head back home."

"And miss all the fun?"

Quinn gave her a look, the protective look fathers always give their daughters when they try to coax them out of doing something.

"Look, I appreciate the invite, it's just-"

Suddenly Quinn was distracted. Precio's teenage assistant had finally emerged from the stairs at the other end of the dining room.

"Invite? You invited me."

"What?" Quinn replied, absent-mindedly.

"You invited me. Are you okay?"

Quinn's mind was adrift, back on the case. The assistant was wrapped in a blanket, still in her tuxedo, but her stage make-up was turning to mud; wet-kitten-pitiful.

"I gotta go." He pecked her on the cheek before checking her glass. "You sure you don't want a real drink? Might be a while."

"Club soda's fine."

Quinn nodded and excused himself. Gwen rolled her eyes. She'd been here before. Waiting on her father while he worked the case. Little did she know this would be the very last time.

Quinn approached the young assistant with a kind smile. She was scared, she knew she was a suspect. Quinn was conducting interviews in the seance room, purposefully, to unsettle nerves. He led her inside and shut the door, where they were alone beside a round table carved with runes. There were sconces on the wall, a Ouija board with a planchette, a crystal ball, silk handkerchiefs, and creepy animal taxidermy that watched them with their cloudy glass eyes. The girl had been here hundreds of times, but this time it spooked her. There were no more games tonight, no more illusions. This was Quinn's castle now.

"How old are you?"

"Fifteen."

"You need to have a parent or guardian present. Is there anyone I can call?"

"No."

"There must be someone? It's after midnight."

"Who are you? My truant officer?"

Quinn was surprised by her gall. She huddled in the blanket, shivering, eyes wide and scared. All the physical signs of an unsettling shakedown, but mentally she was cast iron.

He clicked a button on his phone to record.

"What's your name?" Quinn asked.

"Eleanor Rimbeaux," Eleanor stated with a French lean on the "aux." Quinn saw that she was growing more comfortable and confidant. Her testimony would be null if she didn't have a parent or guardian present. *I gotta call someone.*

"Am I under arrest?" She asked.

"No."

"Am I free to go?"

"If you want," Quinn replied, feeling a little sick to his stomach for even thinking she was a killer. For picking her in front of everyone. *Why her? There are at least seven male suspects.* He hadn't lead her up here in cuffs, but whenever cops took someone away it never looked decent. Quinn had chosen her to be first because out of everyone in the show, she was the one who was closest to him. As his one and only assistant, if anyone had set up poor Precio to fail, it appeared to have been her. And yet there wasn't a trace of actual evidence to tie anyone to the murder. It was like trying to find Alice all over again. Like a broken record that had been skipping for twenty-five years.

Eleanor rolled her eyes and spat out a telephone number. Quinn was surprised, but he dialed it. Eleanor crossed her arms and leaned back in a huff.

"I'm just trying to protect you, Eleanor."

"It's not your job to protect people. You're the person people call when protection fails." Quinn sat back after getting a taste of just how sharp her tongue could be, like seeing a blade slip from a dull sheath.

Within a few rings Serval, Eleanor's grandfather, picked up the phone. Quinn told him the situation and he agreed to come down from the Hills to rescue his granddaughter. He was a lawyer, and made sure Quinn knew as much. Quinn hung up on him.

"Need anything? Soda, sandwich?"

She shrugged no so they sat. The minutes ticked slowly by. Eleanor got antsy. Quinn admired the artifacts around the room. Magician's props and instruments designed to keep the audience's attention away from the truth. The seance room door opened and Jeff leaned in.

"Quinn?"

Quinn excused himself to speak with the medical examiner.

"Two blades were used, one in each hand. Nothing we've collected from the kitchen or the staff could have done this. We're talking extreme velocity and precision with hand-stropped razors. Probably three inches long. I'd need a red hot scalpel and several seconds to cut four arteries so finely, and that's during an autopsy. Your perp did this in one double-stroke on a standing, living victim."

"So what're you saying, Jeff? Someone has knives for fingers?"

Jeff didn't have time to answer. An old, distinguished gentleman shoved his way into the adjacent room, making a scene.

"Where's my granddaughter!" they heard from the steps.

That was fast Quinn thought. Suspicion arose in him like he was being taken for a sucker. He couldn't say why, though, but he felt like he was still in the theater watching the magic show. *Maybe it was a stupid idea to hold interviews in this hokey room.*

"I'm Mr. Rimbeaux, Serval Rimbeaux." Serval proclaimed as he stood at the top of the steps. "I demand to see my granddaughter at once!" He was tan and suave and all right angles. His face was stiff and slimy at the same time. Expensive gold rings adorned his fingers. Quinn looked at Eleanor and for the first time noticed she wore jewelry, too. Silver bracelets and a black leather choker with a diamond stud. He had tried to ignore jewelry on girls because it always sent him back to the one clue in Alice's murder that didn't add up. Not to mention the paradox: a cold, calculated metal or precious stone, meant to signify love, which people rob for, kill for, and give to their wives and mistresses in exchange for playing nice. Alice's jewelry would have broken the case if only Quinn could have connected the dots.

"Mr. Rimbeaux… You're Eleanor's legal guardian?"

"Yes, sir. And I am also her attorney."

Mr. Rimbeaux stormed into the seance room.

"Eleanor, what in God's name are you doing here?"

"I'm a magician."

Mr. Rimbeaux looked aghast. He suddenly noticed the garish decor hanging on the walls, the beasts surrounding him, and the cryptic card and board games scattered about. He seemed off-put.

"Detective, are you attempting to involve my granddaughter in a murder?"

"While I don't believe she committed the murder, Mr. Rimbeaux, I think she knows something."

"Knowing something does not give you the right to hold a minor in custody. Especially on a school night, doubly so for someone with delinquency issues." Serval spoke as if Eleanor wasn't there. "You understand what I'm saying?"

"I think so," Quinn noted.

"She's unfit! Just … look at her!"

"You think she's an unreliable witness?"

"Absolutely! Just look how impressionable she is."

"I resent these comments, let that be known!" Eleanor yelled into Quinn's phone.

"Can we begin?" Quinn asked, pushing to keep everyone in the room talking.

"No, we can not! Not until you answer a couple of questions of my own," Serval interrupted. "Is Eleanor under arrest? And are we free to go?" He watched as Quinn struggled to come up with detailed answers for the record.

There was no concrete reason to keep Eleanor in the seance room. She was obviously not the killer. She was too short to slice Precio's neck, and even in the grainy security footage Quinn felt he still would have noticed her silver glittery outfit in the middle of the turmoil.

Serval rapped his rings on the table like a high-pitched gavel. Quinn found himself looking from grandpa to granddaughter. His detective's intuition was sparking. Someone in the room was lying. Maybe everyone.

"Where were you the moment Precio was murdered?"

"You don't have to answer that!" snarled Serval, furious with Quinn.

"I was backstage, preparing for the next trick."

"What was the next trick?"

"He was supposed to get someone from the crowd, and we would make them disappear. Looks like someone disappeared him first."

Her apathy was unmistakable, but that didn't mean she killed him. Precio was the worst magician Quinn had ever seen, she was the one that sparkled. *Maybe he was holding her back on purpose. Maybe that gives her a motive?*

"Are you resentful of Precio at all?"

"Don't answer that."

"Look, Mr. Rimbeaux, I know it's not to your liking, but I intend to end this case tonight. We've locked everyone in and I'm talking to everyone here."

Serval turned pale. "You mean... The killer's still here? Inside! With my little girl!" His panic was infectious as he scrambled to collect Eleanor from her seat.

"We're safe. There are cops everywhere," Quinn offered.

Serval yanked his granddaughter from her seat and down the stairs as Quinn chased after them, even though he knew he had to let them go. They were fast. Much swifter than an old man his age should be. Much swifter than Quinn even, still a few years shy of the plasticine man in front of him.

"Wait!" Quinn reached for Eleanor, but Serval got her out the fire exit door and into the chilly Los Angeles night. Her silver jewelry reflected under the streetlamp.

"I will not have my granddaughter subjected to a murder investigation that she has no part of. And I suggest you erase that interview as it is tangible proof of police misconduct." Quinn stopped, realizing Serval might be right. He had played by the book his entire career. He was on unfamiliar territory. If Eleanor really had nothing to do with this he was way out of bounds right now. Not only that, the killer was still inside plotting their escape.

"If you would like to schedule a formal interview during more appropriate hours I would be happy to oblige."

"There's no time!" Quinn urged. "It has to be done tonight. Please, just let me ask a few more questions. She knows these people. She knows something!"

Serval forced Eleanor down the stairs. She looked over her shoulder, a guilty grin across her face, before landing on the concrete sidewalk below. They glittered like gods under the streetlight. So much jewelry, silver for Eleanor, gold for Serval. It hadn't seemed so overwhelming before, but there, together, sparkling under the full moon and city lights, Quinn got that feeling again.

It was a game to these people. Attorneys. Magicians. Killers. They were only playing games. Some audiences were just more willing participants than others. Quinn realized if he was ever going to figure this out, he needed to stop being so pragmatic, and start playing the game.

"Can you give me a hint," Quinn demanded. Serval didn't move aside, but he did not leave, either. Quinn searched Eleanor's young eyes.

"This is uncalled for. Eleanor, I demand you not to answer that question."

"It's not murder," she piped up. "It's magic." Eleanor grinned and Serval spun her around and moved her to the valet.

Quinn stepped off the escape platform as he watched the valet bring Serval's Bentley. Eleanor glittered under the streetlamp, the same way she had when she appeared from the falling cards.

"It was a good show," Quinn called out. The admission surprised him.

"Thanks for coming," Eleanor replied with a wink before disappearing into the car.

Serval kept his eye on Eleanor as he closed the door, paid the valet, and hopped in the driver seat, never looking back as he sped away. Quinn watched them, then turned, his coat brushing the banister when he heard a delicate *ping* on the asphalt below. Quinn glanced and saw something silver shining on the concrete. He leaned over and picked it up. It was a silver ring shaped like a serpent. The same type of ring that belonged to Alice.

Impossible.

Quinn felt a single, numbing freeze take hold of his body as he looked at the ring in his hand. The night was beginning to add up, only he wasn't sure how. He had been lured there, of that he was certain. Not by his daughter, as he first thought, but by someone else. Only it wasn't the kind of show he had been expecting. Someone had been steering Quinn to this moment the entire evening, and Quinn felt certain it was Eleanor, though he had no idea how. Quinn grabbed a cop who stood dutifully beside him.

"Chase after that car!"

The officer looked around, confused. "What car?"

The Bentley had disappeared down the driveway and out into the busy streets of Hollywood.

"I want a lineup of every magician in the place. Men only. You can let the women go. And the headliners. And the waitstaff." The cop nodded and sped off obligingly.

Within seconds guests filed out of the mansion as Quinn looked over an employee and guest list with every name crossed off but seven. Over a hundred suspects down to seven in only three hours. And one of them was a serial killer. Eleanor had set him up to finish her show.

Justice is on the way, Alice.

There were six young men lined up on the main stage. All of them too young to be Alice's killer. Something was amiss. *Why would Eleanor give him the jewelry if the killer wasn't inside?* Quinn feared it was a distraction. Yet another turn of the magic trick. He knew he couldn't let it cloud the biggest clue he'd had all night, which was suddenly staring him right in the face. There were seven names on the list, but there were only six people standing in front of him now. Someone was missing from the list.

Quinn radioed to his fellow officers to confirm there was no one else in the mansion except the police, the six men in front of him, and Gwen, upstairs.

Gwen.

Quinn made his suspects wait again. He rushed up the steps.

"Ok, everybody outta the pool," he joked as he waved her toward the exit.

"Seriously! I've been waiting all night. When are you going to tell me why we're here?" Gwen pleaded.

Quinn couldn't tell her the truth: that the twenty-five-year-old case that had haunted his dreams since she was a little girl had lured him there, lured them both, but for what reason he didn't know. And now they could both be in danger. He had to get her out.

"I wanted to surprise you," he blurted without thinking. Her concerned face grew into a broad smile and that glow fired from within. Her eyes were bright with life and spirit. And she was on her third plate of fries even though the kitchen shut down hours ago. The unopened bottle of her favorite bourbon stuck out of her purse, and the club soda with lime has been drained to the ice in her glass.

"Is there something *you* want to tell me?"

Gwen blushed. With all the turmoil she wasn't sure when or how or if she would ever get the chance.

"How'd you know?"

"I'm a detective, remember?" Quinn laughed and before he knew it, they were surrounded by cops, congratulating them with applause.

"Mom didn't tell you, did she?"

"No..." Quinn blushed with the quiet realization that he would be playing with those grandkids sooner than he thought.

"You always were one hell of a detective," she exclaimed. Quinn looked at her with all the pride a man can have, a new spirit and life filling his own void, before the sudden realization that he was back on duty washed all of it away.

"Seriously, you should go. Catch up on sleep while you can. You've got many years of insomnia coming your way." Quinn reached in for a hug and the tears that jumped to Gwen's eyes spoke volumes that pages could not contain.

"Oh, Dad..."

He wrapped his arms tightly around her, his only baby girl.

"Now, please, go. I hate to do it, but I'm serious this time."

"What's going on?"

"We're missing a suspect. Our number one suspect. He's here somewhere, we just don't know where."

"You've checked all the rooms?"

"Every single one."

"No, I mean, like, all the secret ones?"

"What secret ones?"

"Dad... it's the Magic Castle. You didn't think there would be secret rooms?"

Quinn hugged his daughter tightly, then worriedly backed away, acknowledging her tender stomach before waving goodbye. Quinn stormed down the stairs to get down to business. The cops pivoted out of his way as he hustled back to the main stage where his suspects were under guard.

"Which one of you was gonna spill on the secret rooms?" Quinn demanded.

Finally, someone spoke up.

"We don't want to lose our apprenticeships for divulging Castle secrets."

"Yea, like... we know someone got killed, but I didn't do it."

The room grew louder with their defiant pleas. Quinn let them talk over each other for a few seconds. They all suspected the other. One by one they shut up when they saw they couldn't wear him down.

"Each of you will escort two officers to every secret hideaway or passage or whatever you got around here and you will find the missing apprentice or so help me God you'll all be trying to escape San Quentin with everything you learned here."

The magicians and cops snapped to the task. Quinn revolved from group to group, amazed at the hidden extensions inside the maze-like mansion. It didn't take long to find what they came for.

The suspect was found hiding in a crawl space that smelled like bootleg whiskey. Quinn helped a cop haul the small man out only to realize it was the preacher cowboy from the opening act. He dusted himself off and smiled as if they didn't just find him inside a wall. He was taller than expected, once he was all puffed out in front of Quinn.

Quinn had the cops form a circle, enclosing him inside with the cowboy.

"Let the others go," Quinn said. The cowboy was the killer, he could smell it. But he was too young to be Alice's killer. *Violence is hereditary*, Quinn thought, knowing that once he revealed the evidence that connected the cowboy to Precio then he would have complete freedom to investigate the cowboy's family tree. Then he would uncover Alice's killer, and all the others, too. They had to be connected. *But how did Eleanor find out? Did she get too close?*

Quinn circled the cowboy.

"He moves, you shoot him. Got it?" The five cops surrounding them responded in kind by unbuttoning their holsters.

"I didn't do anything," the cowboy pleaded. "I was just hiding … for a trick! I got scared!"

Quinn ignored the cowboy's small talk. He replayed the security footage in his mind. There was such chaos right before the scene, as Precio stepped offstage and fell into the audience, it was impossible to pick out the action and the actors involved until the blood sprayed and people fell away in waves. He remembered seeing the cowboy earlier, in his stunning act, and knew he was agile and capable. And he was just tall enough to match the description. And he was also in the video, helping Precio to his feet, moments before.

Quinn frisked the cowboy and came up with a wallet and cell phone, but no blades. He even checked business and credit cards for sharp edges. The phone had no removable plates and it wasn't in a protective case. Quinn knew the guy still had the blades on him somewhere, that was part of the trick, making an audience believe in movement when nothing moved. The cops had checked everywhere from kitchens to trash cans. The blades must've returned to their sheaths. Quinn tore the fringe leather coat off the cowboy and turned it inside out. Nothing except pockets in the sleeves for cards and ball bearings. No knives.

"Hey, I can be kicked out for this!" The cowboy said, no longer good-humored. Quinn checked the man's dress shirt sleeves and came up with nothing. Quinn frisked the cowboy once more, ignoring threats of sexual harassment. He thought only about the coincidence of the jewelry and this cowboy who almost got away with killing Precio, and he knew they were related. It was too much of a coincidence. But still, nothing added up. The answers were all right in front of him, and yet Quinn was no closer to the answer.

Getting close is part of the set-up, it doesn't afford you an advantage.

Quinn took a step back. The cops tensed, thinking the cowboy was about to do something when Quinn got a premonition. The guy didn't have anything in his coat, up his sleeves, and his bolo couldn't hide anything.

"Hands up," Quinn said and he saw that the cowboy had calluses on the thumb and forefinger of both hands, as if his hands had adapted to working with sharp edges.

"Hold still. I mean it." Quinn got in close and felt the man's shirt. He touched the buttons and around the collar. Suddenly, the cowboy tensed and Quinn knew he had him. The cowboy looked at Quinn, face awash with guilt as Quinn reached his fingers in and found them. Disguised as collar stays were two tiny three-inch steel slivers dimpled on one end for grip, which tapered to an edge sharper than a scalpel. Quinn pressed one into a wood-paneled wall and it gave way like butter.

"Take him away," ordered Quinn.

The police cuffed the cowboy and his mouth trembled. His eyes betrayed something that made Quinn's mind race.

Eleanor isn't innocent either, he kept thinking. *Eleanor had the jewelry...*

"I didn't do it!" the cowboy screamed. "I didn't kill anyone!"

Quinn turned, nearly amused. He held the evidence in his hands.

"Seriously, kid. You went to all this trouble to kill Precio, to disguise the weapon, to hide … And you didn't do it?"

The cowboy looked at Quinn with fear in his eyes. Quinn was on to him.

"There something you wanna say?"

"That's not Precio!"

"What? Of course it is." Jeff scoffs.

"No. It isn't!"

Jeff and Quinn looked at one another, a deep realization suddenly sinking in.

"Precio's alive!"

Something inside Quinn stopped, though the world around him seemed to keep revolving right on past. It almost made him dizzy.

"Tell me everything."

"Precio stole my tricks. He's been stealing them for years! Always the star of the show … It's *bullshit!* Precio was a hack! But when she became his assistant, she told me if I killed him, she'd help me cover it up … only …" he breaks.

"Go on."

The cowboy looks at Quinn, desperately. He has nothing to lose, as he's already lost everything.

"When I cut that man's throat … I realized he wasn't Precio."

Quinn remembered the moment Precio looked at him, urgently, from the stage. He remembered the tricks, such as they were, and his fearful behavior. Suddenly it all made sense. Precio was a terrible magician … because the man onstage was not, in fact, a magician.

"So … Eleanor *helped* you?"

"Who's *Eleanor*?"

"The girl. The magician's assistant. The young girl…"

He shrugged. "Everyone here called her Alice."

A storm of truth surrounded Quinn, but the lightning was so intense he couldn't make his way through the clouds.

"Take him!" Quinn shouted at the man. He turned and raced back to the body upstairs. Eleanor must have known Quinn.

Must've known about his police work. Probably that stupid article they wrote about him a couple months back. Somehow she set this whole thing in motion.

Quinn knelt beside the body and reached into the body bag. Jeff looked aghast as Quinn pulled and tore until something popped and ripped and Quinn's hand came up with Precio's nose.

"Holy shit" Jeff gawked as he looked at Quinn. They both knew what had happened. Jeff had been preoccupied with the vicious wounds that had killed the man, and Quinn had been preoccupied with finding the killer on an evaporating deadline.

If this wasn't Precio then who was he? And more-over, where was Precio? Quinn took the handkerchief from the dead man's suit pocket and wiped away the rest of the make-up. He was much older than the man he was made up to be.

It's not a murder mystery, he thought. *It's a magic show.*

His mind raced with possibilities. Precio was awkward on stage because he didn't belong there. Quinn had met that same awkwardness another time that evening, but he was off his guard and hadn't been able to place it. It was Eleanor's grandfather, Serval. In retrospect, he knew exactly what he was dealing with, and who the body was in front of him.

"This man isn't Precio the magician. It's Eleanor's grandfather." As the words came out of his mouth, he was bombarded with thoughts out of his control.

Eleanor knew about Alice. She had the same Tiffany's jewelry that's been discontinued since before she was born. Tiffany's sterling. The serpents ring.

The killer must have given it to her, the same way he gave it to Alice. Only he didn't kill her. He didn't kill her because he couldn't kill her. Not because he didn't want to... But because he couldn't...

Because he was related to her.

Quinn took a step back with the realization. It was both a huge leap of faith and yet the only logical conclusion.

Eleanor's grandfather was the real killer.

Eleanor's grandfather killed Alice.

The thought penetrated him as the truth unveiled itself.

The man I've been hunting for all this time is finally dead. Eleanor found out. She found out about me somehow. It had to be that article. And she put us all in this place together.

Quinn lifted one of Serval's dead hands and inspected the rings. Tiffany jewelry, a discontinued set released over twenty years ago. Serval must've spent a fortune on jewelry over the years, handing out those expensive trinkets to all his would-be victims. The leftovers passed on to his own daughter, then to his granddaughter. Eleanor had received gifts from her dear old Pop Pop all her life. She must've loved him dearly, until the day she discovered that the gifts he gave her were the same gifts he gave other little girls. She probably got curious as to why her grandfather liked her friends so much but kept her at a distance. She probably wondered why, as her mother got older, their relationship with her wealthy grandparents became more and more estranged, and why they had to struggle just to eat. And eventually her questions gave way to answers her little mind couldn't understand, and when she finally faced it she broke into a thousand little pieces.

Or worse. Maybe, and more likely, she knew all along. Because she was a victim. Just like Alice.

Quinn knew he'd never find out the concrete details, because like any good magician, Eleanor was long gone, her secrets buried safely within. She had set up Serval's death and fled, a disappearing act she had learned from her serial killer grandfather, one of the greatest magicians Quinn had ever encountered.

She must have blackmailed him to get him to put on the makeup. Maybe the cowboy, too, though he seemed to have his own motive. And maybe Precio just wanted the opportunity to play a part in the greatest trick he would ever be able to pull.

None of it mattered. Not to Quinn. Alice's killer had finally been brought to justice. It didn't matter that it wasn't by him. Quinn had served the police force loyally, but tonight it was Eleanor that took care of Alice's killer, bringing justice for her and dozens of other little girls just like them.

"How'd she get Precio to go along with it?" Jeff questioned.

Quinn waved his hand through the air. "Ahh, forget it." The truth was too goddamn convoluted for the public. Eleanor's scheme was as fragile as a spider's web, yet she still managed to tangle everyone inside. His time was up, Quinn thought to himself. He was too old for the dirty tricks of the young.

He dropped the prosthetic nose and grease-paint smeared handkerchief into the body bag and zipped it up. He wasn't pursuing Eleanor and Precio anywhere. He'd had enough. If someone else wanted to do so, so be it, but as far as he could tell she was the victim of a crime too unconscionable to imagine, and Precio was merely her lowly assistant. The real culprit was gone, and Quinn felt a wave of relief wash over him that he hadn't felt for twenty-five years.

Jeff nodded in agreement. He got the idea. The cowboy killed Precio, it was as simple as that. And if the cowboy tried to set the record straight, he'd be the one that looked crazy. After all, who can trust a man that lies for a living?

Quinn sent an email to his chief from his phone tendering his resignation. His retirement was effective immediately. He took a deep breath, shook hands with Jeff, and motioned for the cops guarding the main entrance to let everyone out of the Magic Castle. He took his gun and his badge and handed them over to a cop outside. The cool evening air woke him up with a kissing breeze. He couldn't believe it was over, and yet he couldn't help feeling the excitement of something else right around the corner. It would be the biggest case of his life: He was about to become a full-time grandfather.

As Quinn strolled to his car he reached into his pocket for his keys. He felt the serpent ring Eleanor left behind amongst the scratchy teeth of his keys and he pulled it out. He admired the smooth dragon chasing itself ad infinitum. He slid the ring over his knuckle on his pinky finger and squeezed his fist tight. To his surprise, it was a perfect fit.

About Gabe DiDomenico

Gabriel DiDomenico is hopelessly attracted to horror and crime fiction. He blames this charming character flaw on growing up in Bloomsburg, PA where he enjoyed a safe suburban childhood close to Centralia, the infamous mining town with coal fires that still smolder below the surface. In 2010 he moved far away from his hometown to write from another place with trouble hidden in its bedrock, Los Angeles, California.

For more info visit www.halfhollow.net

MERCY IN THE WEST

by David Beeler

It's been three days since I watched somebody die. It was one of those thoughts that entered the head of Gustavus Murphy with a randomness that seemed to echo life's twists and turns. Gustavus rocked from side to side as his wagon struggled over the muddy, gulch-filled road. He pulled the reigns hard to the right, directing the wagon around a deep puddle left by recent rains. The wheel of the wagon rolled over a pile of bleached horse bones, now partially submerged in the damp earth. A small purple flower grew from one of the eye sockets of the horse's skull. It seemed as though the flower had found some sanctuary, borrowing the skull for protection just as the lumbering wheel of the wagon came along and crushed it, pushing the skull and the flower flat into the damp earth. Along this road of dreams, such was the fate for many. Carved by a litany of pioneers seeking new horizons, Gustavus wondered how many of them had, indeed, found greener pastures.

There was smoke in the distance. He pulled the reins up short, reached behind the buckboard, and extracted a spyglass. He gazed into the distance and furrowed his brow. There was good smoke and bad smoke. This was unmistakably bad.

Gray smoke rose from one of several wagons which had been hastily formed into a defensive circle. *Apaches*. Gustavus stood up on his seat and scanned the area to the horizon with his spyglass. Drawing in a deep breath, he removed his rifle from behind the buckboard and checked that his Derringer was snug in his belt. He snapped the reins and the wagon lurched forward.

On drawing near to the wagon formation, bodies lay strewn on the ground. He leaned over the side of the wagon where hoof-prints too many to number were pressed into the ground. Gustavus noted that none of the hoof-prints had shoes. The small band of pioneers had been completely overrun. The lifeless would-be settlers lie on their backs, their clothing ransacked, and anything of value taken, including their scalps. It occurred to Gustavus that the only "greener pastures" they would find now would soon be growing over top of them.

He heard a cough from behind a nearby wagon. Gustavus climbed down from his bench with his rifle and aimed it out in front of him. His heart picked up its pace as he moved toward the location from where the sound had come. There, propped up against one of the wheels of the covered wagons, was a tall, lean man, struggling to lift his pistol and aim it at Gustavus.

"Whoa, No! I'm not yer enemy!" Gustavus protested in his thick Irish mutter. "Just stumbled upon yer misfortunate scene here."

All the strength the man had mustered to lift the gun fled his arm and it fell like slack rope. Gustavus scanned the area for any signs of potential danger and concluded that the Apaches had moved on. "How is it yer not dead?" he finally asked.

A wildness filled the man's eyes. "They took my daughter. I chased after 'em, shootin'. They shot me up with arrows." Gustavus saw the shafts of several arrows sticking from the man. "Then one shot me with a gun and I fell down the ravine. I guess they didn't think I was worth bothering with."

"Well, it's yer lucky day … Well, not yer lucky day, perhaps, but allow me to introduce myself. I am Dr. Gustavus Murphy—medical practitioner, salesman of fine elixirs and remedies, entertainer, and bon vivant! The last part's French. It means I enjoy a good chin-wag. Stay here. Well, obviously you will – I'm going to get my bag. Dr. Murphy's here to *help!*"

Gustavus returned to his bright red wagon on which gold letters were emblazoned, "Dr. Gustavus Murphy's Traveling Emporium – Elixirs, Cure all's, Stain Remover's, Photographs, and Entertainment!" He continued to scan the horizon for any sign of errant Apaches, but it remained clear. Dr. Murphy extracted a black doctor's bag and a canteen from his wagon then hurried back over to the slouched pioneer.

"Here, some water." He tipped the pioneer's head back and the man greedily gulped at the water. "There. There. Not too much." Gustavus pulled a square brown bottle from his bag. "Now, this is my own recipe: Dr. Murphy's Miracle Elixir. It has morphine extracted from the finest poppy fields in the Ottoman Empire. It'll make you drowsy, but it does wonders to take away the pain, and I'm guessing you are in quite a bit of that right now aren't ya, fella? You could use a proper dose of relief." Gustavus prepared to pour the elixir into a small jigger when the man grabbed his arm.

"Do you think I'll make it?"

Gustavus exhaled, avoiding the man's eyes; he knew the prospects were poor. "Hard to say 'till I get a good look at you. You've got more holes than a sieve."

The pioneer's grip tightened on Murphy's jacket sleeve, "They took my daughter. You've got to find her. She's only thirteen. You *must* find her!"

Murphy leaned away from the man, looking out to his left where the land stretched as far as the eye could see. He looked to his right where the expanse extended to the mountains far off in the distance. "Right," he muttered. He looked at the lean, sinewed man whose tan face had lines plowed into it from years of toil and pegged him for a farmer. His clothes were drenched with blood from the various shafts sticking from him. He'd seen it before – men that should rightly be dead, carried by their will to live for something beyond themselves.

"Please…"

"Yes… Of course. I'll look for your daughter." Gustavus knew from his time as a young physician in New York, through his military service, and now out into the sparsely populated west that there was no stronger medicine than hope. Even though the chances of finding that girl were minuscule, that shred of hope could be the difference between life and death. "In the morning we'll look for her, but first, let's see what we can do to help you, so you can help me find her." The man eased his grip and slumped back against the wagon wheel. Dr. Murphy unbuttoned the man's sopping shirt.

"How does it look, Doc?"

"Like yer pretty good at catching arrows… and you've caught war arrows. They have this little trough carved in the side to encourage blood loss. I was a surgeon in the war—"

"North or south?"

"Does it matter?"

"I s'pose not."

"I've seen soldiers rally from worse and pass from much less. It's often hard to tell. But I can tell you this, no man ever lived full of arrows. They're gonna have to come out. And better sooner than later."

"Alright."

The farmer looked to the doctor for confirmation, but Murphy was suddenly very far away. He spoke absently, "If the good man of the house had known in what watch the thief would come…"

A raven cawed shrill and loud as it landed on a wagon wheel. It then hopped down to peck at one of the lifeless settlers. The pioneer shook his head as he considered Murphy's words, "We weren't ready."

Gustavus regarded the pioneer with a peculiar gaze, then as suddenly as he had gone away, he returned to his former self.

The man's skin was clammy, and his cheeks began to grey. Gustavus poured the reddish-brown syrup into the metal jigger. "I present to you Dr. Murphy's amazing cure-all. This is good for all constituent parts of the constitution, for relieving neuralgia and even helping the ladies with their… timely concerns."

The pioneer smiled a half-smile and said, "No presentation necessary."

Murphy laughed. "Well, old habits. There's been a little bit of the theatrical in medicine ever since I got involved with it. Funny how some things find you, most often when yer not even looking."

ᐓ◆ᐔ

New York. Thirty years earlier.

Shamus, a dark-haired ten-year-old with a perpetual smirk and his sidekick, Joseph, whose red hair and freckles branded him instantly Irish, walked down the bustling streets of New York City, deeply engaged in conversation. They both lived within a stone's throw of the wooden sidewalks they now strode. This was their neighborhood, the infamous Five Points.

Five Points was a basin where the gravity of being poor pulled people from different geographies, ethnicities, and backgrounds to pool in what had once been a swamp, filled in and reclaimed as the city expanded. The number of Irish continued to swell as hordes of them fled the potato famine back home. Newly emancipated blacks landed here when their freedom proved not as free as they'd hoped. Blacks and whites intermingled socially in ways that were unheard of in other places, united in their struggle for survival. But just as desperation banded unlikely groups together, it also gave way to rampant crime, violence, and prostitution. The two lads passed a teenage girl who was showing her wares. One of them called out to her, "Hey Lily, have ye made enough to buy me one of them opera hats?"

"Chance'd be a fine thing, Shamus O'Brien!" As the boys passed by a doorway a bucket of mop water splashed before them nearly covering their tattered shoes. "Hey!" yelled Shamus, "Watch out ye ol- Oh! Gustavus! You nearly got me!"

Young Gustavus laughed, "It's about time ye had a bath. What're ye two up to?"

"Ye want to see something amazin'?" Joseph asked.

"Like a girl's knickers?" joked Gustavus. "Hey, Lily!"

"Shut up and get some money!"

"Ha-ha. I wish," Joseph snickered excitedly.

"No. Not that. Something *really* amazin'. Come on, it's uptown," said Shamus, "This'll blow your stovetop."

After hitching a ride on the back of a wagon, the boys jumped off and stood before a tall building. It must've been at least six stories. Gustavus noticed that the brick had been glazed like tile. He thought this must be something special if even the brick was fancy. Entering into the lobby, Shamus guided them along one wall away from the attendant who was busy talking to a cluster of gentlemen.

Making their way up a long narrow circular staircase, they found themselves in a crowded room. The smell of cigars and pipe smoke hung heavy in the air as Gustavus tried to see what this room was about. It was full of men, but their frock coats and wool trousers created a barrier so Gustavus couldn't see beyond. Only a forest of legs and coats. "Come on."

Gustavus felt uneasy, "I don't think we're supposed to be here."

"It's all right, my cousin works here," Shamus assured. Jockeying between the legs of the men they found a set of small steep steps leading down to the center of the room. The room was a horseshoe-shaped viewing gallery. Wooden rails lined the platforms that stepped down to the center of the room so that standing men could lean over the rail and peer into the pit of the room more easily. In the pit was a small bench-like table and small trolley with tools and implements lying on white cloths.

Shamus hopped down the stairs, weaving between the legs of the gentlemen who seemed to loom large. One gentleman noticed them and scoffed, "What are these boys doing in here?" The three scamps slid past without stopping until they arrived at the bottom of the arena, not far from the table. On Shamus' instruction they pressed themselves against the wall near the stairs. A man strode into the arena with no jacket, his shirtsleeves up, wearing a tan apron besmeared with a great deal of blood. Gustavus shot an inquisitive look to his friends as if to say, "Where the hell have you brought me?"

The man in the bloody apron spoke. "Gentlemen, welcome to Bartholomew's surgical theater. I am Dr. Ruff. I have for your entertainment and instruction three procedures: two amputations, and one bladder stone removal. If you've not been present at a procedure before, there may be some screams, so prepare yourself, but rest assured, these patients are fortunate to be with not only the finest, but the fastest surgeon in New York. In order to minimize blood loss and reduce trauma, it is important to work with lightning speed. Without further ado, bring out the patient!"

Four burly men carried in a writhing man in a bed shirt. He was unceremoniously plopped on the wooden table and swiftly restrained by the four men. A fifth man stepped up and organized the patient's bed shirt, exposing his left leg with a foot that had turned black from gangrene.

The surgeon stepped forward, announcing, "I shall begin with the tour de metre, the 'turn of the master.' I shall then saw through the bone. My assistant, Mr. Greeley, will find the artery and tie it off as I sew the skin flaps shut. Watch your fingers, Mr. Greeley! One of our surgical assistants, Mr. Flynn, lost two of his fingers this morning and is in the hospital himself. You must move swiftly to keep up with me!"

Shamus turned to Joseph, "Jesus, that's my cousin! Flynn's my cousin!" Panicked, he nodded to Joseph that it was the time to leave, and Shamus and Joseph retreated up the stadium stairs to the circular stairwell. Shamus turned to Gustavus and shouted, "Murphy!" but Gustavus was transfixed on the spectacle that was to come.

The surgeon took a long-bladed knife from the small cart, placed his arm under the knee of the rotten footed leg of the patient, and beckoned to the room, "Time me, gentlemen! Time me!" In one swift move, he cut through the skin, muscles, and tendons directly below the man's knee all the way to the bone, in a circle around the entire leg. The patient shrieked like a banshee, startling even the most stalwart and resolute spectators in the cramped surgical theater. Gustavus nearly jumped out of his skin. He wanted to turn away, but he had to watch as the doctor quick as a flash had replaced the knife with a saw and was working through the bone. Gustavus was surprised how much it sounded like sawing wood. The patient rose and screamed from the table, then suddenly went limp, having passed out from the shock of what was happening to him. Gustavus too, nearly fainted as he felt his knees grow weak underneath him. Meanwhile, the assistant, Mr. Greeley, was tying the artery into a knot as it spurted blood on the table, his apron, and all over the floor. No sooner was it tied off then he stuffed it back in the stump where there had been a leg moments before and pulled the skin together as the surgeon swiftly used a whipstitch to sew the skin flap shut.

"Time!" The surgeon yelled as he threw his hands in the air.

"28 seconds!" announced a voice in the front row.

"Huzzah! I beat my own record!" The doctor grabbed the severed leg, held it up and asked, "Anyone care for a souvenir?" A series of chuckles emanated through the crowd.

Turning suddenly and unexpectedly to Gustavus, the surgeon proclaimed, "I think this stow away should have it." And with that, he tossed the bloody stump of a leg with its gangrenous foot in tow right at Gustavus. With reflexive action, Gustavus caught the leg and looked down at it. He screamed and turned for help from his friends when he realized they were gone.

Terrified, he let out a new, louder, more panicked scream. Turning to the stairs to beat a hasty retreat, a sea of gentleman's legs closed like the Red Sea upon the Egyptians. That exit was gone. Convinced that if captured he would lose more limbs for trespassing than the last patient, Gustavus knew he had to get out, badly. The back of the operating floor! The way they had brought the patient in and taken him out.

Gustavus started to the left of the operating table, but one of the burly men stepped in his way. Realizing he was still clutching the leg, he hurled it at the man. It struck him on the jaw with the smack that sounded like a ham hitting a marble floor. The sea of gentlemen behind him let out a wave of laughter. One of the other burly men advanced from the right side of the table. He lunged at the boy, but Gustavus dodged to the side as the burly man slipped in a puddle of blood and contorted wildly one way, then the other, until he grabbed another burly man, pulling them both off balance on to the floor. Another wave of laughter broke from the sea of frock coats. Popping out from under the surgical table, Gustavus encountered Mr. Greeley, the surgical assistant, who came at him with a sneer, "You little—"

Gustavus grabbed the long-bladed knife and yelled, "I'll give you the master's cut! Out of my way!"

Shocked, Mr. Greeley stepped aside. Shocked at himself that it worked, Gustavus dropped the knife and ran out the curtain.

For a moment all was still, except the two burly men who were still making their way to an upright position, both smeared with the amputee's blood. But, even they sensed the lull that had fallen on the room and sheepishly turned to the audience. Then, from behind the curtain a defiant little voice rang out, "Let me down!" The curtain was thrown open and the larger of the two burly men who had carried the patient out entered the arena holding Gustavus by the scruff of his coat. As if it were the finale of a hilarious act, the sea of gentlemen broke into applause.

"Somebody help me! They're going to cut off me legs and arms!"

The room roared with laughter. The doctor stepped forward and lifted his hand. A hush fell. "Well, did you pay?"

Shamed and guilty, Gustavus said quietly, "No."

"Well, all these fine gentlemen paid to be here."

"But my friends..."

"Friends…?" The doctor looked around the theatre. Gustavus knew that any attempt to explain Shamus and Joseph would seem like desperate conjecture.

"Seeing as how you haven't paid, we'll only take two of your fingers as admission." The room chuckled, but Gustavus began to thrash so violently that the burly man nearly dropped him. "I'm only joking boy. Take him to my office." Turning to the crowd, he said, "We will take an interlude while I sort out our interloper and prepare for… a full arm amputation in record speed!" The frock coats applauded as the doctor bowed, then Mr. Greely bowed, then the burly men, en masse. Even Gustavus nodded his head to the crowd before he was carried away.

Gustavus was taken to a room down a corridor that had a massive oak desk covered in stacks of papers and books. A large window cast filtered light over a table littered with glass beakers and bottles with tubes connecting them. Several bookcases lined the walls. The burly man plopped Gustavus down in a padded chair before the desk and stood in the door, arms crossed, glaring at the boy as he scanned the room for potential exits.

The surgeon briskly entered the room. "Thank you, Horace." The burly man scowled at Gustavus, then left, closing the door. The doctor followed Gustavus' eyes as he anxiously watched the door close. "Don't worry, I'll let you go. Unless… you want to stay for the next surgery."

"I… I don't have any money."

"Didn't stop you before." The surgeon smiled as he poured himself a drink. "I saw how you stared, transfixed. Your mates grimaced, flinched, made faces, and ran away, but you… you didn't blanch, not for a second." The surgeon leaned into Gustavus. "You were *fascinated*. Reminds me of me at your age, though, medicine was more primitive then. So, the question remains, do you care to see more?"

"Yes." Gustavus heard the word leave his mouth as if someone else had said it, as if he were admitting a truth about himself that he never knew. And here was a stranger, holding a mirror up, showing him an undiscovered part of himself. The surgeon drained his drink.

"You think you've the stomach for it?"

Gustavus raised the jigger of medicine before the pioneer. "Bottom's up." Tilting the man's head back, the doctor poured the narcotic slowly into the settler. "Let that work on you while I prepare." Deftly the doctor removed several items. "All right. I'm going to extract the shafts, then put an herb poultice in the wound, a little trick I learned from the Indians, and we'll put a bandage on there to keep it in place. Now, I want you to think about your daughter and, oh, what's in my left hand?" As the man looked up to where Murphy lifted his empty left hand, the doctor abruptly yanked the shaft out with his right side, swiftly stuffed the poultice in the wound, and applied the bandage. Pressing down on the bandage, he said, "There. Not so bad. Only four more."

By the time the last arrow was extracted, the pioneer was drained and rumpled. Murphy administered another dose of his formula to the man. The pioneer corralled his energy and spoke, "I have something of value in this wagon, a small wooden box. Inside the cedar hope chest."

"All right, then… I'll fetch it."

Murphy climbed into the covered wagon and, rummaging through the hope chest, found a small wooden box under some clothes. He extracted it, a linen tablecloth, and a fresh shirt for the man before emerging from the wagon. The pioneer's pain was beginning to give way to the morphine and opiates in the elixir. His lids became heavy and his movements slowed as if he was moving through the syrup itself.

Murphy tore from the tablecloth a wide strip that he wrapped around the farmer's torso to hold the bandages in place and then helped him into a clean shirt. Murphy sat with the treasure box next to the pioneer, "Now what do we have here?" He slid the clasp open and cracked the lid to discover a number of Carte vistas and letters. The pioneer reached over and removed a Carte vista of a young girl in a white confirmation dress with blonde curls. "My treasure."

"That's your treasure?"

"Yes."

"For where your treasure is, there will your heart be also."

The man smiled, "Thank you, Dr. Mercy."

"Ha! That's good. *Dr. Mercy*. It's Dr. Murphy, actually. But I like that, yes, Dr. Mercy. You may be onto something, there." Murphy tried it on, "Dr. Gustavus Mercy.... Might just have to repaint the wagon."

The pioneer's speech began to slow, "Blessed are the merciful: for they shall obtain mercy."

"Mathew five."

The pioneer smiled again, "You know your scripture."

"My father was something of a preacher... but he wasn't one for mercy. And nor did he obtain it." Gustavus looked off into the distance, but not for Apaches.

Lightning flashed as young Gustavus lay on the bedroll next to his brother. The shanty-like apartment was small, having once been much larger, but the landlord had divided it in order to eek out a few more pennies from the impoverished renters. It was crowded and smelled of damp brick, mildew, and stewed potatoes. But it was home… particularly for Gustavus' younger siblings. Gustavus remembered Ireland, and although times were hard there, it was open and green and smelled of peat and rain, not mildew and garbage and sweat and smoke. This was where he stayed, but it never felt of home.

"Maybe the rain will wash away some of the smell," Gustavus offered his younger brother, Gabriel. Gabriel was thin and boney and coughed a mean chesty cough.

"Gus, I can't sleep. Every time I start to drift off…" As if to complete his sentence, a coughing jag rudely interrupted him. When it finally played itself out, Gabe sighed, "I'm so tired."

"Hang on. Jess gave me some flowers. She said they use this in Africa to stop a cough." Gustavus hopped off the mat on the floor and retrieved something from the pocket of his jacket. Unrolling a handkerchief, Gustavus offered his brother a wad of crunched up petals. "Here. Chew it. It'll help. I think."

Gabriel took the chaw and, coughing, stuffed it in his mouth. He chewed the wad slowly. "Ugh! It's bitter!"

As Gabriel chewed, "Well?"

"Tastes horrible."

"Yeah, well, she didn't say it would taste good. She said it would help."

"Aww, it's awful." He coughed. "How long till it works?"

"Dunno. She didn't say."

Before the herbs could even begin their work, the door swung open with a crash as a stocky-framed man stood in the door, silhouetted by flashing lightning. It startled the boys, not so much from the suddenness of his entrance, but because their father was on another bender. "Get me some food, Goddamit!"

The boys slept on the kitchen floor, so any hope of rest was gone until the storm of their inebriated Pa had passed. As he stumbled into the small space, he kicked Gabriel, lying on the floor. "Why d'you always have to be in the way?!" Gabe coughed. "Ah, don't over-react, I barely tapped ya." Gabe couldn't stop coughing. His face turned red. "You want something to complain about? I'll give you something to complain about!" His father bent over and grabbed Gabriel by his nightshirt, lifting him off the floor. Gabriel's coughing had triggered something deep in his lungs which was clawing to get out and he coughed even harder. "You gonna listen to me, boy? I told you to shut up!" Gabriel hung like a doll from his father's hand, sounding like he might hack up a lung. "Where's me food!"

Gustavus stood up, "He's got a cough, Da. Cant' ye see? He can't help it!"

Just then their mother flew in from the bedroom holding a baby of several months. "No, Gustavus!" She jumped between them, turning quickly from her son to her husband, "It's all right. Let me get you some food." Three other children drifted in from the bedroom, following her wake. She was a small-framed woman whose former beauty was all but eclipsed by the struggle of looking after her expanding family in ever-hardening times.

"Gustavus, take Gabe into the bedroom."

"Hell no! After I eat, I sleep. In my bed. I don't want 'em—"

A savage cough overcame Gabriel who trembled and contorted under its control.

"I told you to shut it!" Suddenly and ferociously, a huge right hand smashed Gabe in his chest, knocking him to the floor.

Quick as a flash of lightning he was over Gabe with his fist raised again. "You listen to me when I tell you—"

And just as quick, Gabe's mother, still clutching the baby, was between the fist and its mark. "I'll get ya some food! Just sit down!" The mother's fierce intent to protect her child pierced his muddied outrage. She repeated herself in a more soothing tone. "Sit down..."

Gustavus carefully moved to his prostrate brother, pulled him onto his mattress, and dragged it with his brother to the far corner of the room as far away from their volatile father as possible. As Gustavus dragged the mattress across the small space, he saw Gabe cough up a mouth full of blood. "Shhhh... you'll be okay." He positioned Gabe so his parents couldn't see it. The last thing he needed was for his father to come unhinged about Gabe ruining the bed mat with blood. Besides, Gustavus had been at the receiving end of his father's wrath before and had seen much worse. "Gabe, you've got to be quiet." Gabe continued to cough, but the cough's stranglehold had been broken. Gustavus was glad that it seemed quiet enough to not upset his Da.

In short order Ma moved the towering rage of inebriation into the bedroom and Gustavus retrieved the other bed mat, placed it next to his brother, and tried to go to sleep.

Coughing awoke him as Gabe hacked and sputtered. Between coughs he murmured, "Gus...? Gus..?"

"Shh! Shhhh! Don't wake him. There'll be hell to pay."

"Gus, I don't feel right.... I don't..."

His brother coughed, urgently, then immediately stifled it. His breathing had a troubling wheeze in it, and the breaths became fewer and farther between. "You'll be okay, Gabe. All right? You'll be okay."

Gabriel's hand tightened on Gustavus'. Gabe mumbled something, then drew in a sharp breath.

"Mama…?"

Then his body relaxed and the struggle within was set free.

In the filtered moonlight, which shone through the grimy kitchen windows, Gustavus saw a surrender, a letting go. Peace settled over his brother like something tangible. It seemed delicate and yet vast in the way that silence can contain all sound. When the sound and fury stops, the silence abides. Gabriel seemed beautiful, finally at rest. Gustavus was pleased his brother was lying easy now. And yet he was terrified that any more noise would awaken the wrath of his father. He pressed close to Gabriel. He clung to him for refuge, hoping that some of the contentment he saw in his brother's face might rub off on him, hoping that in the morning it would all be some bad dream which would fade as soon as he stirred. Pushing away the tears, he closed his eyes hard and held his brother tight, not allowing his thoughts to turn one way or another. In this twilight of fear and embrace, by degrees, exhaustion crept in, until he was asleep.

In the morning, Gustavus found himself clinging to a cold body. As he pulled away from it in confusion, he saw his brother's half-lidded vacant eyes focusing into the middle of nothing. He saw his death stare. Gustavus jumped back. The comfort he had found in the night now gave way to disbelief, horror— to the cold, hard realization that his brother was dead. He had failed to protect him, if he could have done something to stop the flu in his lungs, to have stopped his father, to have – he didn't know what – but if he had known it, and had done it, his brother wouldn't be dead.

Then, in an unconscious defense against crushing guilt, his mind turned, suddenly kicking into morbid curiosity. *So, this is what a dead body looks like?* He puzzled that the body looked like Gabriel but without his animating force. It reminded him of the statues in the Catholic Church, life-like but devoid of life. He reached out to touch his brother. The skin was cold, firm. Then without warning, an avalanche of emotion overcame him and he burst out sobbing. Between sobs, he implored Gabriel's forgiveness, as "I'm so sorry," poured from his lips over and over again. A new emotional wave broke over him, the need for his mother, and he ran, howling, into the bedroom, "He's gone! He's gone. Mama, Gabe's gone."

His mother sprang up from the bed, "What, child? What are you saying?" Gustavus tried to speak, but could only muster sharp intakes of breath, followed by sobs. His sister, Annie, and youngest brother, Timmy, woke from the floor next to the bed as Gustavus managed to point to the other room. They swept out of the bedroom, leaving Gustavus who stood looking at his father lying in bed.

"Jesus, what a racket," he groaned as he rolled over and covered his head. Rage filled the boy's nine-year-old frame until a scream emanated from him like a boiling kettle whistling on a red-hot stove.

Gustavus' father slammed the covers back, "What the hell?!" Enraged at being rudely awoken, he rose toward Gustavus, but a strange sound stopped him cold. It was a sound one hundred times more arresting than Gustavus' scream, more harrowing than the cry of the amputee in Dr. Ruff's surgery having his leg removed. It was the sound of a mother having part of her soul ripped out.

Trying to fathom why his wife might make such a sound, his father stood motionless, brows furrowed, mind racing. He then moved past Gustavus and into the kitchen where his wife cradled her dead son, rocking him back and forth and weeping. The little ones, infected by the palpable emotion in the air, had also taken to sobbing. Gustavus stood quietly in the bedroom doorway, observing his family as if through an inverted looking-glass. Time seemed to have vanished for him. His father stood transfixed at the scene. Moments passed, maybe hours. At last, his father hung his head and walked into the bedroom. A few moments later he emerged, pulled on his jacket, and left without a word.

꧁◆꧂

Gustavus looked at the pioneer. "He was a piece o' work, my father. Didn't drink another drop after that. Well, for a time." Gustavus paused at the sound of a hawk nearby. He scanned the horizon, to no avail. "It's going to be getting dark soon. I don't think the Apache's will be back. There's nothing left for them, but there's plenty for me. I'll stoke the fire in that smoking wagon. You'll be wanting the warmth when the sun goes down." He looked out beyond a northwestern ridge, at the darkening clouds that loomed in the distance. "Just hope it doesn't rain."

Gustavus got the smoldering wagon to heat back up to a flame, pulled blankets out of his wagon and made two beds by the fire as the sun hid in the west and darkness fell heavy on the land.

In the glow of the fire, Gustavus finished giving the settler a few bites of his food. "You don't want to eat too much. You'd be likely to throw up which won't help. I'm surprised the Apache didn't take more. Some good provisions. Shame they didn't get to enjoy them."

"They were good peop—"

"No, no. Save your breath. Not interested in the dead. I'm only fascinated in the dying."

"I brought my family here. Thought we could make a better life. It's all my fault." His bottom lip quivered and he moaned as he turned his face from the fire toward the darkness. It was clear that he was a stalwart man, unaccustomed to emotions. The moan, although quiet, reminded Gustavus of the sound his mother had made when Gabriel died. It shared the same helplessness. "It's all my fault," the farmer accepted. Then he began to cry, quietly, to himself. Gustavus let him mourn and finished his meal to the crackling sound of the wagon burning and the occasional lament of choices made.

After a spell, Gustavus spoke, "It's time. More medicine." Gustavus reached over and produced a small red box from his doctor's bag. "I know something of guilt. It's partly why I became a doctor." The doctor looked deeply in the fire. "And now I have some doctoring to do with you." He removed a leather pouch from the box. Unrolling the pouch, he removed a glass and stainless steel item.

"Look at this. With one of these I can put medicine right into your blood. A lot of doctors think it's better to place medicine into the flesh, subcutaneous, they call it. I discovered that by introducing it to the blood you won't even have to wait but a minute for it to take effect. An Irishman invented it. With this clever little device, I'll be introducing chloral hydrate to your corpus, which will remove all anxiety, and immobilize your body. You may feel a little pinch, but nothing compared to being shot up with arrows. Now, sometimes, a patient can have an adverse reaction, so I'm just going to put this necktie around your hands to stop you from hurting yourself should such a reaction occur." Gustavus tied a necktie around the pioneer's wrist, wrapped it under his lower back and then tied it again around his other wrist. The pioneer was too weak to do anything but allow it. "Now, as we wait for my elixir to take effect, I'll tell ye a little story about guilt."

"Not long after Gabriel's wake, which we couldn't afford – Tammany Hall covered the costs in a bid for our votes – my father tripped over the Lord and fell off the wagon again. It might've been guilt that tripped him, but then, it might've just been habit. He came in carrying half a bottle of whiskey. My Ma was furious at him for spending money on his drink. I came to the kitchen door as she stood there holding the baby and unleashing on him. He turned away, but not out of shame, he was winding up his backhand, which he unhinged with crushing fury to her jaw. He lifted her up off the ground and over the little table, clearing her good dishes stacked there. God, she loved those dishes. And they were flying across the room: her, the baby, and the dishes. They all seemed to hang in the air for a moment as Ma clawed through the room toward the baby when the dishes landed and broke into hundreds of tiny pieces. The baby was screaming at the top of its lungs as Ma gathered her up and cradled her tightly in her arms. My restraint shattered like the dishes. Rage consumed me. I'd never challenged— never dreamed of challenging my father – who wasn't just tough as nails, he was tougher than the hammer that drove them. But here was the man who'd killed his own son and not said a word about it, a supposed man of God, backhanding my mother, knocking his youngest from her arms. My hand found the nearest thing, a large wooden potato masher. There was a leather thong threaded through a hole at the end of the handle. I charged my father. He straightened up to see me coming and laughed. Right up to the point that I swung the hammer of the potato masher at him. As I was holding it by the leather strap, it created a whip-like snap of the masher, landing flat across his forehead with a mighty crack! He fell like a tree. My improvised hammer was tougher than his nails. He wasn't laughing anymore. For a moment, David stood over Goliath, shocked. The giant rolled on the floor moaning and chuckling, "Good one, boy-o.

Just you wait." And waiting we were not. I ushered my mother to the door. "But your father… I think he's hurt." She wanted to help him. I couldn't believe my fucking ears! "Get the others and get out! You know as soon as he's up, it'll be bad."

"But, he's hurt."

"You just buried one child. You want to bury another?" That seemed to sober her up to the imminent danger she and her children were in. "You know where to go. I'll be right there."

The Beaumonts were a Negro family that had one of the first-floor apartments. They were reliable and dependable. We'd hidden there before. My mother ushered my brothers and sisters into the hall and paused at the door, looking with concern at the man on the floor, slouched up against the hutch, who just hit her in the face with all his might. Disbelieving how she might muster any sympathy for this man, I said sternly, "Go!"

"He doesn't mean it. Don't hurt him!"

"Go!" I screamed, and she shepherded the little ones away.

I turned and stood in the door, still wielding my potato masher-hammer. My father's head swiveled loosely as his eyes found me. He slurred, "I guess it's a right of passage. Every boy has to take on his old man at some point. Exodus 20, 'Honor thy father….' Hehehe. Ye honored me with a pretty good blow. But it's far from over."

I knew he was right. It wasn't over. But it needed to be.

I turned and closed the door as I went down to the Beaumont's.

I always marveled at the tidiness of the Beaumont's house. I don't think they had any more money than anyone else in our bowery, but their abode seemed as though everything had just been cleaned or freshly painted, or both. I knocked on the door. Mr. Beaumont answered, "Come on in. Come." Mr. Beaumont had already gotten blankets out and Annie and Timmy were making beds in the corner of the front room. I could hear my Ma and Mrs. Beaumont talking in the kitchen, the cooing of the baby, and the clanking of a teapot hitting the stove."

"I hear you done stood up."

For the first time I realized I was still carrying the potato masher. I nodded, but where there might have been pride, there was sadness— sadness that I had to take a weapon in hand to stop my demented father, and a darkness that it was not over. The first shot had sailed over the bow, and I had landed, but I knew he would amass his troops and come at me full force. There would be no truce, no terms of surrender, only the utter annihilation of my hubris for having dared to stand up to him. And he would take sadistic pleasure in every inch of ground he recovered from me.

"Do you think you may have knocked some sense into his noggin?"

"Not likely."

"'Twas brave. Brave deserves a beer."

The Beaumonts were kind and accommodating. I wished we could move in there, and live in their clean and ordered world. Mr. Beaumont and I drank our beers in relative quiet. I didn't talk much as my thoughts kept returning to my father.

I bedded down and listened to the clock ticking on the mantle, the occasional clop-clop of horse hooves and wagon wheels outside and the rhythmic breathing of my remaining family. I knew if the war was to be won, a decisive victory had to be achieved tonight. A second attack, an all-out offensive was my only hope. I lay still until the beating of my heart eclipsed all other sounds. The clock chimed two. I knew it was time. He would be passed out and everyone else should be asleep. I took a spare blanket, rolled it up and fashioned my form as if I were still sleeping. I crept out the door and slowly made my way up the stairs.

The door swung open to our kitchen. The oil in the lamp had burned out, but bright moonlight still filtered through the smoke-stained glass of the kitchen window. He lay right where I left him, snoring, slumped against one of the cupboards shelves that had been knocked off its pegs and was now leaning at an angle. I stepped forward and caught a glint of moonlight in the whiskey bottle he still clutched. And suddenly my battle plan emerged. It was all there, laid out before me.

I went to a hole in the wall behind the washstand where Da hid his drink, as if none of us knew about his stash. Luckily, there was a bottle there. I set it next to him. I figured that if I could bind him to that board, the shelf he was leaning against, there'd be little to nothing he could do. So, I took the tablecloth and gently lifted it, sliding the broken shards of plate quietly to the floor, folded the tablecloth into a strip and lay it on the floor near him. I got two belts from the bedroom and lay them on the floor near his head and feet. I then took that wooden plank he was leaning on, and gently lay it and him down on the tablecloth and belts. He snorted but continued to snore. The board with him on it was now laying over the tablecloth and belts. I then tied the tablecloth around his arms, trapping them and did the same around his head and above his knees with the belts. I tightened them. He sputtered but continued to sleep. I was pretty sure he wouldn't be able to move, but I put the cast iron skillet and a long kitchen knife in reach, in case. I took the bottle of whiskey, popped the cork, and kneeled next to his face. I hesitated. There would be no going back from this. But I'd crossed the Rubicon earlier when I challenged him. The only way forward was through. His mouth was slack and open as he snored. I took the bottle in one hand and the potato masher in the other, then pushed the handle of the potato masher sideways across his mouth, so he couldn't close it. He stirred as I up-ended the bottle and poured it all down his throat. He began to cough and gag as the whiskey invaded his windpipe. Suddenly awake and wild-eyed, he didn't understand why he was so immobilized as I jumped on his chest and got right in his face.

"You were right, Da, it's not over. I can't let you live, cause you'd never it let go. You come home spouting scripture about the devil and the sinners we are, and then you beat yer own son to death for what?! Having a cough!?"

"Emy beak! Emy beak!"

I put the bottle down and picked up the knife. He was wily and I needed to be ready for any trickery. I pulled the masher out of his mouth.

Coughing he said, "Let me speak… Yes. I laid my hand to Gabriel, but that was the devil working in me."

"That was the booze, Da, and yer meanness. I have a half a mind to give you the tour de metre across your throat, but it can't look like murder.

"Murder?!" He laughed. He was impressed, but not frightened. "You're going to murder me now, are ye?"

"I should have done it sooner, before you killed Gabriel."

"I didn't mean for him to die. The Lord, Gustavus, the Lord works in mysterious ways. "

"The Lord?!! It was YOU! You killed him! And I was so paralyzed with fear… that I let you."

He tried to protest but as he opened his mouth I shoved the masher handle back across it. "No. It wasn't the Lord, it was you. Just as it's not the Lord who is going to kill you tonight. It's me. Papa. Me." And I turned the second bottle up so it all poured out into his mouth. He began to cough and sputter, and as it was too much –

even for him—he began to throw up. Dropping the masher, I grabbed his jaw and with all my might, held his mouth closed and pinched his nose shut as he writhed, choking on his own vomit. It only took a couple of minutes. When the bucking stopped, all that was left was stillness and the putrid smell of his puke. I checked his pulse as Dr. Ruff had taught me.

Gone.

I stood up and looked at the miserable, drunken figure that had so terrorized me and my family and I felt a surge of power. He could never touch me, he would never, ever, harm us again. I stood over him, basking in my newfound strength.

I went to the pitcher and ewer and washed my hands. I was clean. I was free.

It was time to tidy up the scene. I loosed the belts and untied the tablecloth. I put the bottle in his hand. As I rolled him off the board and tossed the tablecloth back to where it had been, he looked like what he was, a drunk who had had too much, passed out, and choked on his own puke.

ꕥ◆ꕥ

"It brought me satisfaction, knowing that he had died struggling, painfully choking on his own vitriol. That was my first."

"Your… first?"

"No one else knows, except people like you, but they're gone now, so it's our little secret."

The pioneer's head lulled in the direction of Murphy. The drugs were taking their effect. "You should… Forgive… yer father."

"Ha! There's more chance of me finding a leprechaun at the foot of a rainbow."

"God … forgives."

"How nice for him. But you see, my father sort of turned me against God. The more I read the Good Book, the more I saw its contradictions. There is no balm in Gilead."

"God works… Mysterious ways."

"That's what he said."

"In this… wilderness… person found me… a doctor." The pioneer smiled at his good fortune, "God's hand."

Gustavus laughed long and hard. He crouched down so that his face was right next to the pioneer's and whispered. "Then God is a cruel bastard after all. The thief comes for you tonight, and I am that thief."

The pioneer made a sound as if to say, "What?" But he slurred as the drugs overcame him.

"I told you before, I'm not interested in the dead. I am, however, fascinated by dying. And tonight, we're going to explore *your* dying." The doctor moved right to the man's ear. "The Good Lord's not taking yer life tonight… *I am.*"

The pioneer's eyes grew wide, his mind raced. He began to struggle, but his hands were tethered and he could only manage to rock from side to side.

"There. There. I learned pretty quickly that even with a heavy dose of sedation, once people realize what's going on… Ha! Been punched in the face pretty good!"

In short breaths the pioneer argued, "Bible. 'Shalt...not kill.'"

"And yet, the Lord smote thousands and thousands with famines, massacres, floods, and pillars of fire. He even smote his own tribe, the Israelites. God's a good smiter. I guess I am the instrument of his… smoting? Does that sound right to you?"

"You're … not… God."

"I am tonight. The way my father raged against life, I rage against death. If I can control it, beat it at its own game, I can vanquish it. Or, maybe, the fear of it. Because when I take a life, I am amazed at the peace, the letting-go, the final release. Almost everyone who this thief has taken has been peaceful. Nearly everyone. Except my father. His face was grotesque, twisted, and violent. So it is in life, it is in death. Befitting the vicious arsehole he was. But for you, there may be peace."

"I don't want to die... My daughter"

"Yes, yes. I told you, I'll look after her."

The man's eyes well in fear.

"No! I'm not ready!"

"Well, no one ever is. Yet, everybody wants to go to heaven..."

"Yes..." With the thought of heaven, the pioneer relaxed, and a tear rolled over his strong cheekbone and down his leathery face. "I... long... for it."

"Well, prepare your ticket. The smoke of that approaching train is nearing the station."

"Your soul shall rot..."

"Don't worry about me. I suspect you wouldn't make it another day." Gustavus looked into the fire for several moments and spoke absently. "Truth be told, it's the notion. When the notion enters my brain, it's like a snake. Once it bites, it won't let go. The snake injects my mind with its venom, and the only antidote is to see it through to the end." He turned back to the settler and leaned in close to confess, "I find it ironic that the medical symbol is two snakes intertwining around a staff: one snake, the savior; one the destroyer. The destroyer temps me to do what a doctor shouldn't, and yet, I am powerless under its spell."

The doctor pulled away from the settler and took the jigger and placed a white pill in it. He added some water from the canteen and used the syringe as a stir stick. Drawing the concoction up into the syringe, he announced somewhat formally, "Now this is all in the name of science. I'm fascinated to understand that moment of death – what's on the other side when you cross over? Is it peace that awaits us? Is it a great, vast sea of nothing, or is there something religious, like clouds and angels? This is a cocoa extract found in any number of remedies, but this version is very pure. It's called cocaine. It tends to bring some mental clarity, so I'm hoping it will pull you out of your sedative stupor long enough to share with me what you experience when you pierce the veil. What do you think it will be like, passing over? I like to ask people that because it's a different thing to consider when yer staring down the barrel then when yer thinking about it in the abstract."

The frontiersman had managed to remove a small pen knife from his rear pocket and had cut through the silk tie binding his hands. The numbing effects of the drugs were overcome by the adrenals now coursing in his veins. The pioneer's back arched in protest as the doctor moved the syringe to the man's arm. "Nooooo. Nooo."

The pioneer rolled to his side, grabbed a board sticking out of the fire and swung it at Murphy with all his might.

As the board struck the doctor, fiery cinders sprayed across his face. The syringe flew into the air. From his knees, the pioneer lifted a makeshift club overhead and it came crashing down just as Murphy rolled away. Another shower of embers spewed from the red hot end of the board as Murphy came up with his Derringer pointing at the pioneer.

Defiance was in the pioneer's eyes, but he'd spent his last effort, and he knew it. He slumped back on his knees.

"So, I could shoot you. I could leave you to die from your wounds, or I could offer you a peaceful transition."

"I… have no concern for myself."

"Then there ye have it. Think of science. No one in history has been able to stop someone from dying. But I want to try. Before you can cure a disease, you have to understand it."

Sadness hung on the pioneer, not for his demise, but for the plight he brought his family. "I failed… I failed my brother. I failed my wife. I failed… my daughter."

Gustavus considered the man kneeling before him. "Believe me, I understand your grief. Think of me as Hades ushering you across the River Styx. All I ask is to understand what you experience."

The pioneer slumped further, "I think…. I think…." He fell to his side, depleted.

Dr. Murphy moved him to a more comfortable proximity of the fire's edge. "You gave me quite a start there. Didn't think you had a surge like that in you. Now, need to find that syringe." Murphy took a board from the fire as a torch and searched for the needle. A glint of the stainless steel caught his eye. He wiped the dust off. "Don't suppose a dirty needle will make much difference now."

The doctor got back down so his face was only inches away from the pioneer. He spoke intimately, "Now this will either sharpen your thoughts or kill ye. But please, try to share what's happening."

The pioneer's breathing changed to short quick breaths. "Promise… You'll help my daughter."

"Yes, yes. I told you… I'll keep an eye out."

The pioneer's breaths grew faster.

"Wait… I didn't give you the injection! You can't go now! What are you experiencing? Speak to me. What's it like?"

The pioneer drew in an audible breath, filling his lungs deep.

"What do you see?"

The pioneer exhaled a long slow breath and ceased to breathe. The doctor checked the man's pulse.

Crestfallen, he leaned back from the dead man. "Damn it," he sighed. He regarded the man lying next to him. "There it is. Eternal peace." He stood up and looked at the man with a tenderness with which a parent regards a sleeping child. He then drew his blankets next to the pioneer. "I'll just lie here with you for a while, 'til you're cold," and he cradled the pioneer 'till the flames of the fire died to embers.

The bright morning light climbed over the hills as Gustavus woke up. Smoke still curled from smoldering bits of the burned wagon where the pioneer lay. Gustavus went to his own wagon, removed his camera and proceeded to set it up. He took his time getting the contraption assembled until finally there was a loud pop and a small cloud of smoke and a picture captured the pioneer, forever memorializing that moment in time. Then he closed the pioneer's eyes, which stared straight up at the bluing sky. He broke down his photo equipment and loaded it back into his wagon.

Dr. Murphy dragged the pioneer over to where the other dead settlers lay. A raven cawed and took off. A buzzard flew up but quickly descended back down to its meal.

"I'm sorry I don't have the inclination to draw an earth bath for all of you, that's too much digging. You'll have to be content with joining the natural cycle of things as the coyotes, buzzards, and other critters make a meal of you."

Having gone through the belongings of the pioneers and removed anything of value or use and loaded it into his own wagon, Gustavus set back out on the trail, keeping a look out for Apaches. He hadn't gone far when he saw a figure in the distance on the road. Gustavus removed his revolver and checked the Derringer in his belt. "Whoa." Pulling the horses to a stop, he slid his looking glass open and was shocked at what he saw. "Well, I'll be…" He scanned the horizon with the glass, then snapped the reigns and continued.

In short order, he approached a girl in what had been a lovely pale blue dress. Her face was streaked with dirt and her blonde curls were tangled and wild.

Gustavus reached into the pocket of his waistcoat and removed the Carte vista given to him by the pioneer. The picture was of the same girl, but younger, innocent, untroubled. The girl before him had feral eyes and looked as though she might either claw him to pieces or turn and run away.

"Rebecca?" Rather than being reassuring, hearing her name made her suspicious.

"How do you know…?"

"I found your father and before he died, he asked me to find you." Gustavus extended the photo toward her.

"So, he's…?"

Gustavus nodded. "You could say he's found peace."

The girl stumbled sideways as though something had slammed into her.

"Allow me to introduce myself, I am Doctor Gustavus Murphy— medical practitioner, salesman of fine elixirs and remedies, entertainer, and bon vivant." He reached out, extending a hand to help the girl up onto the wagon. She reached out her hand reflexively, but then withdrew it.

"It's all right. You can trust me. I'm a doctor."

About David Beeler

David Beeler was born and raised in Kerrville, Texas. He is a classically trained actor, having attended the Royal Central School of Speech & Drama in London, which he funded by writing and producing plays in Texas. David lived in the UK for a decade, primarily as a theatre actor. *Booth*, a one man show written and performed by David, won a *Fringe 1st* award at the Edinburgh Festival, as did an ensemble piece about John Wilkes Booth, entitled, *Our Brutus,* which was also nominated for the Independent Theatre Award. *Our Brutus* transferred to London and landed David a writing commission from a West End Producer, as well as his first writing agent.

On moving to sunny LA, David's script based on Glen Miller was short-listed for development by American Zoetrope. David joined the sketch comedy troupe, Lester McFwap, which had a TV pilot green-lit, while also co-writing with his comedy duo *Dave & Tom* with Tom Konkle.

In addition to being a writer and actor, he is an award winning photographer, videographer, and producer, and he also enjoys building furniture and architecture. However, David considers his greatest achievement to be his co-productions with his wife – their two sons, Chayim "Kai" and Ryder.

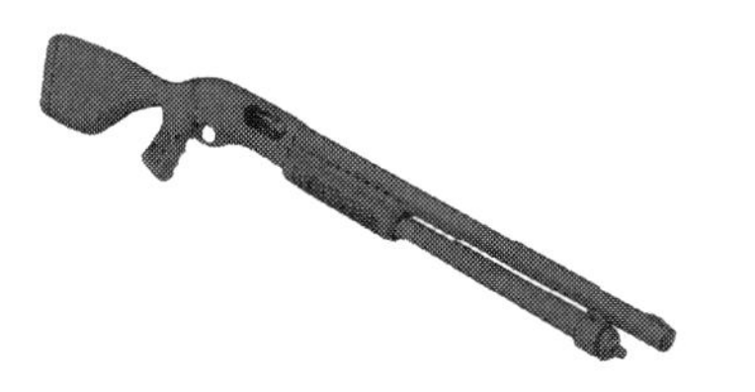

LAST NIGHT IN QUARTZSITE

by Casey Mensing

Shawna wasn't surprised Tommy kept pressing her to go home with him. She enjoyed knowing how badly he wanted her. Having him half-mad with lust would make everything go smoother. The promise of satisfaction delivered without innuendo. "Mind-blowing sex like you've never experienced in your life" as soon as the job was done and they were on their way to L.A. Her words. Her promise.

Tommy was a young coyote, yipping and snarling at the scent of her. The way she filled out her tight tank top; she was calling to him, titillating his imagination with her siren song. If only Tommy had paid attention in English class when they were studying Greek Mythology. Tommy tried to play it cool, focusing on the tattoos along her arms. A rose with a thorn-strewn stem. A tear-shaped drop of blood hung from the pointed tip of each thorn. But Tommy chose to comment on the phrase, *You have to die a few times before you can really live,* which appeared on the inside of Shawna's left forearm.

Shawna quickly realized it was going to take even less effort than she thought to lure Tommy into her plot. She was surprised he commented on the Bukowski quote on her forearm. She wasn't surprised Tommy had no idea who Charles Bukowski was. Usually, it was the images that caught the male gaze. She knew it was his way of playing it cool, pretending he wasn't staring at her tits, which she had been pushing in his direction since she'd laid eyes on him three days ago, long before she rolled out her plan to rob the gas station and hit the road to Los Angeles. Tonight. Together.

Tommy was desperate to get out of Quartzsite. His daddy had been a drunk until his mom left. Then his dad found Jesus and started scratching out a living in the local gem trade when he wasn't scratching out a living playing the lotto. Meanwhile, all the girls in town were looking for husbands, but Tommy wasn't interested in being tied down. Then he met Shawna last night, and he thought he'd found his perfect woman. Beautiful, wild, and most importantly, passing through to something better than this shit hole had to offer. He hadn't thought too much about when or how he would leave town before then, just that he would. But for the rest of the day he could hardly think of anything else, which was just the way she wanted it.

Shawna had Tommy pay for the drinks while she got the car. She wanted to hit the gas station that night because the weekend cash would still be in the safe. Plus, she reminded him as soon as they pulled off the job they could leave town. It was clear to him that she couldn't wait any longer to have her way with him.

With a swagger in his boot, Tommy strolled up to the bar and paid the tab. He had tried to convince Shawna to swing by his place for a quickie, explaining that it would relax them both before they hit the gas station and rolled out of town, but Shawna dismissed the idea.

"Be patient love. Just think how much hotter it will be once the money's in hand, and we're safe."

Shawna knew Tommy wouldn't stop trying to work his way into her pants before she got what she wanted. She had him pay the tab while she got the car just so he would cool off a little. Shawna also wanted to make sure the shotgun and .38 she had in the car were loaded and ready to go. Her plan was to drive them from the bar to the gas station, then out onto the open road, westward bound.

By the time Shawna drove them over to the gas station on the outskirts of Quartzsite, Tommy was rearing like a young buck, hopped up and ready to go. He jumped out of the black Mustang as soon as she got it parked, clutching his gun tightly. He was ready to rush in, grab the cash, and flee. Easy breezy. Tommy burst in through the double glass doors while Shawna hung a few steps back with the shotgun. The place was empty except for the cashier.

Shawna let Tommy take the lead figuring it would be more intimidating to see him come rushing in than her, standing all of 5'2", even if she was wheeling a shotgun. Unbeknownst to Tommy, Shawna knew right where the security cameras were and exactly where the blind spot was, so to anyone who happened to look back at the recording, it would look like Tommy was flying solo. Tommy had his pistol trained on the face of the dead man behind the counter, but all he could think about was making Shawna keep her promise afterward.

Anton wasn't in the mood for this shit. He'd grown tired of living the vampire life working the graveyard shift at the gas station. He'd come out to Quartzsite six months ago to hide out for a time and try and forget his past. And he was doing a pretty good job of it, too, except for the occasional reminder of that redneck hiding in that bunker outside town that's got about twenty grand that used to be Anton's, but he'd get his in due time. This morning Anton had been told he needed to find a new place to live because his landlord was coming back to town and he wanted his trailer back. Anton didn't have a lease, so he was shit out of luck. He also got a call from his brother that his estranged wife was looking for him. His brother had promised that he hadn't told her where he was, but he knew she'd find him, eventually.

Shawna held the single barrel shotgun like an extension of herself. Calm and experienced after hours spent blasting buckshot into the hills back home. This did not go unnoticed by Anton.

Tommy white-knuckled the .38. He had his finger on the trigger, but his thumb was nowhere near the hammer. Tommy knew he had to take total control. Make the cashier piss himself in fear, turn Shawna on, and make off with the cash without a shot fired. Maybe pistol-whip the cashier if he had to. Whatever got the job done.

"Alright, asshole. Everything from the register, the safe, and that March of Dimes box into this bag."

It was clear to Anton that Tommy had no intention of using the gun. He also knew the brunette in the black hoodie and faded jeans with the red-lipped smirk was in charge. Tommy continued to bark orders, but Anton kept his focus on the shotgun-wielding woman who was clearly aware of the security camera's blind spot.

The roughneck no fear attitude Tommy flexed surprised Shawna. He talked tough on the way to the gas station, but she thought he'd lose his nerve once they entered. She didn't realize how wrong she had been.

Tommy tossed a canvas bag awkwardly onto the counter with his left hand. "I'm not fucking around, man! Pop that register before I pop you!" Tommy kept the pistol steadily pointed at Anton as he moved around behind the counter filling the sack with the cash from the drawer and the March of Dimes box.

"Didn't I say the register, the safe, *then* the box?"

"You did. But seeing as how the box is next to the register and the safe is behind me, I thought I'd save you two some time by not backtracking. But if you want to hang around a little longer I can make some coffee. It's up to you."

"I could end you like that, smart ass!" Tommy shouted at Anton. Tommy moved toward the counter, lining up the barrel with Anton's right eye. "Now get the fucking money and keep your mouth shut!"

Shawna worried that Tommy would go too far, and they'd end up with a sack of blood-stained bills for their trouble.

Anton eyed his aggressor, then calmly snatched the sack off the counter. He was hesitant to turn his back on Tommy and the girl. He was confident he was safe from catching a bullet, at least until the safe was opened. But as soon as that door opened and the cash went in the sack, it was anyone's guess how this might play out.

I hope he doesn't pull a gun out of the safe Shawna thought to herself as she clasped the shotgun tight. The way Tommy was pushing and threatening made her nervous. She figured Anton to be the type to put a bullet in Tommy even if it meant taking one himself. He was the type to say something stupid like, "It's the principle of the matter."

Tommy just wanted it to end. He wanted the money, the girl, and a new life in L.A. Everything he'd been promised in the last few hours that he'd been waiting for his entire life. He'd kill for it if he had to, but he didn't want it to come to that. Disappearing after an armed robbery was a whole different thing than dodging a murder charge.

Anton wanted to shoot Tommy in the face. He wanted nothing more than to watch his head explode all over the bags of Hot Cheetos he had shelved a little over an hour ago. Unfortunately, he didn't have a gun stashed in the safe or anywhere else behind the counter. So, he calmly put the cash from the safe on top of the register money and the March of Dimes collection. He thought it was pretty shitty to demand the March of Dimes collection. Only a real bastard stole from expecting mothers and babies.

Shawna sighed with relief when Anton tossed the bag on the counter without any trouble, but she still worried about Tommy. Now that he had the cash in hand he might decide to put a few bullets in the cashier. She wasn't prepared to do time on account of someone else's megalomania.

"Get out from behind the counter." She couldn't believe the words were spilling from her mouth.

Tommy turned to her, in shock. "What the fuck are you doing?"

Fuck me, Anton thought to himself.

"He's coming with us," Shawna demanded, though no one was more surprised than her.

Shawna was out the door first, shotgun by her side. Tommy pushed Anton out in front of him by jamming the barrel of his gun into Anton's back. The three moved conspicuously toward the black Mustang out front. Shawna opened the driver's side door, pulled the seat forward and nodded for Anton to climb in. Anton hesitated, just long enough to make eye contact with her for the first time, just close enough to smell the essence of citrus and cigarettes on her breath.

Tommy's pistol poked him hard in his kidney and Anton climbed in behind the driver's side. Shawna and Tommy got in the front seat, Shawna behind the wheel, and the car pulled out onto the highway heading west.

Tommy was anxious. His fevered mind was consumed with the dirty promises Shawna had made hours before. But he couldn't for the life of him figure out why Shawna had decided to bring this guy along for the ride. *Maybe she wanted to kill him? Maybe she got off on that?* Right now only one thing was for sure: they had to get rid of their new passenger before anything was gonna happen with her.

"Come on, baby, let's dump this guy out in the desert and find somewhere to go. I want you so bad," Tommy pleaded.

"You'll get what you want. Be patient." She gave him that lustful look of hers, all doe-eyes and soft lips. "I promise it will be worth it."

Anton admired the way Shawna carried herself. The calm, no bullshit way she controlled the situation. The sexy way she kept that moron next to her in check. It was a turn-on, for sure.

"Where are you taking me?"

"Shut up!" Tommy was torn up with lust. His hand roamed up Shawna's leg, but each time it neared the warm part between her thighs Shawna forcibly removed it. She was growing tired of being pawed at, but she knew they weren't done yet, so she refrained from smacking him on the nose the way one would a misbehaving dog, however intense her urge.

Tommy grew angry. He and Shawna should be in a motel somewhere, not escorting this smug asshole in the back seat to God knows where. They'd have to kill him. Every minute that passed bore the thought even further in his brain. Or maybe Shawna was even more twisted then he thought. *Maybe she wanted to torture the poor bastard*. When it came right down to it, he really didn't know anything about this woman, or what she was capable of. All he had really thought about was that she was hot and that he wanted to screw her. He took Shawna's hand off the gear shift and placed it on the growing bulge in his pants. If he wasn't getting anywhere pawing at her, he decided he'd play it another way.

"Not now, hon," Shawna replied, giving him a toying squeeze before removing her hand. Shawna used her playful, flirty voice. The one she used the entire time they were at the bar to lure Tommy into this situation. Right now, she needed to keep him calm and obedient. She worried about Tommy's aggression. She always went for the hotheads.

Anton began to worry that Shawna might lose her hold on Tommy. The kid was unpredictable, that was certain. He wished that the pistol Tommy had in the waistband of his jeans would discharge and blow his manhood clean off. It'd serve him right. All in due time, he thought. Surely it wouldn't be too difficult to convince Shawna that the best thing for everybody would be to put a bullet in Tommy's head and end his suffering once and for all.

Tommy grew distant in the front seat. The uncertainty weighed heavily on him. He was never one to have patience. When he was a kid they gave him Ritalin to calm him down. But as he grew up he realized ADHD wasn't his problem, it was that he felt trapped in Quartzsite and he never felt alive. *Life was for living, not existing* was his favorite motto. Now was his chance to truly finally live, and yet something, or more to the point, someone was in his way.

Shawna could sense Tommy's growing agitation. He had stopped molesting her, or even speaking. Earlier in the night he was full of nervous jokes and flirty eyes. Now he was staring out of the passenger's side window as malevolence slowly crept over his face.

"It's okay, baby."

"You lied to me," Tommy seethed, breaking his silence.

"I didn't lie," Shawna cooed.

"No. You lied. I did everything you asked. We got the money. We're on the road. And I don't know what you're doing with him, but I'm over it."

"Insurance."

"What?"

"If we left him at the station he would have called the cops the second we drove off. Then we'd have state troopers all over us. Do you think they're gonna pull us over and play nice? This is Arizona. They'll shoot us dead before we even get out of the car."

Tommy looked at her, a dumb expression across his face.

"And we couldn't kill him and leave him at the station. Do you really want to add a murder charge to your resume? At your age? Cause I sure as hell don't. So he stays with us until we cross the state line, then we drop him off in the desert. Alive."

"This was not part of the plan," Tommy whined. "And what's to stop him from ratting us out later?"

"By the time he makes it to anywhere with a phone, we'll be long gone. And who really cares about some gas station in the sticks anyway? Shawna looked back at Anton and flashed him a beauty queen smile. "No offense."

"None taken," Anton replied. He let out a sigh and lay back in the seat as he wished for a cigarette, even though he gave them up years ago, when he noticed the car was decelerating.

"What the hell's going on? Why are we slowing down?" Tommy screamed, accusingly. Shawna and Anton glanced at one another, but neither answered.

Shawna forced the car over onto the side of the highway. The car came to a complete stop and shut off.

"Shit," Anton mumbled to himself.

"Why did the car stop? What are you doing?" Tommy asked incredulously.

"Did you put gas in it like I told you?" Shawna asked in a tone usually reserved for children.

Anton smirked.

"Are you serious? We're out of gas? You never told me to put gas in the car."

"Maybe if you listened to me instead of staring at my tits all night you would've remembered."

Anton couldn't help but laugh.

"Shut the fuck up! Next time you laugh I'm going to shove this gun into your mouth and fire every last bullet into your head."

Anton stopped laughing.

Tommy looked around in horror. They were surrounded by an all-consuming darkness. He turned to Shawna for answers.

"Well… What do we do?"

Shawna popped the door open while the other two exchanged looks.

The trio climbed out of the car and surveyed their surroundings. Nothing but cold, dry desert. "What do we do?" Tommy reiterated.

"Gimme a sec." Shawna snapped, agitated.

"We don't have time for this!" Tommy barked. "Let's just take him out in the desert and put a bullet in him, then try and hitch a ride."

"There's nothing around here. And who knows how long it'll be before another car comes by."

Anton got up on top of the trunk and looked around.

"Get down!" Tommy shouted as he waved his gun at him.

"Look over there. Looks like a house." Anton said, coolly ignoring Tommy's threat.

Shawna and Tommy looked in the direction Anton pointed.

"Maybe we should check it out," Shawna suggested.

"Yeah, alright." Tommy conceded.

Anton climbed down from the car and nodded at Shawna.

"Grab the shotgun and keep it on him," Tommy said to Shawna. Shawna followed his orders. She knew it made the young buck feel good to be in charge. The three of them crossed the highway into the scrub brush, rock, and darkness.

"Stay in front," Tommy demanded. "Try to run and I'll put a bullet in your back."

"And they say chivalry's dead," Anton quipped.

Shawna bit her tongue as Tommy tripped and quickly skipped to play it off.

After a little under a mile of silent marching, the three reached the dark house. There was no sign of life, no cars parked out front, only the paint chipped Buick behind the closed door of the detached garage.

Shawna tiptoed around the side of the house. All the windows were dark, nothing but silence inside and out. Even her footsteps along the sun-baked dirt didn't make a sound. Shawna neared the back of the house when she saw the light of a television flickering through the blinds in the window. She took a deep breath, turned around, and tiptoed back to the front of the house where Tommy held Anton at gunpoint.

"All good," Shawna reported.

Tommy nodded, eagerly, as he pushed Anton toward the front door. Anton looked at them, suspiciously.

"Are you sure this is a good idea?" Anton pleaded.

Feeling his resistance, Tommy shirked him off onto Shawna.

"Make sure he doesn't take off."

Shawna trained her shotgun on Anton while Tommy marched up the front steps. He quietly tried the door, the handle turned and it opened. Tommy stepped cautiously inside the house and motioned for the others to follow.

The front room was dark as they entered. Instinctively, Anton wanted to flick on the light and make sense of the place, but the sound of the TV coming from the back of the house froze him. He looked at the others to see if they heard it.

Shawna sensed doom. The house began to vibrate with fear and anticipation. She wondered if her entire plan hadn't just been a massive misjudgment which was about to collapse on top of them like a giant house of cards. She had played out all the angles in her mind as she had walked around the house. She felt confident she'd covered all the bases, but right now that moment of self-assurance felt far away. In its place was a layer of sweat and goosebumps that did nothing to cool her burning nerves.

"We should get out of here," Anton warned.

Tommy was too full of adrenaline and youthful immortality to heed him. He marched from the darkness of the front foyer into the hallway, toward the faint glow of light.

Despite his strongest reservations, Anton couldn't help but follow. He saw the light of the television coming from the room at the end of the hall. He watched with bated breath as Tommy's hulking silhouette stormed toward the flicker and flash.

Fatalistic curiosity got the best of Shawna, too. She moved in behind them but played it safe by pressing her body against the wall as she braced for impact.

Tommy's eyes were fixed on the light at the end of the hall. His gun was locked and loaded. His white knuckles quivered as they aimed straight ahead when a man appeared in the doorway opposite them, blocking the flickering glow with a heavy load in his hand.

"Drop it!"

A blast of light exploded from the back room like the television burst apart. Tommy caught the discharge in his left shoulder. A second shot missed him completely, sending drywall everywhere. Tommy got off a shot that hit the man cleanly in the gut and he doubled over. Rallying, Tommy charged the man, who rose before they both got another shot off and tumbled helplessly to the ground, where they bled out silently staring at one another.

Anton and Shawna stood motionless. The scent of blood, viscera, and burnt gunpowder filled the house. Shawna held her gun out in precaution as she backed into the foyer and out the front door, nervously checking all around her as she went. Anton stood in wonder debating whether or not to check and see if they were both dead. Realizing they probably were, and that there was nothing he could do for them either way, he turned and casually walked out of the house, closing the front door behind him.

Anton stepped out of the house to meet Shawna who glared at him with a wild-eyed smirk. She had done what she'd set out to do. The gas station robberies. The cash in her trunk. Twenty-odd-grand sacked away somewhere on the property. And the fool she got on camera, the kid who's gonna get pinned for everything not only got himself killed but took out the prick that sent her ex-husband to jail so years ago. Things were finally starting to look up for Ms. Shawna Fuller. She held her shotgun at eye level and aimed it at Anton's chest.

Anton was unarmed and uncertain of how she intended to play this. That smirk. Danger and pleasure. Anton fell for her because of it. Some shithole town in Tennessee. He was only passing through. Shawna was hustling a couple of guys at the bar, offering empty promises in exchange for full drinks. Anton studied everything about her. He was confident he wouldn't be leaving that bar or that town without her. He was right.

"I'm a fair person," Shawna said. "I'll give you a chance to run."

"Run?"

She cocked the barrel and Anton took off. He could feel the gravel scatter beneath his boots as he zig-zagged through the desert like an iguana. Adrenaline surged from fear and arousal. Another of their twisted little games. Only this time Anton was afraid. He had reason to be. He'd left Shawna sleeping in a motel in Miami. Not a word of goodbye, not even a note. He wasn't even sure what compelled him to drive off that morning. Thought he could save her, maybe. Thought he could save himself. He knew unequivocally he still loved her, lusted for her like no one else. Yet there he was, racing through a desert in Arizona as he searched for higher ground to take a stand, once and for all.

Anton tucked himself behind a large cactus to catch his breath. The cold desert air felt like fire on his skin and his lungs ached. He saw the flash over the ridge when suddenly the top of the cactus he was hiding behind exploded, sending chunks of flesh and spines everywhere. Anton got up and rushed toward a group of boulders. The next scattering of buckshot struck the dirt and rock only a few feet behind him. Anton dropped to the ground, pressing himself into the earth as he tried to be as still as possible even though rocks and the spines of jumping Cholla dug into his skin. Everything went quiet. He began to stand when found himself face to face with Shawna's shotgun barrel.

"Bang," Shawna said, her shotgun aimed right between his eyes. "I got you."

"You've always had me," Anton replied.

She dropped her weapon at Anton's feet.

"Then why did you leave?"

Anton looked at the gun, then held out his arms. "We're together now."

Shawna sat down in the dirt next to him. He put his arm around her and they let their bodies fall into one another. The clouds overhead slowly passed, and they embraced under the moon.

"Guess we better get in there and get what we came for," Anton said at long last.

"Do you think it's still there?" Shawna questioned.

"My twenty grand? It better be!" he exclaimed, a wide smirk across his face.

Shawna laughed. It was good to see him riled up again. Maybe this time it would last.

"Where we headed after this, Mr. Fuller?"

"Anywhere you want, Mrs. Fuller. Anywhere but here."

About Casey Mensing

Casey Mensing is a prolific author and screenwriter who has written such imaginative books as *Last Fair Deal*, *The Unimaginable City*, and, *I Am Ahab*, a collection of short stories released in 2018, and a follow-up *Poems and Short Stories* published by East French Press in 2019. His screenplay *Division Street* was an Official Selection of the KinoDrome International Film Festival. Casey currently resides in downtown Los Angeles.

PLASTIC CRAP

by Ethel Lung

Auntie Chu's apartment was burgled. Not a big deal. It was common to have your place robbed every few years if you lived in Taiwan; it happened to everyone. The conversations about your house being burglarized were always super causal:

"Were you home when it happened?

"No."

"That's good."

"Did they take anything valuable?"

"Nope."

"That's awesome!"

Then we high-fived.

We all knew how to safeguard our valuables. Grandma knew not to put money under her mattress but to tape it under her chest of drawers. Mom knew to wear her jewelry 24/7 so the burglar would have to kill her to get their hands on the family gold, and a respectful burglar would never kill a lady. And dad locked his precious plastic model airplanes in the glass cabinet.

Yes, these model airplanes were dad's most valuable items. But unlike grandma's cash and mom's jewelry, they were, in fact, completely worthless. I never could understand why he wasted so much time with each one, only to abandon them to his sacred glass shelving unit in the living room once they were complete.

I remember he would always have to lie on the couch after inhaling too much of the toxic glue he used to create each perfect miniature aircraft. And every few months he would go to the hobby store to see if there were any new releases of P51s, B25s, or F6s. If he got a new one, he would start building it right away, painstakingly putting it together with an X-Acto knife, tweezers, and a tiny paintbrush before passing out on the couch for the rest of the day.

My sister and I always thought they were stupid. He never let us help, and we were never allowed to touch them. We were only allowed to look at them through the locked up glass cabinet.

Whatever! Their stupid tiny wheels fell off all the time anyway. *Stupid airplanes.*

So anyway, instead of giving away cash, jewelry, or my dad's model planes, we let the burglars have semi-valuable items like American VHS tapes, faded jade jewelry, and used leather belts – the ones with polished nickel square buckles with the designer logos on them. These thieves of the night knew their fashion and we knew how to support the burglar industry.

Plus, we knew the burglar's system. Dad's friend told us they would go up to the rooftops so they could hop down to the top floor balcony, slide open the unlocked glass door and collect their VHS's and belts. Once they were done, they'd climb back up to the rooftop and jump to a neighboring rooftop or just descend into their next victims' balcony. These hooligans always struck either at the witching hour when a bear attack couldn't wake you or right after you left for work. This ensured that they'd have sufficient time to leisurely sieve through your drawers and closets. I always imagined them dressed in color block jumpsuits and dope high tops like The Reebok Pump, galloping like cheetahs through the city, or like Brazilian parkour geniuses. They'd have sacks filled with stolen treasures on their backs, hundred dollar bills flying into the dark sky as they leaped through the air. I've been told I have a vivid imagination.

But all that changed with the burglary of Auntie Chu's apartment. They didn't take anything – high five – nothing at all, but the giant, steamy twist was that the robber left a substantial pile of shit in the middle of the living room. Literal shit. A 'fuck you' present for not having anything valuable enough for them to take.

That was the new trend. Residents in the cities were getting human feces "F you's" left and right. It was as if all the burglars got together for a happy hour and decided, "Hey, let's not only rob their homes but let's poop there, too! And not in the toilet, but…wait for it…on the floor!" I mean, who was that trendsetter? Or was it just one burglar with super active bowel movements doing all the shitting around the city? How could he produce so much waste? How much did he have to eat to be ready to defecate on the spot like that? Did he ever get performance anxiety, or fear someone would walk in on him? How long had he been doing this? Did he bring a book with him? I had a lot of questions. It seemed like taking a dump at your victim's house was a lot of work.

Regardless, the shit was a game-changer.

Auntie Chu had her carpet steam cleaned twice, but it didn't matter. She might have gotten the poo out of her carpet, but she never got it out of her mind. Eventually, she couldn't take it and she had her whole carpet replaced. She couldn't stand the thought of having remnants of criminal particles in her brilliant white carpet, and I got it. That shit was never coming out. And for a minute I even wondered if the carpet companies and steam cleaner salesmen were in on it, but I kinda doubt it. They're not exactly the fashionable belt crowd.

So now everyone in the city had to remember to lock their doors and windows, and most important of all, leave a few hundred bucks out to dissuade any bowel movements from the robber. Suddenly, you weren't scared of being robbed so much as not having enough in value to satisfy a nefarious criminal with a premeditated tummy ache. This once symbiotic relationship between burglar and victim had now evolved into a fearful distrust between victim and perpetrator, all thanks to the fecal fuck you.

Eventually, our time was up. Mom picked my sister and me up from school on an unmemorable afternoon. I was in second grade. We lived in a fairly undeveloped area in KauShong, the most southern city of Taiwan. Apartment buildings were still being erected around our high rise. Lumber, rebars, loose nails, and broken glass littered our block. Kids played without supervision, but we all got our Tetanus shots. One kid had a nail going through her foot, her sneaker soaked red while we helped her get back to her mom, climbing eight flights of stairs to her apartment. My sister was almost impaled by rebar once, but no one sued the construction company because there was never anyone on the construction site during the day. The apartment buildings being built had all the windows installed overnight. New families were moving in when no one was watching. It all happened under the blanket of darkness.

So mom picked us up and we climbed the four flights of stairs to our apartment. That was the part I dreaded each day, walking in the dark, dirty staircase where every large and poisonous spider in Taiwan decided to call their home, where they would make these elaborate webs across the ceilings. We stayed close to the inner rails of the stairs to avoid surprise attacks from any creepy crawlers. My sister had one land on her face one time, no lie. Each and every day we navigated through those arachnid death traps. But this day was different.

Mom dug her keys out from her purse to open the door but she paused. She told us to wait outside.

"Don't move."

Mom pushed the door, which was already ajar, even wider. We could barely see inside. Our couch was flipped over. Mom told us again not to move and to wait, then shut the door in our faces. My sister and I looked at each other. We didn't move. We didn't speak. We waited. What was mom doing? What was taking her so long? Why was our couch flipped over? Did dad get home early to rearrange the furniture?

Mom finally came out. She took us into our apartment and told us we got robbed, that the robber had left, and that we were safe. My sister and I said okay casually since, remember, it wasn't a big deal. I looked at our living room, but it didn't feel like our living room anymore. Everything was there, but nothing was in the right place. It seemed like someone picked up our apartment, shook it really hard and threw it back down. The couch was not the only thing flipped upside down – the coffee table, lamps, bookshelves, pictures on the walls, everything. Everything was torn down, ripped or flipped.

My sister and I reached for each other's hands and held on tight as we walked toward my mom, who was in her bedroom, looking through the mess while talking on the phone. She moved frantically, but her voice was calm. She was talking to the police. Mom and dad's room was in worse shape than the living room. The mattress was thrown against the windows, which made the usually bright room dark. Mom turned on the lights…all the drawers were taken out and the contents were dumped out, clothes were ripped out of the closets. It looked like the robber intentionally threw the clothes everywhere. Nothing was left untouched. Even the toilet's water tank was opened.

Mom rummaged and peeled through the piles of debris on her dresser. She paused and sighed, then jumped up and down in joy. She found her jewelry! She gave us big hugs. The robber must have missed the jewelry under her pile of dirty clothes on the dresser. She was relieved she didn't lose the jade necklace grandma gave her and immediately put everything back on, after scolding herself for ever taking it off to begin with.

The kitchen was a disaster. Plates, bowls, pans, and chopsticks were littered on the floor, a lot of them broken. The refrigerator was wide open, with all the food taken out. A torn Napa cabbage was all the way in the living room. My sister and I looked at each other, then down at the cabbage. What was a torn cabbage doing in the living room? We headed toward it. Someone had taken a monstrous bite right out of the side. But that was it. One bite. Then, in unison, as the thought hit us simultaneously, my sister and I looked at each other once more. Our eyes widened with fear. We didn't say anything. We knew what the other was thinking. The burglar hadn't taken anything – only one bite from the cabbage. We were doomed.

We slowly started peeling through the wreckage in our living room. We stood in the cleared area and worked our way out, taking cautious steps as we moved books and broken glass, keeping our eyes on the ground the whole time. We piled everything against the living room wall until the floor was empty and stood back, satisfied. My sister and I even hugged each other we were so ecstatic, when Mom came in and asked what was up.

"We didn't find any poop in the living room!" We were elated, but only briefly, as a dark current ran between us as the realization hit that it could still be lurking somewhere else in the house.

"Of course not," mom said, casually dispelling our fears.

"But how? What do you mean?" we asked, astonished. "They didn't take anything!"

"Yes they did," mom pointed.

My sister and I looked at each other, confused, before following our mother's gaze to the broken glass cabinet against the wall. It was empty. We turned to one another in disbelief and giggled. Suddenly, I envisioned the burglar leaping through the dark night with his satchel on his back, soaring from rooftop to rooftop; only instead of fashionable sacred treasures, he was hauling a bag full of worthless plastic crap. Maybe they weren't so bright after all.

Dad was devastated when he got home. His life's work, ruined. But eventually he found solace, largely due to us persistently reminding him that his paltry model airplanes once saved us from some pretty major shit.

About Ethel Lung

Ethel Lung hails from Houston, Texas, but escaped to Los Angeles to pursue her lifelong dream of acting, until she came to the realization that she sucked at it. Turning her love of film and storytelling in a new direction, Ethel began writing screenplays where she quickly found herself as part of the Fox Writer's Initiative as well as the Nickelodeon Writing Program. Her work has been featured on various comedy series on Disney, Nick at Nite, and YouTube Red.

Ethel currently lives in Los Angeles, CA where she continues to develop content with her writing partner Tiffany Lo for film and TV. In her spare time, she enjoys soup, lecturing her children, and pretending to like Crossfit.

GENUINE

by Suzanne Crain Miller

After

The most God-awful sound… it was the most God-awful sound I've ever heard to this very day. I thought I was dreamin' 'fore Janet ran into my room an' woke me up. So I go out there, stumble around in the dark with a campin' flashlight, wishin' I'd a worn a helluva lot more than flip-flops, when I saw it: a silver hubcap. Then a front fender bent so as you could hardly tell what it was, an' pieces of glass sprinkled like glitter on a birthday card all over the ground. An' there it was, up ahead, wedged in a grove of pine trees… that bitch's Mercedes. I stood still. My heart was risin' in my chest. That's when I heard it, even though a few hours later I'd swear I never heard nothin' at all. Only I will ever know it, but I did. A meager "Help" from just beyond the pine grove 'fore everything went silent again, 'cept for the crickets scratchin' their furry legs together an' cars whizzin' by a fair piece away.

Before

When your life's like mine, what you don't want is time to think. You do about all you can to steer clear a anything that'll give you any blank space in your day to roll around in your head what it is you gotta shoulder. I do pretty good at keepin' busy. Only time I cain't escape is when Janet calls out, "Can you get the mail, hon?"

Well, then, an' those few seconds when I lay my head on my pilla' for I can cut my phone on.

So here I am, headed out for the mail again, an' this highway's always busy. Every day I gotta wait for ten minutes or more just to get across to my own mailbox. Used to be easier. Only certain times a day it'd get crazy, but now, it's nonstop. My life's turned into plannin' when I can block out a time to go get the damn mail, an' hardly any of it's ever for me.

Most of us blame it on that company done moved in the old Felton warehouse down the road. Nobody seems to know what they're doin' down there. My neighbor Sharnice says it's some kinna' tech startup, but she don't know. Probly got the buildin' cheap seein' as it's twenty miles from town. Sharnice really gets goin' 'bout all the changes 'round here. She goes off about how city folks don't mind commutin' to our neck of the woods if they can get them a real deal.

If I go for the mail 'round five o'clock I see 'em all drivin' by like a parade. Mercedes, Lexus, Grand Pri's, every kind a hot shit car you can imagine. Bet they're makin' huge car payments. Some a the drivers are older. They been workin' for years to get what they got. Some of 'em are young. Kids startin' 401k's an' college funds for babies they don't even got yet.

Wonder what they think about us; all of us livin' in these here trailers an' cinderblock houses they whiz by, too proud to even look. Probly hate it that their boss moved 'em out this a way. Probly feel like they're forced to waller with pigs. It's damn near certainty they hate comin' out here as much as we hate 'em comin out.

Finally. A break in traffic an' I'm gettin' across this here road to the mailbox. Won't be nothin excitin'. Nothin important. Bills, bills an' more bills. Oh, an' some notices remindin' me a unpaid bills. More to add to those stacks a old ones already on the kitchen table.

Janet helps me with 'em some, with her disability check. While I'm at the Quick Stop, she's like my own personal secretary, sortin' the bills an' labelin' 'em with these sticky post-its she likes to get from Dollar Zone. She'll make calls an' tell 'em our sob story to get extensions that she schedules out between her favorite soaps. I've told 'er more than a time or two that she shoulda' been a soap star what with how she can pull out the tears when she's talkin' to the bill collectors.

"Naw, I couldn't be no actress. Difference is, hon, I ain't actin on the phone. It might sound like drama to those on the other end, but it's our life."

What can I say, she likes to embellish.

Goin' on three years Daddy's been dead. Didn't leave much to speak of. Instead of a last will an' testament, I got Janet an' this here trailer to keep up payments on so Janet has a place to stay. An' I'll be honest, a handicapped stepmom itn't much of a inheritance.

But she ain't all bad. We like to sit up nights an' talk about the good ol' days, back before she met Daddy, an' watch talk shows she's saved on the DVR while I'm workin'. She likes to give advice to the people on the shows even though they cain't hear her. On holidays, we'll sit on the big couch drinkin' together an' swappin' heartbreak stories. So far hers beat mine seein's how all my limbs work an' I ain't been widowed, but there's still time.

For some reason she's gettin' under my skin a little more than usual today. It's my first day off in weeks an' I'd like nothin' better than to sit home, watch HBO, an' eat a whole bag a salt an' vinegar chips. Figure's Janet's itchin' for a night out. Guess three years is long enough to be in mournin'.

Fixin' her face up while I get a bath, she's chatterin' on about gettin' laid. Not somethin' you wanna hear about from the woman who used to do your daddy. There ain't no explainin' that to her though. She's about as loose-lipped as they come, wants to talk about every damn thang.

I slip my red spandex dress on as she wrestles with the zipper on her hot pants.

"Whew girl!" she breathes heavy. "Your daddy used to adore me in these. Couldn't peel him off me every time I wore 'em."

T.M.I. Janet. *T.M.I.*

My silver earrings are turnin' yellow. Tends to happen to most a my Dollar Zone finds. They'll last one more night. Well, not if Charlie comes home with me. He's got this thing about lickin' ears an' earrings. Some kinna turn on for him. Don't know if I'm in the mood for him tonight or not. Depends on whether or not somebody takes Janet home. Cain't have her showin' me up.

We walk outside, get in the car, an' 'fore we can even back out the driveway a silver Mercedes comes whizzin' right behind us, nearly takes out our trunk. I blare the horn, but the car's long gone.

"Damn it! There she goes again!" Janet hollers. "That bitch's always racin' aroun' here like there's a fire somewheres."

Seen the driver for myself, several times. One a those new office workers, works later than the rest of 'em, then tears up the road to get home. My horn don't register with people like her. Her kind's so up their own ass they don't even know they bother anybody. They don't even care. Couple a times when I been on my way to get the mail, she's all but run me over. Crazy bitch.

I let Janet rail about her the whole way to Shay's so she'll get it outta her system, but I'm not gonna let it ruin my night. Shay's has cheap liquor, good music, an' Sally, the bartender, knows everybody in there by name.

Never understood why they called it that, though. Shay's is such a strange name for a lounge. Guess at one time or another somebody named Shay done owned it. Now a Mexican fella owns it.

His wife hangs out in the back with their baby. One night I happened to be goin' to the bathroom an' walked by the kitchen. There she was, tit hangin' out for all to see, lettin' the baby just go to town. I couldn't believe it, but then Daddy used to always say them Mexicans got their own set a manners, though I cain't really tell they got any. Course, I only ever met a couple, so what do I know?

"Janet's a live one tonight, boy!" Sally shouts over the bar as she hands me another beer. I look out over the dance floor an' watch as Janet shimmies all over some cowboy I don't recognize right off. It's clear she's been at home thinkin' 'bout struttin' her stuff, watchin' all those soaps, dreamin' 'bout when a man'll feel 'er up again. Her jeans look like they're painted on. Any minute that zipper could bust right open even though she eats like a parakeet; ain't much over a hundred an' ten pounds drippin' wet. I smile at her, take a drag on my cig, an' watch as she does her thing out on the floor.

A hand's on my shoulder. I look up an' see Charlie. He sits down next to me.

"How'd you get her outta that trailer? I was beginnin' to think she was a permanent part a your couch," he jokes.

"You an' me both. She decided it's time, I suppose." I drop the cigarette in my empty water cup an' the cherry sizzles. "How's your week been?"

"A'right. Store's been slow. I done re-did the stock room about ten times."

"That bad, huh?"

"'Fraid so. How 'bout you? Quick Stop been busy?"

"Cain't have a slow day there if I wanted to. Even when we're slow, we're busy. Chris keeps tryin' to make us do all his dirty work for him, an' Ol' Man Scott's still after me about that cruise. Every day he comes in about lunchtime buggin' the crap outta me." We can't keep our eyes off Janet as she twitches out on the dance floor.

"Didn't his wife die last year?" Charlie asks.

"That's why he's askin'. There they went an' saved up their whole lives for this cruise to Jamaica, then she up an' has a heart attack!"

"That's sad. Cain't blame you for not wantin' to go though." Charlie agrees.

"I ain't about to go on no cruise in no dead lady's place. Fuckin' creepy." I throw back a shot an' take a quick swig from the sweaty beer. The label's half torn off. Real carefully I peel the rest off.

Music blares outta the old speakers, which keep switchin' back an' forth from country hits to eighties pop. Those Mexicans seem pretty behind on the times, but they have surprisingly good taste in music. Charlie's kinna giddy tonight. He introduces Janet to several a his buddies. I can tell he's hopin' she'll go home with somebody. He knows what'll happen. Me an' him ain't no regular thing or nothing. We just like to be there for each other, like we're each other's fallback, an' right now neither of us got anybody better to fall back on.

11:30. Janet's still slow dancin' with Meyer Brimly. She's got that look in her eye. I interrupt 'em for a second to give her my keys, wish her luck, an' she grabs my hand like she's gonna change her mind, but then she sees Charlie waitin' by the door an' she lets go, grinnin'. I don't rightly think she's ready, but she'll get into it once Meyer gets her goin'. I'm just glad to have my house back, if only for a night.

I leave her my car, an' Charlie an' me take his pickup back to my place. Sure enough, if he ain't the most predictable son of a gun, he starts lickin' my ears like some puppy the minute we get in the house.

"Hey now, give me a minute. I gotta pee." I lie.

He puts his hands up like I'm a cop who just walked in on him robbin' a bank, then flops down on the couch an' turns on the T.V.

"I'll be right here when you get back," he says.

Part of me wishes he wouldn't be, but the other part is kinna glad he is. I walk down the hall to the bathroom. Starrin' myself down in the mirror, I think about how it's only been a couple weeks since me an' Brian broke up. Then there's the fact that Charlie hadn't been split from his Manda any longer than that. Maybe we'll just talk. Maybe that's all I feel like doin'.

When I walk back out, Charlie's helped himself to some a my chips an' has his feet up on the table. I sit as close to the other end as I can, knowin' the distance'll help. I put another cigarette up to my lips an' light it.

"Somethin' wrong?" Charlie pesters. "Most a the time I gotta slow you down."

I take a drag an' think about that myself. He's on to somethin'. I don't feel right. Tired I guess. Tired a havin' the same job day in day out. Tired a havin' to worry about Janet. Tired a him bein' my fallback guy. Won't do no good to say it though.

"Naw, I'm fine. Guess I'm just tryin' to be more of a lady tonight. Tired a bein' a quick lay. Maybe I want you to work for it." I answer with a grin.

He sees this as the go ahead that it is an' we go through our motions. Forty-five minutes later we're layin' back on my sweaty bed, takin' drags off the same cig, smoke curlin' around our faces. For a split second, in the haziness, Charlie's kinna handsome. Not like Brian, but in his own way.

"So…what's Brian's deal?" he cain't help but ask, stretchin' out longways so he can get a better look at me.

"Same ol' same ol'. Found another girl who's more his type he told me, Kristina from over there in Tigerville. He said me an' him were fallin' into a routine, gettin' borin'." I mutter.

"Routine? Hell, ain't that what's s'posed to happen? You're s'posed to settle into some kinna life with somebody after a while. Cain't be fuckin' like rabbits an' road trips to the South a The Border all the time! An' you not bein' as much his type, well, he was always one to be into the cheap girls an' cheap you ain't so consider yourself lucky." he nearly shouts.

"Me? Naw, *I'm not cheap*." I elbow him. "I just sleep with you an' pretty much anybody else who comes knockin'."

"Awe, that itn't cheap. That's lonely," he states, tracin' one a my breasts with his oil-stained finger. "You'll quit all that when you find the right one. For now, you're samplin' the goods."

We drift off to sleep at some point. I wake up to Janet's voice fillin' my ears from out in the kitchen. Sounds like she's talkin' to Meyer. Givin' him the boot already. That's Janet for ya. Woman loves drama.

Charlie sleeps in cause he knows Janet won't care, but I head on to work. I clock in at 11:00 an' get ready for a long haul. Jeanie's already here askin' me how my night went. She's always wantin' to know. Ain't got any life herself, a real momma's girl. Got herself a scholarship to one a them fancy universities when she graduated high school, but couldn't bear to leave. So here she is, sittin' at the Quick Stop with me.

On days like today, I look at her an wish I'd a gotten me a scholarship. Man, I'd a gone in a flash. Wouldn't have to ask me twice. That's how life works though itn't it? I got the guts, but no brains. Jeanie got decent brains but no guts.

Day's goin' on pretty dull 'til twelve o'clock hits an' there he is, right on time, the recently widowed Mr. Scott. Lord knows.

"Hey there, Mr. Scott. How's it goin'?" I ask tryin' to sound like I care. "Gonna have the usual?" It's a habit, even though I already know the answer.

"Oh, I guess so. Maybe two a those pies today, though. Hurry along the heart attack, right?" he cackles all weird, reachin' over the counter for the first pie.

"Come on now, Mr. Scott. You know you ain't gonna have no heart attack. You're fit as a fiddle." I reply handin' him a plate with a second pie on it.

As I watch him eat on that pie with only his bottom dentures on, in my mind I'm pretendin' we're on that cruise he keeps on about an' we're eatin' at one a those fancy buffets, drinkin' fine wine. An' he's settin' there gummin' his steak, an I'm tryin' to cut up the rest of it in small enough pieces for him. A pretty picture it ain't.

After strollin' round the aisles for a while, he finally stops near the postcards. Studyin' them careful like, I can tell he's revin' up to say what he's got on his mind. Bet my paycheck I know what that is, too.

"None a these here postcards got a beach on em, heh? I bet Janet sure would love to get a postcard from Jamaica," he fishes, still steady flippin' through the stack a cards with all the historical sites to see around here. Meaning we got tons a copies a all three sites.

I try not to pay him any mind, count the cash in the drawer to make sure I ain't got to change it out for a hundred yet. Mr. Scott keeps on with the postcards for a bit then strolls over and starts talkin' to Jeanie. I hate havin' to keep tellin' him no. Not cause I mind hurtin' his feelin's. More cause he's wearin' me down a little more every time he asks. Guess most people wouldn't give a trip with some geezer a second thought. They wouldn't do it in a million years. But me? I keep thinkin' how it really wouldn't be so bad screwin' him if I'm layin' on a beach while I'm doin' it. Jeanie's tellin' him one a her borin' ass stories about her mama's reactions to medicines. With that, Mr. Scott decides it's time to go. He winks at me as he walks out. I wave an' smile.

"You're crazy for not takin' that man up on his offer!" Jeanie scolds as she wipes hot dog grease off the counters. "I'd give anything to go to Jamaica."

"Shoot Jeanie, lay off me. You know good an' well you wouldn't even be able to step foot on the god-damn boat." That shut her up.

From the way she's bitin' her lip, I can tell she's tryin' not to cry. She hustles off into the back room. Done offended her. *Great.* All I did was tell the truth. I'll have to make it up to her somehow.

I give her time to cool off, an' I start arrangin' bags a corn chips an' corn nuts in a pyramid that won't stay, I know, but I got nothin' better to do. A light shines in my eyes from outside, somethin's reflectin' the sun, blindin' me. I move over an' can see from the window it's the silver Mercedes. The car door swings open. I hold my breath a second. Been waitin' to see the driver up close an' personal. First time whoever it is has slummed it an' come in here.

A girl about my age struts in dressed in designer duds, got her a high dollar blonde dye job. Looks like she's had one a those Brazilian Blowouts Jeanie whines about wantin'. The kind where they do some kind of special treatment so your hair gets straightened. Looks like one a Janet's soap stars, but classier. She's diggin' in her purse. Pullin' out a wallet, she rushes over to the drink cooler an' pulls out one a them health shakes we hardly sell any of. I won't dare tell her it's more than likely way past its expiration date.

"Those any good?" I ask her.

She doesn't even look at me, but looks past me at all the bad checks tacked to our bulletin board behind the register. It's clear by the look on her face, a look like she's had a corn cob stuck up her ass since the day she popped out a her momma's cooch, she's not gonna be a Quick Stop regular.

"I don't care what it tastes like. 60% of this country is obese because everyone is worrying about what tastes *good*. It's fuel. Plain and simple," she rattles off.

"Okkaaay," I whisper under my breath.

"Can you just ring me out please? I'm not here to chit chat," she fumes.

I want to fly over this counter so bad! I want to open up that shake, hold her mouth open, an' pour it down her throat 'til she gags. Just her luck, I actually need this job, so I just smile back an' ring her up. Her mouth curves into this little grin like she's won some contest I didn't know I was in but she's been preparin' for her whole entire life. She knows I won't do anything. She pays, slings her hair over her shoulder an' leaves. Through the glass door, Jeanie an' I watch her pull away.

Cain't help but wonder where she's headin'. Bet she's got a nice house or one a those new fancy apartments they built out a the old mill downtown. My thoughts drift to what makes us so different. How is it she's drivin' a Mercedes while I'm stuck with a beat-up old Ford that only works half the time?

"Good genes," Janet informs me as I'm goin' over it back home. "Some people are born with the best genetics. You know, what your mama an' daddy pass down? You an' me, well, we better count our lucky stars we didn't get more a our parents genes than we did, right?" she blabbers on, steady paintin' her toenails hot pink out on the porch. Takin' this as truth, I accept it an' head in to get changed out a my work clothes.

I fold my work pants an' pile 'em on top a all the other pairs fallin' off the shelves. Between me an' Janet, we must have fifty pairs at least. That Mercedes driver was wearing some kind of expensive pants for sure. They were all glossy like a peacock's feathers. Our pants are cheap. Most of 'em're pretty tacky colors. Closest thing I got to any like hers are my black velvet ones. They're just knockoffs though. Ain't no real brand name to speak of. I want some like Mercedes girl's. Maybe I'll get me some like'at next paycheck.

The week rolls by an' 'fore I even know it, it's Friday again. I nearly call in sick to start the weekend early but I decide to go on in. Better not leave Jeanie high an' dry. Hate it when she does that to me. As I step out Janet tells me she might actually go grocery shoppin'. I try not to act shocked. I'm just glad she's feelin' like joinin' the land a the livin'. Wouldn't dare go against it.

Walkin' up to the door a the Quick Stop, I see Chris's car out front. *Just great*. He's probly already countin' Oreos, fillin' the drink machine, an' gripin' 'bout how sales ain't what they used to be. Overall he's an okay guy, but I don't think he ever dreamed a bein' a thing but what he is; some micro-managin' store manager, an' he eats, drinks, an' sleeps it. Thinks bein' a boss is the only way to come up in the world, don't even matter what kind you are. Even if it's the boss a some no-care employees at the local Quick Stop off route 47. He can have it. I just wanna get paid. Don't have any desire to be overseein' nothin'.

Mornin's kinna borin' though. Chris hardly says two words to me, an' leaves after only a couple hours. Wonder what burned his biscuits? I head to the bathroom in back to take a break when *Dang it!* Lookin' in the mirror I see my earrings have turned from anything resemblin' silver to a brown kinna copper. I situate my hair so they don't show that much an' laugh at myself for bein' so vain. Why's it even matter? Ain't nobody lookin' at me. All I ever do is come here day in day out. Hang out at Shay's on occasion. To hell with it. Gold, silver, copper… *whatever*. Who's lookin' anyhow?

‘Fore I know it, it’s already ‘bout closin’ time, an’ I’m ready to get the show on the road. Jeanie asked to cut out early on account a her mama not havin’ a nurse around tonight, so I’m left alone to close up. I knew I shouldn’ta came in. I count minutes for the next little bit an’ at ten to midnight I call it. I nearly got the door locked when she pulls in. Her silver chariot screeches to a halt behind me as I turn the key in the lock. I pretend like I don’t see her an’ pull the keys out. Ain’t no way Mercedes bitch is ruinin’ my Friday night. Whatever she needs can wait. She flings her door open an’ hops out.

“I’m glad I caught you,” she blurts, all smiles, real relieved like. “I really need to use your phone. My cell isn’t charged and the office doesn’t like for us to make personal calls. My husband thought I’d be home hours ago.”

Lookin’ her over, I glory in the fact that she needs me. For once in my life, I’m in control, an’ damn, it feels good.

“I just locked up.” I deliver with my own big grin.

Her smile droops to a frown, but she tries to keep herself under wraps. She knows her brand a rudeness won’t get her anywhere.

“It’ll just take a second. I promise, then I’ll be out of your way,” she pleads.

I stand starin’, makin’ her fidget. Best fun I’ve had in a long time. I know I’m the bigger person, an’ of course I’m gonna open it eventually, but just for this second, she can wait on me.

“Isn’t it kind of early to be closing? I thought you were open ‘til midnight?”

She’s got me by five minutes, but damn. She just can’t go a second without bein’ a bitch, can she? I unlock the door an’ tell her to hurry up. She barely grunts a thanks as she rushes past me around to the side of the counter where she snags the phone. She’s real careful not to put the grimy thing on her ear. She just holds it close enough for her to talk. Cain't say I blame her.

I shuffle the display around on the counter while I listen in. Tells her hubby she had some work dinner an' they've still got some files to go through then she'll be home, not to wait up. By the sound a her voice I can tell it's not the first time.

Their conversation quiets an' she apparently wins him over with a whisper. Her giggle seals it. I try not to be overly nosy. Must be nice havin' somebody to call. Somebody who cares when you're late. Sure Janet cares, but mainly cause I pay the rent an' she'll be out on her ass if I'm not around to bring home a check. Somebody bein' dependent on you's a far cry from somebody dependin' on you.

The suit Mercedes bitch has on fits her to a T. Even standin' there, leanin' on that counter talkin' on a gas station phone she looks like some model in a magazine. Probly look that way even if she covered herself with mud. I'd die to see her parents. Genetics have been good to her. Honey an' brown hair, tan skin, waist no bigger around than a dinner plate. Looks like she's from some foreign country, like she's doin' us all a favor just by gracin' us with her presence.

As she hangs up the phone, I notice she has on the same earrings as I do.

"Hey," I call out to her like some kid, movin' my hair away so I can proudly show her mine. "We got the exact same pair. Dollar Zone, right?" As soon as I say it, I realize my mistake. An' by the look on her face, I must be downright insane to think that this woman has ever even stepped foot inside a Dollar Zone.

With a wicked grin, she laughs, "A – no. I didn't get them at the Dollar Zone. I've never even heard of the Dollar Zone, but I'm certain with a name like that it's bound to be a real gem." She turns to give me a better, clearer look at her shiny accessories. She's got a small bruise on her neck, partially covered by her collar, with the beautiful dangly earrings accenting her whole look. “These are *genuine* sterling.”

She reaches a hand up near my face an’ I flinch. She stops to look at me, then delicately inspects my earrings. “These are fake.”

Not knowin’ what to do, I nod like some hypnotized idiot. I ain’t surprised she’d say this, but I’m in total shock she touched me. In some sick way I feel honored she’d leaned in so close. Puttin’ her purse up on her shoulder, she marches back out to her car an’ drives off.

As I lock up the store, a spotlight outside catches one a my earrings an’ it shines bright orange in my reflection in the door. I take a close look an’ realize they practically look like brass. Guess I’ll toss ‘em out. Oh, screw it! *Genuine…* Who cares? They still look about the same as hers, or did for a few days anyway. Christmas is comin’ up. Maybe Janet’ll get me a genuine somethin’ or ‘nother?

A few weeks go by without much eventful happenin’. We have a good Thanksgivin’. Lots a leftover turkey an' stuffin’. Charlie came to our place after he ate at his parents, helped finish off some pie. Still no regular girlfriend for him yet so I been fillin’ in. Ain’t half bad bein’ his regular thing, but I won’t say nothin’ about it to him. Just gonna go with the flow for fear that bronco might buck.

Janet’s done told me she wants some makeup for Christmas. She made sure I know she don’t want no K-Mart junk neither. Sittin’ home watchin’ her *Days of Our Lives* she’s done made up her mind she wants some a that expensive stuff from a department store. She says it’ll make her look more like Susan Lucci. I’ve picked up some extra hours at the station an’ I got enough dough to splurge so today Charlie an’ me are gonna drive into Fort Worth an’ get her an Estee Lauder gift box.

Takes us nearly an hour to get into town. So much traffic. No way I'd live here. Not with all these other people. Wouldn't even come here at all if it weren't for the fact that they got all the best stores.

We walk into Saks 5th Avenue. Never has made sense to me why they call the ones that ain't in New York that. We're a hell of a long way from 5th Avenue. Charlie sure as shit don't belong here. Cain't take him anywhere. He's puttin' his fingers on every piece a clothin' in the place like a little boy. I'm glad he wiped that chili from his corn dog off his face before we got inside.

"Cut it out Charlie!" I hiss.

He turns red an' stuffs his hands in his pockets. Don't take long to find the makeup counter. Everything's a lot higher than I'd expected. I still got enough if I don't get Charlie anything. He won't mind anyway as long as we can screw. That's about all that's on his Christmas list.

The lady behind the counter pours on the charm. She can tell we don't know what to buy. I tell her a little bit about Janet's skin color an' the kinna clothes she likes to wear. Finally, she pulls out a eyeshadow set that looks exactly like Janet: gaudy as hell.

We're about out the door an' ready to go home when I spot the jewelry counter. Knowin' full well I don't got no business lookin', I go look anyway an' there they are…my earrings, only genuine. Eyein' me, the clerk pulls them out so I can get a closer look. I hold them up to my ears an' look in the mirror. They look real pretty an' they sure are light!

"They certainly are becoming aren't they?" the clerk flatters.

I look at the tag as I lay them back on the counter, blinkin' because I'm thinkin' it has to be a mistake. $150.00!

"Come on. You can't have none a them in this lifetime," Charlie chuckles, pullin' on my arm.

All the way home I'm thinkin' 'bout those earrings…so light an' dangly. They looked real good on me, just the way they looked on that Mercedes Bitch. Why is it she can have them but I can't? She probably don't work any harder. Sure, she works a lot, but so do I.

Wouldn't you know it, itn't but a day after our trip to the city an' here she is, in the flesh, runnin' in to buy one a her health shakes. An' there they are again. My earrings hangin' so nicely off her ears - a *genuine* slap in the face.

"You get those at Saks?" I ask as she stands at the counter diggin' for her wallet. "I mean I a…I…just saw some like 'em when I was there yesterday."

There's that wicked grin. Doin' anything but takin' her money was a big mistake.

"And here I was hoping to get a quick lunch and avoid all this, but since you asked, yes, I did get them at Saks. But not the one in Fort Worth. The real one, in New York."

I glare at her, astonished.

"Now, can that be the end of this little convo?"

Jeanie drops the candy she's stockin' an' stares like the whole thing itn't real. She probly hasn't seen nobody this rude before. I do my best to bite my tongue.

"Just bein' polite. Sorry"

She laughs at me. Right to my face. The whole world is a joke.

"It's okay. I don't blame you. You don't know any better. But, you'll get the hang of it. Once you realize that people like me don't need to have their day disrupted." She slings her purse over her shoulder on her way out.

Mrs. Pruitt steps up to pay.

"Some people." she scorns, shakin' her head as we all watch the Bitch's car zoom out a our parkin' lot.

I ask Jeanie if she can mind the register an' I race as quickly as I can to the break room. Sittin' on a crate of juice, I have the best cry I've had since I don't know when. Don't exactly know why I'm cryin'. Maybe cause she's a bitch? Maybe cause she's right? I don't know. Maybe it's cause I won't ever have any *genuine* anything an' I know it. Jeanie comes in after a half-hour an' tells me to go home. I never took her up on anything so fast in my life.

It's nearly 4:30 a.m. when Janet comes runnin' in, shakin' me.

"Get up! Somethin's wrong!" she's goin' off.

I roll over, pushin' her away. "Go on now."

"I'm serious! Come on!" she keeps on.

I sit up an' push myself up off the bed. Won't be a bit a peace 'til I go look.

"It was this loud noise a some kind. Awful! Right out there!" She fills me in, handin' me a flashlight as we head down the hall.

Stumblin' out in the yard in my nightgown an' flip flops I shine the light out in the field. At first, I don't see anythin', but as I get on down near the ditch, I see a hubcap lyin' near the road. There's tire tracks deep in soil around it. It's followed by a front fender bent so as I can hardly make out what it is, then pieces of glass sprinkled like glitter on a birthday card along the ground. Then, there up ahead, a silver car wedged between a grove of pine trees. I stand still. Feels like the whole God damned earth stands still around me.

It bein' so early my mind don't register whose car it is 'til I see a purse lyin' in some brush. I've seen that purse… Mercedes Bitch! The best I can figure she's done ran off the road in the middle of the night.

"Help!" I hear real quiet like, an' only once.

I run over to the driver's side but there's no sign a her. Her door's still shut. The windshield's broke clean through. She must have been thrown. I shine the flashlight, searchin' all around. Finally, I see her about twenty feet away, heavin' on the ground.

Leanin' over her I watch her chest go up an' come back down. She's hurt real bad. Janet calls me from the porch. I open my mouth to yell for her to call a ambulance, but the beam of my flashlight crosses her earrings. There they are, her genuine sterling earrings. I look at the injured girl lyin' there starin' up at me, impaled on this here stick, bleedin' to death out here on the freezin' ground, an' the moment is clear. Carefully, I reach down an' pull her hair back, tryin' not to get blood on my fingers. One of her eyes, bloodied an' swollen, opens. She looks right at me an' I freeze. Her lips move. She's tryin' to say somethin'.

Turnin' back to Janet, I again open my mouth, but then I see her neck. The bruise I saw before isn't just a bruise… It's a hickey.

"What's goin' on?" Janet shouts, steppin' off the top step over toward the woods.

I look down at Mercedes Bitch again. Her eye closes. She knows what I decided, maybe before I did. Crouchin' down, I slip both earrings outta her ears. She won't be needin' 'em where she's goin'. An' without even thinkin' another thing about it, I put 'em in the pocket of my nightie, an' what do you know? They're *genuinely* mine.

Her chest gets still. She stops breathin'. She goes stone-cold quiet as if by takin' her earrings, I've taken her power. Like Superman without his cape or some shit. The minute I took 'em she quit breathin'. Man, that's creepy. Cuttin' off the flashlight, I run through the weeds just as Janet comes down the steps.

"Ain't a thing out there. You're probly dreamin' again. You been takin' your Ambien?" I distract her, pattin' her back, leadin' her into the house.

"Well, I thought I did. I –"

"See, you don't take that, you know you have those crazy-ass nightmares. I'm gonna start settin' a reminder on your phone," I tell her.

She gives one last glance out into the field, shrugs an' goes inside.

After

Loud bangin' on the door is our alarm clock. Throwin' on my robe I go to the door. It's a policeman. I'm too groggy to get tense so I open the door.

"Mornin' ma'am." he starts. I stare back. "Sorry to bother you, but there was a crash out there by the road last night and we're wondering if you might a heard or seen anything to speak of?"

Reachin' up, I rub my neck. I feel the cold silver against my hand. I've got the earrings on! I'd forgotten I put 'em on this morning, after I wiped the blood off. I try to be calm. For all he knows these are mine. He don't have any reason to think different unless I give him one.

"Naw. Sorry I cain't help you, officer. Didn't get in 'til late an' I sleep like the dead soon as my head hits that pillow."

Starrin' out over the field he continues, "Well, alright, ma'am. Had to check seein' as you're the closest place to it. Real bad thing. Best I can figure the woman fell asleep at the wheel. Been dead a couple hours or so. Young, pretty gal, too."

"Damn shame," I add.

"Sure is." he agrees. "Sorry to wake you. Have a good one."

He tips his hat as he goes back out to the scene. Soon as the door shuts, nausea takes hold. Tears get close to fillin' my eyes 'til I see Janet standin' in the doorway. She can't take her eyes off me, squintin' like she does when she thinks she's got your number.

"Nice earrings," is all she says.

"Thanks," I reply. "They're genuine."

About Suzanne Crain Miller

Suzanne Crain Miller is a novelist, screenwriter, and poet who lives in Carrboro, N.C. with her husband Chad, and their lab, Slim Shady. For her daily grind, she is a managing editor for several journals and an art teacher volunteer at a local women's shelter. She is part of the Heron Clan Writing Community, and speaks about suicide prevention whenever and wherever possible.

For more info visit
www.tattooeddaughter.wordpress.com

FIRST TOOLS
by Nicholas Zeman

I knew cars would bust you. Insurance receipts, license plates, everything registered with the government. Once you were in a car they had you, there was no getting away. Learned that from the Contra Costa county case—the "Original" Night Stalker. I learned a lot from him. But the main thing was the bicycle—people are so bamboozled by the automobile, they don't see the advantages of any other mode. The ONS saw the versatility of the bicycle. I went down to the library and read up on it. These detectives want to be famous so badly they write books to tell you how to get away with murder. Blinded by the almighty dollar. Sold their souls, if you ask me. This idiot detective from Hercules wrote about one of the most prolific and successful burglars, rapists, and murderers in the state's history and tells you that in almost every case he escaped on a bicycle over terrain where an automobile could not follow—down creeks beds, over trails and paths and through parks. Now *there's* some source material for the burgeoning up-and-comer. The Sacramento police were helpless against this sick fuck as he raped their friends, sisters, mothers, daughters, and wives.

You could disappear on a bicycle in virtual silence— here one second gone the next. Especially at night, and especially if you know the streets. Make sure the chain's got plenty of grease, and the tires are full of air, and then, what can they say? You're just a guy on a bicycle, that's it. Some nondescript pedestrian. I remember sitting in the stacks late at night, reading about it, thinking about him, and daydreaming about my own exploits, for when the time was right. I was inspired by the ONS. Not the part about raping women in front of their husbands and then bludgeoning them to death, Jesus. He was a sick fuck. But he kept silent. And he was intelligent. In a sinister kinda way, he sort of reminded me of me.

You come to know the city a little differently from behind the handlebar of a bicycle, and I'd become a master of it. The bicycle and the city. I'd gotten so fast, you should have seen my legs. I couldn't even wear shorts, my woman was so jealous. Every time I left the house, if I was in shorts my girl thought I was going out to fuck someone else. Lucky for her I have an over-arching principle that I live and die by which is, simply put, a grown man doesn't leave the house in shorts.

I guess you could say I have a lot of rules about things, the way I dress, the things I do, the people I spend my time around. And well, that relationship didn't last. Just like all the relationships before. They can't handle the discipline it takes to maintain my routine.

I couldn't work construction anymore. It was killing me. I wondered why I ever studied engineering to begin with. Thinking I could design and build great things; I realize now the only people who get to do that are the ones that are willing to get on their knees and beg for it. Or they were born with it to begin with. Talent means nothing. You should see some of my drawings, some of my stonework! I was the top of my class! And now, there's nothing to show for it but bile oozing through the sewers, rising in the streets, and climbing up the back of my throat. I've grown to have an impenetrable hatred. The world is a sick place filled with sick people. It almost makes me sick. I've come to hate real estate brokers, property developers, and landlords the most. These devil-worshipping land barons build the cheapest piece of shit they can get away with in order to extort the most money possible from the maximum number of people they can. I saw what they did to the architects and engineers over the years. I've been watching. And perhaps I could have handled their ruthlessness more readily if they had shown themselves to have any style at all. A man on his knees doesn't have the balls to take risks, not like I do. So I quit. It was the biggest risk I've ever taken in my life, until now.

It takes a while to prepare for something like this. You must educate yourself. Find out what worked in the past. Find out what didn't. Sometimes the only way to learn is from practical experience. But it's easy to plan an event. What really matters is the getaway. The event is easy. The break-in. The robbery. But it's the getaway that's most important. And as much as I'd thought about it, the getaway had posed a problem for years. A car was just too risky, it could only be used in very specialized applications. The Blake Brothers—they used a note to rob a bank, and they even got away with it. Except they used their own car to do it and somebody saw the license plate. Didn't take long to track 'em down after that. I took a long hard look at that bank they hit, too. I saw how it was built. I know why they liked it. They were on to something. It was the car that fucked 'em.

But banks were too risky, especially for a self-made start-up. I needed an entry point. Home invasion. B&E. That was more my style. I decided I would only go after cash; trying to fence electronics and jewels and shit just wasn't for me. Dealing with some crooked pawnbroker or cheap jeweler haggling over the price all the time? Hell no. Those are some of the most grim and depressing people in any city anywhere in the world. The cash trail ends with me. And after speculating long and hard about other modes of transport—

the imminently dangerous and overly loud motorcycle, for instance, or the surveillance-filled Metro— it was no wonder the trusty bicycle eventually arose as the clear and safe choice.

My education came quickly, but was not without surprises. One of the most interesting things to me was that people actually believe locks keep you safe. That they keep people out. When in reality locks, like people, are particularly vulnerable to malice. Once you get to know them, they aren't really all that different. All it takes is a couple pricks to bust them open. So you get a tool kit going. You can call it anything you want. The bike's a part of my kit. And my multi-plier pocket tool, with my screwdrivers and knives and pliers on it. I've got a set of pins, different sizes and lengths and pliability. A couple other tricks up my sleeve. Little tricks of the trade I picked up in my research. And then I waited. I didn't know what for. Until it happened.

I saw the guy's kit that night. Impressively small. Core essentials, really. Somebody had done their homework. He would have cleaned me out if RD hadn't come to pick me up that night. I knew I'd be drinking, and I hate parking in Hollywood, so I let him drive and deal with it. But he wanted to come home early so he could smoke because he couldn't do it at his house. Thought his neighbors were watching him. Told me my neighbors were watching me. Then we parked down the block and walked up the steps only to get stuck in the hall when my key wouldn't turn in the lock. A wasp fought its way out of the hall light.

"Did you pay the rent?" RD questioned.

That's when we heard something. Something inside. Like it was heading out back. I told RD to stay put while I raced down the stairs, giving him a good head start by the time I finally made it outside. I looked around the crummy parking lot, searching the cars, waiting for someone to leave. A kid on a bike rode by, glancing at me with a smile before disappearing across the street. I continued to search the empty parking lot for the perp, even kneeling to look under an unrecognizable pickup truck parked near my balcony with no luck.

When we finally got inside we found the sliding glass door to the patio wide open. And there was his kit, right on the fake hardwood floor. Must have fallen out of his pocket during his departure. Twelve pins of differing lengths, shapes and flexibility, much nicer than my own. I thought long and hard about how he had targeted me. I guess all of those hours at work, or sitting in the library, or riding my bike, or of thinking about breaking in to someone else's home landed me here, a strange irony. But it was enlightening.

I broke down his every move, knowing burglars rarely move on a job without some intelligence. Had somebody been watching me? It's pretty hard to watch somebody, it's a lot of work. I considered the likelihood that he went out that night with his kit but didn't know exactly where he was going to strike until he landed at my door. But it didn't seem plausible. I couldn't figure it out. Why me? I looked around my place just to confirm everything was intact. He was good… but not good enough to get away with anything. Not that night. I moved out the next day.

I found all kinds of articles about burglars checking people's mailboxes and then searching for the names they found online, or cutting the power to people's homes while they did surveillance. Most of the stuff was obvious, but there was one detail I found fascinating. I didn't realize that you committed a burglary in stages, not all at once. See, you cut the power and force a door at 3 am one night and then you leave. Then you come back the next night right after dark and everything is set up. You leave clues for yourself to see if anyone has been there. You stash the bike maybe between 150-300 yards away. You go the last little bit by foot. Your escape route is already planned. Sammy Gravano and John Gotti planned Paul Castellano's murder for seven months. They organized an eleven-man hit squad that dressed in white trench-coats and black Russian hats for the occasion. I always kinda liked Sammy The Bull. I watched him on 20/20. He said of all the nineteen murders he committed every single one of them was against another criminal or a gangster, and that he never hurt anyone who was innocent. Now that right there is my kinda fella. A man of principle.

It wasn't long before I started spying on policemen. I've always hated policeman since I was 15 years old, back when I started smoking pot. My idiot mother locked me out of the house one day, the same day I had invited some friends over to hang out in my room and listen to my rare collection of Legendary Stardust Cowboy singles. I had to get a ladder and climb in through the attic window. A near-sighted neighbor thought I was a burglar and called the cops who came ready for a burglary and ended up arresting all of us for possession. Some of my best friends said I set them up, that I was a snitch. A Narc they called me. A fucking Narc. I hated those Louisville pigs after that and I've hated them ever since. Then there was the time the shifty meter maid pulled a gun on me when she thought I was going to let my dog's fecal waste lay in the park without cleaning it up, but I was just going to get an earth-friendly biodegradable sheet from the metal dispenser to pick it up, the raving bitch. And then of course there was the time I was questioned outside the library after a long night's worth of research for being a rapist and a stalker. After an hour of questioning they finally let me go, explaining I fit the description of "a tall white guy in a hat."

My time was coming. I had outgrown the library. I'd been watching A&E for weeks. It was time to go deeper. I needed to hit the streets. I got a transistor radio, and I found these two fat pigs and--listen to this!--I told them I was a newspaper reporter for the L.A. Times and my boss told me I had to follow the calls but I couldn't figure out how to decode 'em, and if they could just help me out… Where were the calls coming from, you know? I told them I couldn't track anything for the paper if I didn't know the codes and I'd be fired. And then, the kicker, I told them how smart they must be to have all those codes memorized. And after about a four minute conversation with these two nitwits working the Broadway corner of some fucked up Chinatown parade on a bright Saturday afternoon, doing absolutely nothing on the taxpayer's dollar, they told me every single code in the book. And I've got a mind like a steel trap. They told me how to know which calls are the closest to me and what station I'm talking to. They told me how to know which district a call from each street would go into if I was on the job. They told me everything.

I did a lot of test runs after that, made fake 911 calls about prowlers or burglars on certain buildings and I tracked the whole thing—time of the call to emergency, emergency to police dispatch, all of the associated codes that the dispatcher gave the street cops, the station they were deployed from, the response time to the crime scene. I watched them from rooftops through my binoculars as they stormed into buildings I had made phony calls about. This one time I even saw the cops who told me how to read the radio codes respond to one of my phony calls. That's when I knew I was ready. It was clear; I was playing chess and when everyone else was playing checkers.

I made sure I had everything mastered before I set out, and binoculars were by far the hardest thing to perfect. Sure, you think "Idiot had to learn how to use binoculars?" but it's not about using them, it's all about the vantage point. *Invisibility*. You couldn't just stand outside a coffee shop and peer through a set of binoculars, especially at something you had marked. Nobody could see you do it. No camera, no pedestrian, nothing. You try it. You couldn't do it. It's all about patience, foresight, a frame of thought, a line of thinking, focus, organization, and mental health. And my senses were as keen as ever. All I needed was the perfect target.

I decided a while ago I'm not wasting my efforts on your average son of a bitch. I don't have time for them. I'm looking for the worst of the worst. Those that seek out and prey on people who are weaker than themselves. Those who prey on the innocent. Those are the people I'm after, and I'm not too far away from them now.

Pedophiles. Land Barons. Lecherous Scum. The murky waters run deep in Los Angeles. Sometimes I find it amazing that something like a city is even possible with all the corruption and depravity behind the curtain. It didn't take long for me to chose my first target. Franklin D. Spinrad. He tried to have me evicted from an apartment once. It was rent-controlled. He didn't like that. I guess after a few years he thought I'd outstayed my welcome. There were a bunch of us. We had to fight it in court. I remember hearing somebody at the courthouse say

"The only reason I haven't sued for abuse of process is because I can't afford the retainer to secure legal representation which was intentionally created by his actions. He fraudulently filed a lawsuit against me solely for the purpose of obtaining a default judgment against me in an effort to destroy my credit and obtain monetary gains for his and his client's benefit."

He was an ass. But he was easy enough to watch, the arrogant prick. He was in court for a couple weeks. He made victims out of the desperate by extorting thousands of dollars from immigrant carpenters with six family members living in one-room apartments with large pots of rotten tripe boiling in garlic and tomatoes all day, smelling up the entire block so they can feed their entire family for five dollars. Five bucks will buy you a lot of tripe the day before it expires over at Jay's. And if the poor carpenters didn't want to be thrown out of their little tripe boiling ratholes for being five days late on the rent, now they had to pay.

"It's gonna cost you $1,000 to see this case dismissed," Spinrad told thousands of Hectors and Guadalupes on the third floor of the courthouse on Hill street. I can already tell I'll be spending a lot of time in that courthouse, casing future victims. It attracts a healthy dose of evil, that courthouse, full of accusers and killers and liars. And most of them are wearing suits. It's like the marbled gates of Hell.

And you should see where this old bastard lives. I followed him home from the courthouse one day. Nice place. Up in the hills. Makes a living throwing people out of rat holes they go into debt trying to rent. Then he just jacks the price up and does it all over again to the next schmuck that shows up at his door. Somewhere along the line I became one of those schmucks. I'm nobody's bitch anymore.

Since I quit the architecture firm I've seen a lot more of these glitches in the system. I have a lot more free time on my hands so I started refinishing old furniture. It's a chance for me to use some of my design skills, and a good excuse for collecting all the odd tools I've been putting together. Eight and twelve-inch mill files. Heavy-duty pliers and wire cutters. Electric drills, saws, and other odds and ends I've purchased over the last few months. I turned my storage unit into a shop. Gives me a private place to do my work, and RD pays me a couple bucks a month to keep his shirts in some storage bins, which helps offset the cost.

I tell people I'm an upholsterer, when I tell them anything at all. A lot of times I tell them I think it's rude to talk about work or what you do for a living. But I'm really more like a skip tracer, following people, finding people, setting up scores, scouring routes and paths and getaway possibilities on my bike. I read the crime reports every day. I read every newspaper in town. I love the newspaper. Just today, Murrieta police Sergeant Don Weller told the LA Times that burglars have been using a new technique, tripping circuit breakers.

"The bad guys will go out and turn the power off to the residence, and they'll stand outside waiting to see if there's any response from the inside, and if there isn't a response they'll make their way into the house."

Those burglaries are still unsolved.

It never made any sense to me why cops would talk with the papers about what frustrates them. I guess they're making excuses and trying not to look like idiots, but by telling the public about all these professional burglars and their mastermind techniques, they're just schooling a whole new wave of criminals! It's like the idiots with their books! Everybody's got such a big mouth these days. Nobody can keep their fucking trap shut.

Some might say that I'm like that, too. But I consider myself to be more like Percival, here only to show others everything that I have seen. And I have seen the wicked as well as the righteous. I can see everything in proportion to the whole of the entire universe now that I changed my thinking. I am seeing things clearer than I've ever seen them before. My mind is razor-sharp. I've been fasting for a week, and the purification I have felt is overwhelming. Isolation has lead to enlightenment. I can look into a person's eyes and tell what's in their soul. That's how I knew Spinrad was the one, just from looking at him. From the quiver of his lip to the way he talked out of the corner of his mouth. It was all a part of the spiritual diet I had been following.

So I watched, and I waited, and when the time came, I took it. Spinrad was at an event, I made sure of that. But his staff was still there. I parked the bike safely beside a neighbor's house and made my way into his vast yard on foot. The night was cool and clear. I climbed the wall in a corner outside the view of the video cameras and glided along the shadows until I spotted the lattice framework on the side of the house. I sprang across the yard, darting between trees, bushes, and gazebos until I could touch it, and I quickly tiptoed up the feeble woodwork to the upstairs balcony. I rolled over the top and lay down, waiting for a moment to catch my breath before slowly standing and seizing the moment.

My delicate fingers squeezed into the soft leather gloves I'd had in my pocket, and I drew my tools out from their roll into the moonlight on the luxurious Beverly Hills balcony. I drew two pins delicately from the roll and slipped them into the lock, where I could feel them scratching across the mechanics inside. Within moments I caught the lever, ever-so-carefully lifted it, and the deadbolt was at my mercy. I turned the door handle and removed my tools from the door without making a sound. Not a shadow was cast as I swung the door wide and stepped inside Spinrad's felonious estate.

It smelled rank. Worse than corruption. Something more sinister, like death. I was in his private office, exactly where I had planned to be. I hurried to the desk, unsure what I was looking for, quickly unlocking doors with my pins and sorting through files before closing them back. I went into the closet.

The closet had rows and rows of jackets, suit pants, other expensive designer clothing, and a safe. I entered the six-digit code, the only logical six-digit code, followed by the pound sign, which is typical for this make and model, and the door swung open and it sparkled.

Diamond necklaces passed over. A hundred-thousand-dollar watch, skipped. Passports and paperwork, all overlooked. But there was an envelope, and what looked like eighty to a hundred-thousand dollars in cash rubber-banded in the back. I helped myself, shoving the money into my fanny pack, quickly checking the envelope to find a series of high-dollar bonds when someone stepped in the room. A maid carrying a load of laundry.

I looked at her, and she glared at me, her eyes wide with fear and surprise when I ran at her, pushing past her before she could scream, and I disappeared into the bedroom. A butler, having heard the screams of the maid, appeared in the doorway, cutting me off, and so I turned myself out onto the balcony and leaped over the side.

I landed on the ground with a great whooph! knocking the air clear out of myself, but the sight of a fully grown man racing toward me helped me pick myself up and run. I sprang back over the wall, leaving my attacker trapped like a fenced dog.

I ran down the street to my getaway. I could hear the sirens growing louder in my head. The screams from the mansion seemed to alert the neighbors, who began to pour out of their homes. At long last I reached the tree where I had left my precious bike only to find, to my horror, that it was gone. I looked around, but there was no sign of it anywhere. I must have lost time in my moment of disbelief because the next thing I recall was being slammed to the ground and the cacophony of the arrest. The sirens wailed around me as the police ran from their vehicles, screaming. Rotating blue and red lights blinded me as they flashed within their strobing bulbs.

And then something strange happened. There, in the middle of it all, a teenage kid strode by enjoying the cool breeze of the calm night, gliding past the scene atop my bicycle. And he looked at me with a deliberate grin, and he smiled.

About Nicholas Zeman

Nicholas Zeman is a writer in Los Angeles, California. Originally from Louisville, Kentucky, Nick studied comparative literature and art history at the University of North Dakota in Grand Forks. He has published over 600 articles in various business and financial journals in the U.S., England, and the Netherlands. He has also published art reviews and scholarship on Abstract Expressionism in such publications as the *High Plains Reader* and the *Grand Forks Herald*, as well as artinfo.com.

SKY RIDERS

by Will Wallace

In moments like this, it was always the silence that struck Tommy the most. He smiled as the cold air licked his face and fluttered the stray dirty-blond locks that poked out from under his aviator's cap. Three thousand feet above the calm waters of the Mediterranean Sea the air was still, and visibility stretched to the horizon in every direction. Wisps of white clouds dotted the air, reminding him of the cotton fields he ran through as a child. Below, the warm water was as inviting as a bath at the end of a long day. It was beautiful along the coastline. But up here, Tommy was exactly where he was meant to be. Up here, Tommy was free.

The radio *crackled* and a voice brought him back to reality. "You still with us, Tommy?" The voice belonged to Ennio Giovanni, Tommy's boss and mentor. Tommy smiled and keyed his mic.

"I'm here, I'm here," he said into the handset. "Just having a look around. Thought I saw something."

"Daydreaming you mean, mon amie." It was a woman's voice, her accent caressing each syllable like a long lost lover.

"Why dream, Cecile, when the real thing is so much better?" Tommy replied.

"Come back down, Tommy. We're still on the clock," Ennio said.

"You got it, boss." Tommy returned the radio handset to its hook and pressed the ignition button on the console.

With a growl the engine of Tommy's triple-winged, green *Triceptor* came to life. Tommy eased the throttle forward and felt the power return to the plane as he took the yoke in his gloved hand. The vibration Tommy felt through the body of the *Triceptor* was a comfort. Though he loved gliding in silence, the roar of an engine was always music to Tommy's ears.

The gauges looked good, pressure was normal. Tommy shifted his weight in the cramped cockpit, trying to make himself a little more comfortable on the ratty seat. Reaching out of the cockpit, Tommy patted a hand against the side of the *Triceptor* like a loyal horse, right on the image of a double-winged seaplane set against a blood-red sun, supported by the words Dinamico Accompagnatore Impresa. "Come on, baby girl," Tommy cooed. "Time to get back to the party." Tommy shoved the yoke forward and the *Triceptor* dove through the sky.

Flecks of water collected on the lenses of his flight goggles as the *Triceptor* rocketed through a bank of clouds. Though he was surrounded by white, Tommy knew exactly where he was. He glanced at the altimeter just as it hit 2000 feet. Tommy yanked back on the yoke and the *Triceptor* burst through the cloud cover into the bright sunlight. Tommy throttled back and the engine quieted to a rhythmic purr. He wiped the condensation from his goggles with the sleeve of his flight jacket. Then he saw her.

Four massive propeller-driving engines pushed the long hull of the luxury skyliner through the crisp sunlight, the wind whipping long bright blue banners emblazoned with the twin-propeller seal of Martin Aviation. An elegant framework of brass and wood lattices crisscrossed around a thick fabric envelope that surrounded the massive gas-filled balloons keeping the great ship aloft. Scattered along the latticework, small observation platforms dotted the ship. Atop the skyliner, at the nose of the envelope, the cockpit shined brightly in the sun. Lovingly painted in large elegant letters along the hull beneath the tall windows of the cockpit was the name *Elizabeth.*

Cruising a few hundred feet above the *Elizabeth*, two prop-driven seaplanes flew in tight formation. Each of the seaplanes carried the same seal as Tommy's *Triceptor*. Tommy throttled forward and the *Triceptor* fell in line with the two other seaplanes. Tommy glanced across the way and grinned at the seaplane running alongside his own.

In her mauve *Faucon*, Cecile Dubois handled the yoke with a casual indifference that belied her true mastery of the plane and the engine that powered it. The end of a cream-colored silk scarf, tucked into her leather flight jacket, snapped lively in the wind, giving more fuel to the rumor that Cecile was a famous actress who had escaped to Italy in order to outrun a tumultuous past. This idea was, of course, ridiculous, but with a smile and a shrug, Cecile would never deny the possibility that it was true.

"Welcome back to Earth," Cecile teased into her radio. "Miss me?"

"Impossibly" Tommy replied, feigning heartbreak. Cecile laughed from her cockpit.

"Anything to report?" Ennio's voice interrupted over the radio.

Pulling up the rear in his beige *Sirocco*, Ennio Giovanni kept an eye on the cyan waters below the *Elizabeth*. With dashing good looks and the dark olive skin that came with old Italian blood, it had not taken long for Ennio to drum up enough money from family and friends to open a small escort company right in the heart of Paradiso da Pilota, the cluster of islands off the coast of Naples inhabited by an assortment of aviators, smugglers, pirates, and scalawags. Now, nine years later, Ennio had one of the largest hangers and two of the best pilots money could buy on his payroll.

"Another beautiful day in paradise," Tommy detailed.

"Bene, bene," Ennio said with a smile. Italy was God's country and the adventurer couldn't imagine living anywhere else. Taped to the control panel amongst the levers and gauges of his seaplane was a sharp black and white photograph. In it, beaming a wide smile was Elena, Ennio's whirlwind of a daughter, leaping into the air, hugging a terrified Calico cat as it flailed in her arms. Behind Elena stood her father, his arm curled lovingly around the waist of his wife, Lucia. Ennio often remarked that Lucia was the only woman he'd ever loved, but the truth of the matter was that Lucia was the only woman who had the fortitude to put up with his aerial exploits. Standing to the left of Ennio and Lucia, Cecile heaved with laughter as the struggling cat knocked a pint of beer from Tommy's hand, sloshing the foamy liquid in his face. The perfect moment frozen in time. Both Cecile and Tommy had the same photograph taped to their consoles. Ennio flashed a grin as the memory sparked through him. He keyed his radio again. "Tommy, since you're in such high spirits, why don't you and Cecile give the good people a show. Remind them we're still up here."

"You got it, boss," Tommy replied. "Think you can keep up, Ceci--"

Before Tommy could finish his sentence the *Faucon* shot like an arrow toward the skyliner below. Instantly, Tommy threw his stick forward and jammed the throttle full steam ahead. The *Triceptor* roared as it dove after the other seaplane, chasing after Cecile, matching her wide arc towards the bow of the *Elizabeth*. A grin crawled between Tommy's ears. He knew what Cecile was thinking. The passengers on the skyliner were definitely in for a show. And for once, they didn't have to pay extra for it. Ennio knew the goodwill it brought, and his co-conspirators certainly didn't mind the fun.

Tommy eased back on the stick, nudging his foot pedals to the left as he joined Cecile in a series of tight spirals across the skyliner's bow. As the two seaplanes rolled back and forth, Tommy spied tourists on the *Elizabeth's* main observation deck crowding the windows for a better look at their aerial acrobatics. Though he was impressed with the engineering of these great ships, Tommy would never fully understand their appeal. Sure, the amenities were nice and skyliners could take you to some exotic and hard to reach places, but at the end of the day you were still in a giant tube. You couldn't even feel the wind in your hair. But any objections Tommy had about how rich people spent their money were beside the point. All that mattered right now was keeping them entertained and, more importantly, safe.

Just because something is outlawed, or even eradicated, doesn't mean it always goes away. Piracy was no different. It simply evolved to fit the times. Gone were the days when pirates would appear out of the fog like specters to waylay lost ships and plunder their holds of valuable cargo. Nowadays a new breed of pirate was screaming down out of the clouds and forcing aviators to land their planes. Usually, the unlucky pilots and their passengers would be robbed, their planes stolen, and then they'd be left to fend for themselves. Others weren't so lucky. The more brazen of the pirates would board luxury and cargo skyliners to hijack and strip them clean. As piracy grew, so did the demand for added security. Escort companies appeared overnight to scoop up lucrative contracts. Many of these companies fell away, but those with the skill and the armaments to deal with the pirates flourished. And if Tommy and his compatriots did their jobs right, it would mean an exclusive contract with Martin Aviation and all of the privileges that come with it. Just because Dinamico Accompagnatore Impresa was a sought-after escort company didn't mean it was always easy sailing. If they won this contract, they'd never need to take a spotty job out of Athens or Istanbul again. Gone would be the question of whether the people who hired you would skip out on the agreed-upon payment. Gone would be the anxiety of spending what money they did earn on repairs to their planes, or worse, funerals for pilots. If they won the contract, Tommy and his friends would essentially become company men for Martin Aviation. But Tommy didn't care. All that mattered was keeping the *Triceptor* flying and the wind in his hair.

Tommy shook his head to clear his thoughts. *Stay focused* Tommy told himself as he came out of the spiral and leveled off. Wide-eyed passengers waved and shouted through the windows of the observation deck. Tommy couldn't hear them, but he and Cecile smiled and waved back as they disappeared from view.

Wind whipped through the open-air platform at the stern of the skyliner. Strapped securely to the iron-grated deck, a Spotter scanned the clouds behind the *Elizabeth* for any potential threats. He wore a brown canvas set of coveralls with the Martin Aviation logo stenciled on the back. Atop his head was a matching skull cap and goggles. Letting his binoculars fall to his chest, the Spotter turned and walked to a metal roll-top desk ratcheted to the deck. The safety lines that kept him secured to the *Elizabeth* slid along a series of guide rails cut into the deck.

At the desk, the Spotter pulled a lever and rolled back the desk's covering. Inside was a large thermos. He flicked back the lid and fingered out a thick straw. After a few deep pulls from the straw, the Spotter felt the strong coffee warming his belly against the chilly air. As he reached again for the thermos, something flitted past a cloud in the distance beyond the *Elizabeth's* stern. The Spotter replaced the thermos in the desk and returned to his position on the platform. Binoculars pressed to his goggles, the Spotter scanned the clouds. He lowered the binoculars again.

A brass canister dropped into the receiving mechanism nestled beneath a spider's web of pneumatic tubes that rose to the ceiling, turned and snaked away through the skyliner. First Officer Clemmons retrieved the canister and read the message inside.

"Captain Brisbane, sir," Clemmons called across the bridge.

"Mmmm," came a reply from an elderly, uniformed gentleman standing before the large windows at the head of the bridge.

"A message from one of our look-outs," the young First Officer said as he stepped across the bridge. The elderly man held out his hand. Clemmons handed over the message.

Captain Brisbane pulled on a pair of reading glasses and scanned the message. His white hair was close-cropped under his captain's hat in the old military fashion. A beard, similarly white, covered his cheeks and jaw-line with a neat mustache culminating in two points under his nose.

"A lookout has spotted something in the clouds to our stern," Brisbane said in a voice that could easily belong to a smiling grandfather as he bounced a granddaughter on his knee. But in his uniform, with the Mediterranean sun shining off of the gold epaulettes on his shoulders, the voice commanded respect and obedience from his crew.

"Make a note in the log," Brisbane said as he folded his reading glasses, "and have our escort check it out."

"Yes, sir," Clemmons answered with a salute. Brisbane returned the salute and moved back to his spot in front of the large windows.

Clemmons ducked through a small hatchway and into the radio room where a Radio Operator sat before a wall of radio sets. He pulled off his headset as Clemmons tapped his shoulder and handed over the message.

"Have the escort look into it," Clemmons told the Operator. He nodded and turned back to his wall of radios where he activated a transmitter labeled 'ESCORT CREW.'

"Escort, come in," the Radio Operator's voice crackled through the static on Ennio's radio.

With a gloved hand, Ennio flicked a switch on his radio and picked up the handset. "Escort, here. Go ahead, *Elizabeth*."

"One of our spotters has reported a possible sighting in the clouds above your position to our stern. Please investigate."

"Will do, *Elizabeth*. Escort out."

"So you were daydreaming," Cecile accused over the radio.

"Not daydreaming," Tommy replied. "Scanning the horizon for potential threats."

"Sure, sure, petit garcon."

"Always with the name-calling," Tommy replied with a grin. "You're lucky we're-"

"Save it for later, bambini," Ennio interrupted. "You have work to do."

"I'm on it, boss," Tommy replied dutifully, but before he could push his *Triceptor* back to a higher altitude, a single blood-red seaplane broke through the cloud cover like a fiery angel of death. It was a Scorpione, a known, if not expected threat. The seaplane swung low in a wide arc before Tommy and his companions. Sharp barbs glittered in the sun on the Scorpione's fuselage, invoking the namesake of the gang the seaplane belonged to. But what drew Tommy's eye wasn't the seaplane's red body scorching across the crystal blue backdrop of the Mediterranean; it was the man standing atop the Scorpione, Il Macellaio. *The Butcher*.

Thick leather straps attached to the belt at his waist kept Il Macellaio secured to the top of the seaplane where the two wings met. Standing there, he reminded Tommy of the barnstormers he adored as a child back home. Their aerial exploits always brought a smile to his face. But unlike those daredevils, Il Macellaio wasn't there to make the crowd on the *Elizabeth* 'ooh and ahh.' He was there to make them scream. Il Macellaio looked back over his shoulder at Tommy and sneered, his wiry dark beard snapping in the wind.

Though their seaplanes were often held together with no more than spit and scrounged parts, the Scorpione gang was the most feared band of pirates in the Mediterranean. Most gangs settled for forcing wayward planes and smaller skyliners to land in order to rob the tourists of any cash or valuables. But the Scorpiones were bolder and more brazen in their approach. They didn't only rob their victims. The Scorpiones kidnapped, sold, or ransomed anyone they came across that would bring them a buck. But if the ransoms were too small, fingers and ears would be sent back to prove the Scorpiones were serious. They were the wolves of the air, but like wolves, they hunted meager prey. Until now. Until now, no pirate gang had ever gone after a prize as large as the *Elizabeth*. The Scorpiones were moving up in the world.

As if he sensed what Tommy was thinking, Il Macellaio raised a Lewis machine gun with a meaty arm and bellowed his war cry. Instantly a dozen blood-red seaplanes broke through the cloud cover and surrounded the three escort planes. They chugged back and forth, making a show to intimidate Tommy and his friends.

Il Macellaio bellowed again and his seaplane dropped like a stone towards the skyliner below. His comrades repeated the cry and pushed their sticks all the way down. Like a swarm of red wasps, the Scorpiones buzzed about the *Elizabeth*, drawing the attention of crew members and tourists alike. Cecile and Ennio watched from their seaplanes as the Scorpiones darted here and there. Cecile looked across to Ennio.

A look of quiet consternation washed over Ennio's face. "Stay loose and keep them away from the hatches." He broke formation and threw his *Sirocco* into the flight. Cecile grinned and did the same, her *Faucon* taking off like a shot after the nearest Scorpione. Tommy howled in delight as his propeller blades chopped through the air, speeding after Il Macellaio.

Officer Clemmons watched as a wave of brass canisters fell into the wire baskets beneath the pneumatic tubes at the back of the bridge. "Sir," he exclaimed, but Captain Brisbane cut him off as he strode across the bridge barking orders.

"I'm well aware of the bloody situation, Officer Clemmons," the Captain shouted, his grandfatherly tone was replaced with the cadence of military precision. He watched as the red seaplanes surrounded the *Elizabeth*.

"Three escorts against a dozen pirates?" Clemmons asked, sweat dappling his forehead.

"Management says they're the best in the business," Brisbane replied. "But all the same, best not to be caught with our trousers down. Inform all gunners at once."

"Yes, sir!"

Brisbane turned to the two Pilots at the front of the bridge. The Pilots gripped the two large wooden ship's wheels set parallel to each other. Both wheels were from British warships that had been sunk in battle during the last century.

With a measured voice Captain Brisbane said, "Keep us steady, lads."

The Pilots nodded to Captain Brisbane, replying in unison "Sir," before glancing at once another in nervous accord.

Brass shell casings sprouted in the wind before falling thousands of feet towards the blue water below as Il Macellaio fired his Lewis machine gun at Tommy's approaching *Triceptor*. He cursed his gun when the bolt kicked back, the magazine empty. Il Macellaio ripped the circular magazine from his weapon and threw it to the wind. Fifty yards behind him, Tommy ducked, holding on tightly as he piloted the plane into an evasive barrel roll.

Cecile's mauve *Faucon* zipped around the stern of the *Elizabeth*, hot on the tail of another Scorpione. She glanced to her right and saw the glass ball turrets dotting the skyliner come to life. Each of the turrets housed two heavy machine guns and Gunners ready to take over should Cecile and her companions fail.

The red seaplane dipped and weaved before it dropped into a steep dive. But Cecile kept pace with her prey, jamming her stick down to match the Scorpione's dive. Easing into range, Cecile lined up the Scorpione in her gun sights and squeezed the trigger between her legs. Hot lead exploded from her single machine gun. Bullets splintered the Scorpione's tail, chewing it to pieces to expose the flimsy wood frame beneath.

Cecile took aim again, this time riddling the exposed engine between the wings above the pilots head with a spray of bullets. Sparks showered the Scorpione pilot and his engine coughed and sputtered as the old wooden propeller slowed until it abruptly came to a stop. Slapping his unresponsive controls, the Pilot lifted himself out of the cockpit and glared back at Cecile. "Diavolessa," he exclaimed before leaping from his burning plane. Cecile cackled as she pulled her *Faucon* back into the fight. A patchwork parachute opened below her and disappeared into the sea.

Tommy gritted his teeth as he tried to keep up with Il Macellaio, all the while dodging the fire from his Lewis gun. Breaking through a bank of clouds, Tommy found himself a thousand yards above the *Elizabeth*. He looked down to see a horrific picture: Scorpiones swarmed the *Elizabeth* as she hovered closer to Naples. At the same time Cecile and Ennio did their best to keep the blood-red seaplanes away from the great skyliner. But something didn't sit right with Tommy. They hadn't made any attack on the skyliner. It was as if they were waiting for something.

He keyed his radio. "Be on the lookout. They're holding back for something."

Cecile shot back over the radio. "I can assure you, they are not holding back."

Ennio's voice crackled through the radio. "She's - merda!" The *Sirocco's* engine roared as Ennio put the seaplane through its paces. "Cecile's, right. They're not playing around."

"But something's wrong. Why haven't they converged on the skyliner? Or shot up with the cockpit to force it to land? It's—" but before Tommy could finish his thought, the answer to his questions broke through the cloud cover.

Amidst the swarming Scorpiones, two four-engine transport planes appeared. These heavy-duty haulers carried ten Scorpione pirates, each adorned with a tight leather body harness and a submachine gun strapped to their back. As the two transports rose in elevation towards the *Elizabeth*, they split off and took positions on either side of the skyliner. As the Tail Gunners kept an eye out for escort planes, the Grapplers on each transport stood from their platforms and aimed bazookas at the skyliner.

Boom! Boom!

Two rocket-propelled grappling hooks screamed towards the *Elizabeth* as coils of heavy cable unwound at lighting speed between the Grapplers feet.

Thunk! Thunk!

The grappling hooks plunged into the metal hull of the *Elizabeth*, each a stone's throw from an access hatch that lead into the skyliner's interior passageways. The teeth of the grappling hooks bit deep into the metal hull as the cables went taut, tethering each of the transports to the massive floating ship.

Setting aside their bazookas, the Grapplers on each transport pulled on their goggles and connected their body harnesses to the cables with D-rings. They tested the cables and found them secure. Taking deep breaths and giving themselves the sign of the cross, the Grapplers stepped forward and leaped from the sides of the transports.

The D-rings *sang* and sparks flew from the cables as the Grapplers zipped down, landing on either side of the skyliner. Instead of submachine guns, the two Grapplers unslung portable blow torches and lit them, their flames turning to blue jets. The Grapplers flipped dark shades across their goggles. They angled the torches against the hinges of the access hatches and blazed through the metal.

"Shit," Tommy hissed. "They're gonna take her!"

"Waiting until we get to Naples is too risky. It makes sense," Cecile continued.

"We can't let that happen," Ennio finished.

Tommy glared through the windshield at Il Macellaio, who grinned, his gold tooth reflecting the sun through an otherwise black tangled beard. "Roger that, sir."

Glancing back, Ennio saw Tommy break his pursuit of Il Macellaio and drop like a comet towards the skyliner and the transport planes. Tracers slipped past the *Sirocco's* wings. Ennio looked over his shoulder where he spotted two more Scorpiones on his tail. He jammed the throttle forward and banked away from the skyliner with the two red seaplanes in close pursuit.

Crouched near the hatch, one of the Grapplers worked the blue flame until the first hinge broke away into a handful of white-hot pieces of metal. Smiling, the Grappler turned his torch to the second hinge. *Clang! Clang!* Sparks flew inches from the Grappler's head, sending him sprawling onto the hull of the skyliner. Removing the shades from his goggles, the Grappler saw Tommy's *Triceptor* cruising ten feet alongside the *Elizabeth*. Tommy leaned out of the cockpit with his trusty Colt .45 in hand. *Bang!* The bullet ricocheted off the hull, inches from the Grappler.

"Ah! Quell'era vicino!" the Grappler shouted back.

Tommy laughed and aimed again, this time at the barbed grappling hook holding the transport to the skyliner. *Bang!* The hook swung loose from the hull. Switching hands, Tommy trained his pistol at the transport above him. The Tail Gunners tried desperately to point their machine guns at Tommy, but he was too low. The Scorpiones frantically shouted at the transport's Pilot, but it was too late. *Bang! Bang!* Bullets shattered the windscreen of the transport's cockpit sending glass everywhere. The Pilot covered his face and yanked the stick to the left, away from the gunfire.

Tommy waved goodbye to the Grappler as the transport banked hard to get away. "Merda!" the Grappler shouted as the cable went taut and yanked him off the side of the great ship.

Tommy watched the Grappler sail away like a puppet on a string. "One down. One to go." He banked the *Triceptor* under the belly of the *Elizabeth* over to her starboard side. He popped the spent magazine from his Colt and slid in a fresh one, then thumbed the slide release, kicked the breach back into place and loaded a bullet into the barrel. Pulling back on the stick, the *Triceptor* rose into position beneath the remaining transport, but he wasn't alone.

Cecile's *Faucon* dropped into position right in front of Tommy, her backwash blasting into his windscreen.

"What the...," Tommy snarled as he regained control of the stick.

"Can't let you have all the fun, mon ami," Cecile called from her cockpit. Tommy smirked as he pulled the *Triceptor* away from the skyliner. Cecile blew him a kiss as he took off once again after Il Macellaio.

Cecile pushed her throttle forward, inching the *Faucon* closer to the skyliner. She lined up the grappling hook with her sights and squeezed the trigger. Bullets tore into the skyliner's metal hull, dislodging the grappling hook, and leaving a field of pockmarks and bullet holes behind. The remaining Grappler looked from the loose grappling hook to the *Faucon*.

"Oops," Cecile said with a hand over her mouth. Looking above her, she pulled back on the control stick and the *Faucon* shot towards the transport. The Tail Gunner sprayed a futile burst of fire, but it was too late. The transport Pilot spied Cecile's *Faucon* heading straight toward him and banked away hard just before the collision, taking the last Grappler with it.

From his Scorpione, Il Macellaio saw the transport planes arcing away from the *Elizabeth*, the Grapplers dangling from their cables. All around him Scorpione's limped and streamed black smoke from their engines. He started the raid with a dozen seaplanes, but now less than half remained operational.

"Bastardi," Il Macellaio growled, his eyes on the opposing seaplanes of Ennio, Tommy, and Cecile as they all made wide loops only to level out right in front of him. He fired his Lewis gun into the air until it locked up, and he heaved it overboard in anger. Il Macellaio turned, grabbed his pilot by the jacket and yelled over the engine. "Get us out of here!"

Uncapping the final brass canister in the wire baskets, Officer Clemmons turned to Captain Brisbane with his report. "All intruders have been successfully repelled, sir."

"Thank you, Clemmons," the Captain replied, a smug grin hidden beneath his mustache. "It would appear these escorts were money well-spent."

"Yes, sir," Clemmons returned with a smile.

"Tell our new security detail to expect a telegram from the Rome office. Contracts should arrive by post within the week," Brisbane announced as he took a seat in the Captain's chair. Clemmons saluted and moved off to the Radio Room.

The Navigator turned from his station on a small platform at the bottom of the bridge that afforded him an unprecedented view of the surrounding horizons. "La Grande Isola coming into view, Captain."

"Excellent timing," Captain Brisbane replied as he checked the elegant hands of the clock above the Pilots' station. "Take us down, lads," the Captain commanded as he took his seat. "Three degrees at the bow and one hundred feet, if you please."

"Aye, aye," the Pilots said in unison, their movements a ballet of synchronized motion. The large wheels running parallel to the *Elizabeth's* keel were eased forward as the gauges on the center console showed the pressure in the balloons beginning to dip.

Tommy watched as the *Elizabeth* tilted slightly and began its descent towards the Mediterranean and, further still, La Grande Isola, the island oasis off the coast of Naples. He eased back on the control stick and his *Triceptor* rose to join Ennio and Cecile in formation above the skyliner. Both the *Faucon* and the *Sirocco* looked no worse for wear, aside from a few bullet holes. No more than usual. As he turned to see the few remaining Scorpiones disappear towards the horizon, Tommy keyed his radio. "That's worth an extra beer tonight, right?"

Ennio grinned, "We'll see. Gotta make sure we scored the deal, first."

"You don't think we got it?" Tommy questioned.

"Of course we got it," Celine confirmed.

Tommy rode in silence before offering his thoughts. "You think Il Macellaio's pissed?"

Ennio sighed over the radio. "I told him we needed to put on a good show, and that's exactly what we did."

"We did, indeed!" Celine confirmed.

"As long as they get their cut, everything will be fine." Ennio smiled like a confident father to his nervous son. Then, he jostled the yoke, causing his *Sirocco's* wings to dip up and down in a wagging motion. Cecile copied him in her *Faucon*. Never one to be outdone, Tommy tipped his *Triceptor* into a barrel roll.

"That's it, miei amici!" Ennio cheered. "Now let's go grab that drink!"

Engines roared as the three seaplanes shot towards the water below like screaming eagles. Tommy kept his grip tight on the control stick as he inched the throttle forward. To his left, Cecile winked at Tommy as her *Faucon* pulled ahead. To his right, Ennio kept pace with his team before throttling to the lead.

The three seaplanes leveled out just above the warm waters of the Mediterranean as they sped towards the brightly colored buildings of Naples. Tommy eased back on the stick to fall behind Ennio and Cecile as the warm wind licked him in the face. Life had been good to him in the new pirate markets of the Mediterranean, and things were about to get even better.

About Will Wallace

Will Wallace is a screenwriter most prominently known for his work on the award-winning series *Teen Wolf* on MTV. He is currently developing new projects for film and TV, as well as a comic book series. *Sky Riders* is Will's first published short story, which he plans on adapting into a larger novel.

Will is a graduate of the University of Alabama and keeps the "Roll Tide" spirit alive in Los Angeles. He sometimes runs marathons and is the father to Mersenne, a 3-year-old Tortoiseshell cat who hates car rides and rules his life with an iron fist.

For more info visit willwritesgood.com

BEHIND THOSE VEILS

by Shawn D. Brink

My terror began a few months back, and every day since has been hell. Morning after morning, I arrive at work, approaching the Basic I Solutions building, forcing one foot in front of the other, wanting to turn and flee, but knowing that such is not an option.

The building itself is ordinary. Modern in construction, made of common materials: brick, mortar, steel, and glass. The building's not the cause of my anxiety, it's those within that I find disturbing.

You see, the other employees, they're not who they portray themselves to be. Their disguises are excellent, I'll give them that. At first, even I didn't notice their ruse. Even now, I recall my new employee orientation, the Human Resources representative looked so normal, pleasant; attractive even.

But now I see them for who they are, and as a result, everything in my life has somersaulted into chaos. I can actually pinpoint the exact moment when my eyes were opened to the truth. It was a chilly day, the 15th of October. It had been drizzling that morning as I came into work. I remember because the cold moisture on my skin had acted as a much-needed eye-opener.

I hadn't slept well due to nightmares. I get those from time to time, but rarely so intense that they ruin my sleep.

I sat down at my desk that morning and started to work. "How are we doing today?" I heard the voice of Mr. Denning.

Mr. Denning was the CEO of the company. With his salt and pepper hair, expensive suits and power ties, he was capitalism's poster child. I was sure he had no desire to hear about my sleep deprivation problems, so I stuck with the generic, socially acceptable answer. "Just keeping busy, sir," I answered.

"That's what I like to hear. Say, can you please ensure that this memo gets distributed to all the employees?"

"Yes sir," I said as I reached out my hand to take the paper from him, keeping my eyes on my monitor in an effort to multi-task.

"It needs to be distributed no later than ten."

"I'm on it, Mr. Den..."

I froze in mid-sentence as I caught sight of the hand that was passing me the memo. It wasn't human. I looked up from that hand and gazed at the appendage's owner. Denning had changed.

My mind scrambled for answers. Denning wasn't wearing a costume, he couldn't be. The sight of him was beyond what any costume-maker could conjure. Neither was I hallucinating as I felt sure my imagination was incapable of such a creation.

"Are you okay?" Denning asked, his voice rich with concern.

I nodded, but on the inside I was far from okay.

"Just make sure the memo goes out, please."

I took the paper from his grotesque hand, saying nothing. But he didn't move on. Instead, he hovered over me, just long enough for me to catch an odd mildew smell emanating from his person.

"Are you sure you're alright? You look a little under the weather."

Somehow, I found my voice. "Yes. Yes, I'm fine." I sounded robotic, but at least I was talking. Under the circumstances, it was the best I could manage.

Denning stared at me for what seemed to be an eternity, and it was all I could do to keep my emotions bottled up. Finally, he turned and walked away.

As soon as he was out of sight I bolted for the restroom and locked myself in one of the stalls. I don't know how long it took me to get a grip, but eventually I calmed down. I didn't want to go back out there, but I had to, if for no other reason than to get home at the end of the day. But until that time, I would have to face this new fear and try my best to overcome it.

So there I was, that fateful drizzly day, sitting in the bathroom, my discovery made. After a time I collected myself, washed my hands in the sink for good measure, and exited the bathroom when it hit me full steam ahead. It wasn't just Denning. All the other employees at Basic I were in the same condition. I personally checked out each and every one of them, walking by their work stations, trying not to stare, trying not to freak out.

Why did I suddenly see them in this way? It was so bizarre, so sudden, as if someone had strapped a pair of x-ray goggles on my head and flipped the 'on' switch. It was impossible to undo. I could still see their human disguises which before had appeared so genuine, as if their fake masks hung over the real beings like veils.

I use the term 'veil' because that's how thin and transparent their disguises appeared through my eyes after that unforgettable day, October 15th. Under those gossamer covers, they hid their true selves, which were all mucus, veins, pus, and bulbous mass. And after that day, I couldn't rationalize how anything that grotesque could be anything but evil. I took note regarding how much I hated them. Even though they hadn't done anything against me per se, even though I had no proof that they were truly evil, I knew with a deeply seeded and innate passion that I hated them through to my very core.

And then, a terrifying thought hit me. *Was I changing as well?* I ran to the restroom several times before the end of the day to stare into the mirror over the sink where I examined my face thoroughly, but I remained as I always had been.

A sense of loneliness settled in my veins, my assumptions being two-fold. One: I began to believe that I was the only employee at Basic I Solutions who could see through the intruders disguises. And, Two: I believed there was a large probability that I was the only one at Basic I Solutions that was genuinely human. I couldn't be sure, but with every delivery, and every new client meeting, I became more and more confident that my intuition was dead on.

See, my job as receptionist requires that my desk is in the large front lobby. As such, I deal with a lot of vendors and delivery personnel. I watched them as they came and went, I studied them as they interacted with various Basic I employees, and never did any of them indicate that they saw anything out of the ordinary. For them, it was just business as usual. And none of those who entered the building as visitors wore veils. They appeared to me as normal a human being as any single human being can be.

For me, however, things were far from normal. My days were filled with terror, which I had to keep bottled up. I dared not alert my employer to the fact that I was onto them as I felt certain that my safety lay in remaining below their radar.

My options were limited. I couldn't go to the police. What could I report to them that would keep me out of a padded room and custom-fitted straight jacket?

I thought about simply abandoning my employment and living off the grid. You know, like those people that go primitive, hiding away in some abandoned shanty out in the Arizona desert or something. But no. I'm no survivalist. I probably wouldn't last a day out in the wilderness. Besides, sudden job abandonment would surely raise red flags here at Basic I Solutions and I had no way of knowing the extent to which they would hunt me down. All I knew was if they were capable of this level of deception, of convincing real live human beings of their authenticity, they were capable of most anything.

So, I continued my act of obliviousness as long as I possibly could. I made it through the second half of October, November, and into December before things began to unravel.

Two months of constant anxiety had taken its toll. The circles under my eyes had grown deep from lack of sleep due to nightmare hauntings. The tips of my fingers became raw from constant chewing. I avoided weighing myself, but the bagginess of my clothes suggested I was shedding pounds at an alarming rate. Living in a perpetual state of suspense can be an effective diet plan, I noticed. But as the weeks rolled along, I knew I couldn't keep up this charade, not for the long haul. Something would need to be done to alleviate my stress.

And then a thought germinated in my brain. If I couldn't escape the situation, I would simply have to eliminate it. My plan was criminal, but one born of self-preservation, and therefore, in my mind, justified.

Extermination. It was the only way.

But *how?*

I came to the conclusion that I would need to get them all at once. Like bedbugs, if one pair escaped, then I felt certain they would just multiply and come back more resilient than before. So, I began a period of intense intel-gathering, looking for anything unusual in the inner-workings of Basic I Solutions, anything that I could use to my advantage. And, as luck would have it, something turned up fairly quickly. In fact, it was so obvious I couldn't believe I'd never noticed it before.

One early December night as I was gathering my briefcase and coat to leave, I glanced back inside and realized that when I left work every night, I was always the first to leave. And when I arrived in the mornings, most of the lot was already full of what I assumed were other employees' vehicles. I began to develop a hypothesis, and to test it, I randomly marked a few of the cars' tires with chalk. Three days later I checked the marks. The cars had not moved. I made a mental note: the creatures not only work at the Basic I Solutions building, but they reside there, too.

This new info was encouraging. But how could I use it against them? I racked my brain before the answer finally came to me. If they all remained within the Basic I Solutions building, then the best way to eradicate them would be to destroy their nest in one decisive attack. And what's the best way to quickly destroy a building? A *bomb*.

But I was no terrorist. I had never before committed such a crime and had no idea how to make such a weapon.

That day, I began a rigorous campaign of self-instruction, my main concern being that the authorities would somehow catch wind of my internet searches and come knocking on my door. What would I tell them if their investigation led to my apartment? The answer eluded me.

Moreover, I discovered that the best bomb-making material was beyond my ability to obtain. I was no physicist, nor did I have the black market connections to get my hands on yellowcake uranium. But alternatives did exist. Effective explosives, I discovered, could be made with things like fertilizer, fossil fuels, and other common household ingredients.

The Basic I Solutions office was a three-story building constructed back in the 1960s by a very imaginative architect. With all of its angles and curves, it looked like something out of an original Star Trek episode.

It wasn't an overly-massive building, but one that made maximum use of its space. The best thing about its design, from my point of view, was the fact that the entire structure was supported by a massive central beam like the main pole of a circus tent. That beam, coincidentally, was located directly behind my reception desk, right in the center of the building. Logic told me that this would be an optimal place to plant my little creation.

Over the following weeks, I began smuggling in the various components. I'd always enjoyed reading crime novels over my work-breaks and had always kept a backpack with me for the purpose of carrying those books. Now, that backpack came in handy as a way to conceal my contraband.

This process took time as my backpack couldn't carry it all at once. Plus, I had to be strategic with my loads as I was working with volatile components.

Secrecy was the key. My pending crime had to remain unnoticed by everyone, especially the monsters that lived at Basic I.

One of my main challenges was space. My bomb needed to be powerful enough to take down the entire building. This meant that the device would need to be somewhat larger than a breadbox. Considerably larger. That's where my desk came in.

Bit by bit, the contents of my drawers and connected file cabinet were removed and put in boxes which I kept under my desk. This made my days more and more uncomfortable as my leg room grew less and less, but I considered this a small price to pay considering the magnitude of my future crimes.

A challenge came in connecting all the components. I can't tell you how many times I had to drop my pen for an excuse to wiggle under my desk and connect the contents of all the drawers with the proper wiring. Every connection had to be true, failure in this would mean a dud on fireworks night.

And now I've brought things up to the present.

I smuggle in the final components: batteries and the detonator. These items weigh heavily in my backpack, making me uneasy. How would I explain them if I was caught? The answer's clear, I wouldn't.

As soon as I'm at my desk, I quickly and carefully remove my pack, maintaining just enough composure to avoid flinging it into the desk, or the chair, or the pole. The contents are too valuable. I can't risk damaging the goods.

From that point on, it's a waiting game. I try to do my work, even though I know that whatever I accomplish won't be worth a hill of beans tomorrow. Still, I attempt to get things done, if for no other reason than to avoid suspicion.

I stay at my desk over the lunch hour, pulling out a sandwich that I had in my backpack right alongside the illicit paraphernalia. I bite into the sandwich, turkey with habanero cheddar on rye. It looks fairly mild, but the pepper gives it kick, like me.

It's hard to wait, but I force myself. Deliveries come and go throughout the day, per usual, and vendors arrive and leave; all of them human. I don't want to have everything set up and risk setting off the device prematurely. Collateral damage is to be avoided at all costs. Plus, I want everything to look normal. I want their realization of my crime to come a second too late, at the joyous moment their disgusting bodies are ripped apart by the explosion and buried under the rubble of the Basic I Solutions building.

I find myself glancing at my watch too often, a nervous twitch I suppose. With force, I keep my eyes on my work. I must avoid suspicion at all cost.

Finally, it's fifteen minutes to six and the last FedEx delivery guy is here. Only it's a girl. I wonder if it frustrates her as I fumble through the signing for the delivery. Those people always seem to be in such a rush, and I wrote my name so slowly. My nerves were so tightly wound I had to concentrate extremely hard to make sure I didn't pierce through the paper with my nervous scrawl.

I try breathing exercises as I watch her exit through the glass double doors of the building, hop into her delivery truck, and speed off like a bat out of hell. *In through the nose and out through the mouth. In through the nose and out through the mouth...*

I unzip my backpack and peer inside. The items are all there as I knew they would be.

I glance around and everyone is busy at work. They never pay any attention to me anyway. I remove the final two components from my pack, open my top left drawer, and insert both batteries and the detonator. I hook up the final connections and instantly the red LED on the detonator illuminates. The device is ready.

I look at it momentarily feeling as Dr. Frankenstein must have felt when those first volts shocked his creation to life. My creation, however, is capable of far greater destruction than Mary Shelley's creature, of this I'm almost certain. Ever so carefully I slide the drawer shut, and I wait.

The clock strikes six. It's closing time. I shut down my computer for no good reason. At this point, it doesn't matter. The whole thing is going to be blown to smithereens in minutes. Still, I can't help but do it, being the creature of habit that I am. Also, I suppose leaving my computer on might be a red flag to the enemy, something out of the ordinary.

I get up from my chair and grab my backpack, but only get a step away before I realize I've made a serious oversight. Retracting my steps, I open the detonator drawer just enough to see that red LED shining out. I look at the two black buttons on the detonator casing. They stare up at me like a set of dark beady eyes. I poke the eye labeled 'initiate'. The red LED turns off. A green one turns on. The device is live. The 20-minute countdown has begun.

For a second or two, I stand there staring at the ominous green glow. My pulse quickens and a shiver escapes as I contemplate the fact that there's no going back.

I slide the drawer closed again, careful to avoid sudden movements. I don't want any connections coming loose due to carelessness.

I adjust my backpack. The straps feel strange on my shoulders, what with the lack of weight pulling on them. The thought occurs to me that I should have had other things in there just so that it doesn't appear empty. What if somebody notices that it was weighted down when I came in this morning? Would the fact that it's not now raise their suspicion? I know I can't go back in time and rectify such errors. Still, I mentally kick myself for being such a novice criminal.

I push my chair in as far as possible. It doesn't slide in all the way given the fact that the space beneath is filled with boxes of items that once filled my drawers and file cabinet. I take a deep breath and try to stay calm for just a bit longer.

I've progressed too far for turning back, not that I wish to. I don't know what the creatures are exactly that live in the Basic I

Solutions building, but I hate them and feel a duty to both God and country to undo their existence.

The bomb in my desk is silent. This is the digital age, no tick-tocking required. Still, in my head, I hear the seconds sounding off as they pass into infinity, counting down to oblivion; *tick – tock – tick – tock – tick – tock.*

Immersed in my thoughts, I progress away from the bomb towards the front entrance of the Basic I Solutions Building. Inside of me, the tick-tocking booms. It's all I can do to keep from screaming out as my anxiety builds.

The front entrance looms closer, and like a jailbird running through an open pasture, with every step I can sense my freedom nearing.

As I reach out and grab the door handle, I feel something on my shoulder, something wrapping around the strap of my backpack, something impeding my progress along that Freedom Trail. Mr. Denning speaks.

"Before you leave, I was hoping to have a word with you."

I turn and behold the hideousness of the CEO. His veil hides nothing from me and it's all I can do to appear natural.

I look away from him, choosing instead to gaze through the glass of the exit doors, longing for the safety of the other side. I consider wriggling free from my backpack to flee, leaving Denning literally holding the bag. But how far would I get? Could the creatures venture into the parking lot? Or are they absolutely confined to the building? I shouldn't be presumptuous about their capabilities. They've fooled too many people to give up now.

Besides, bolting would surely raise suspicion. I have no reason to think they have knowledge of what I've been up to and I certainly don't want to give them cause to search my desk.

"Can it wait until tomorrow?" I inquire.

"It's rather important," he counters.

"I have an appointment I must get to."

"It will only take a minute."

"But I…"

"I must insist," came Denning's firm interruption.

I feel his grip on my pack tighten ever so slightly. With reluctance, I release my grasp on the door's handle and turn back.

Inside my head, the tick-tocking is louder than ever. I certainly hope that whatever Denning wants to discuss won't eat up too much time.

I try to look him in the face, but all the grossness that his veil fails to hide makes the task nearly impossible. Still, I manage just as I had in past instances, if for no other reason than to remain under the radar.

My nerves tingle as I'm escorted back to my desk. The whole way, he refuses to let go of my pack's strap which lends to the idea that I am a fattened calf being led to the slaughter.

As we near my desk, I try to avoid looking at it because I know what it is. I know what it's capable of doing. Inside my head, the ticking grows still louder.

He pulls out my chair, having some trouble as one of the front legs get caught on the edge of a box stowed there. He spins the chair around, releases his hold on my pack, and motions me to sit.

So I sit, still wearing my backpack. Behind me is the bomb. Towering before me is Denning who's leaning against that central main-support beam. Talk about being between a rock and a hard place. Inside my head, *tick – tock – tick – tock – tick – tock…*

I glance at my wristwatch hoping not to look conspicuous. The second hand moves along. Time is running short.

"Mr. Denning," I blurt. "Can't this wait until tomorrow? I'm on a serious time-crunch."

Mr. Denning's fake face smiles, but his true face snarls. "No. I'm afraid that it's very important we speak right now."

The expression on his real face puts me on edge. "Okay," I say.

Denning moves away from the support-beam, planting his thinly-veiled claws upon the arms of my chair. He leans in so that his face is only inches from my own, forcing me to view him in exquisite detail. Every pulsing vein, every bulbous growth, every drip of pus is presented in high definition for my viewing pleasure.

It's all I can do to keep from vomiting. I swallow hard, keeping it all inside, knowing I must maintain the façade for just a little longer.

"Something has been brought to my attention," Denning says, his countless needle-teeth jutting out of his throat just enough to flutter the veil as he speaks.

He can't know, my thoughts tell me.

"Something of the utmost importance."

There's no way he could possibly know.

"Something that needs to be rectified immediately."

There's no way!

"And how we handle it will determine your future here."

It's impossible!

"Why are you trying to sabotage Basic I Solutions?"

Shit. He knows.

"I don't understand sir," I say, reaching for that final thread of hope even as it's being yanked from my reach.

"Cut the crap," Denning says.

Neither the veil-face nor the real one is smiling now. As for me, I feel the color leave my skin as the tick-tock sound in my brain increases its momentum.

"Do you mind opening your top left desk drawer please?"

I remain unmoving, frozen with fear.

"Allow me," He says after a pause, reaching for the drawer's handle.

I use this opportunity to slip out of my chair. It's time to split, but I don't get far. Denning has me by the pack again, and his grip is beyond human.

He flings me back into my seat. "I would strongly advise against trying that again." The spittle that isn't dangling from his lip spatters across his veil. It smells ghastly, unlike anything I have ever smelled before. Like death. Or fear. My eyes water as my nostrils take it in, but I don't dare wipe it away. Fear anchors me.

He reaches for the desk drawer again, only this time I stay put, and he opens it. There, in plain view, is my detonator with the green LED shining bright as day.

He looks up from the contents of the drawer and eyes me. "Turn it off."

"I can't," I mutter.

He shakes his misshapen head as he pushes the switch. The green light extinguishes as the red re-ignites, but in my head the ticking never ceases.

"You can't, huh? Then what was that?" Denning speaks with barely more than a whisper. "Why create a device of destruction that you can turn off?"

I say nothing.

"I asked you a question?"

I shrug. "I dunno."

"Don't be so hard on yourself. Your little mission was doomed to fail. We've been side-stepping little plots like yours for eons and have become quite adept at detecting them. Yours was a decent, if not better-than-average attempt at destroying everything we do here. So, I guess I should offer you a congrats."

The terror within me is overwhelming, but my need to keep Denning talking overrides it. If I can just keep him talking, then he isn't carrying out whatever diabolical end he has planned for me. And the longer I can stay my execution, the better chance I have of getting out alive.

"What are you?" I ask.

Denning regards me momentarily with his insidious eyes "Does it matter?"

"Of course it matters. If something is going to show up and start impersonating my entire species, I would at least like to know what they are."

"We're the scourge of your Earth and the author of mankind's demise. That's all you need to know."

"Where did you come from?"

Denning scoffs.

"You think yours is the only planet in the universe that has life?"

Honestly, I had never given it much thought.

"Because you're not. Our kind has traveled from planet to planet for time beyond memory. Of all the lifeforms we've encountered, yours does have a certain acumen, for sure, but your tendency to self destruct shouldn't make you too hard to overcome."

A sinking feeling grows within me. "How many others have there been?"

The veiled creep leans over me. "Millions. Hundreds of millions."

"But… Why?"

"We at Basic I Solutions represent one of a handful of scouting parties who've traveled from our current home in search of replacement planets. When we find one strong in natural resources and populated with a weak native species, we send out a signal to the others. And that's what we've been doing here at the Basic I Solutions building. We've been scouting. And we've been signaling."

Bewilderment strikes. Information overload. Crazy, ridiculous information. Yet, as I stare past Denning's veil I know with certainty it's the truth. The fact that I was blinded for so long is much harder to face.

"When the others arrive, Earth will become — how do you humans say it — 'not big enough for the both of us'. Of course, we may not need to exterminate you. It'll take over a century in Earth years for Basic I's signal to reach our planet and another for our ships to arrive here. By then you may have destroyed yourselves. Although we would prefer you refrain from using those nuclear weapons that you're always threatening against each other. We don't want you damaging our planet any more than you already are."

Denning's real face grins, his needle-teeth puncturing his veil. "But perk up, bud! We always hire one native at our shell-company. We need the specimen for analysis so as to determine the best method of species eradication. I'm sure you've blocked it from your memory, but we've done many experiments on you over the course of your tenure here; many, many experiments."

A strange feeling overwhelms me. A scar on my arm suddenly makes sense. I'd noticed it a few weeks back and planned to see a doctor, but my recent obsession with bomb manufacturing had disrupted that plan.

"One of the unfortunate side-effects of all of our poking and prodding, we've discovered over the millennia, is that our test-subjects tend to become aware of our true selves. We think it has something to do with the subconscious trauma that the subject endures on our experiment tables." Denning runs his alien hand along my scar and my brain instantly floods with memories of reoccurring nightmares. "And you have endured much."

For a moment, I contemplate my pending death, and even welcome it. What's the point of going on anyway, knowing that humanity will be wiped out in just a few generations? All the anger and resentment and hatred toward them I've been fostering all these months, it finally makes sense.

"I would be willing to wager that you've been confused lately, that you've had a vague sense of fear. Of *disgust*." He laughs. "It's funny how your simple human brain blocks certain memories which it deems too harmful for the frail psyche of the Homosapien mind."

I had always considered my acts against Basic I to be criminal. Sure, I had felt they were justified, but they were criminal nonetheless. Only now that I know the whole truth, I no longer think that way. Denning and all of his kind, they're the criminals, murdering entire populations, destroying planet after planet, leaving only desolation in their wake, using me as a guinea pig.

"How would you feel if we let you live?"

I don't know how to respond. My first reaction is that Denning's toying with me. Why wouldn't he kill me? I mean, if crime novels had taught me anything at all, it was that the one who knows too much always swims with the fish. And I definitely knew too much.

"Don't get me wrong. I'd love to kill you here and now, but we can't have some bloodhound detective sniffing around Basic I, now can we?

I don't immediately respond.

Denning leans in, pressing his face into mine. I can feel heat radiating from him as his alien flesh presses against my human tissue. Only the thin veil hangs between us. "I said, now can we?" His breath blows over my skin, making it crawl.

"No," I whimper, his closeness bringing nightmare-flashbacks into crystal-clear focus.

He backs up a few inches, reaches over and closes the drawer, hiding the glow of the red LED. "Good to hear," he chuckles as if we're suddenly the best of friends. "Honestly, even with the hatred you've developed, we never thought you'd have the guts to try something like this."

Denning speaks the truth. I'm not gutsy, but I had to try something. I've hated them with a passion for some time now.

"That's why you got the job after all, because you tested healthy enough for our experiments and submissive enough to be a minimum security risk."

Denning gawks at me. His friendly smile remains on his fake face, but disappears from the real one.

"Be advised, we'll be watching you very closely. Be a good employee and come to work tomorrow as you normally would. Keep up the charade and you'll be rewarded."

My eyes must have given away my thoughts.

"Doublecross us and you'll be punished in ways you can't even conceive. Ways even worse than what you've already endured." Denning pauses. The silence is stifling.

"Do we have an understanding?" He continues.

"Yes," I answer. My insides are churning within. I have the feeling that the end is near regardless.

Then, Denning backs completely away from my chair. I use the opportunity to stand, but I don't flee. I don't know if I've been given permission to do so.

"Tomorrow when you get in, you'll have some extra work to do."

I want to run away so badly, but I overcome that compulsion. Instead, I stand my ground, refusing even to wipe his residue from my skin.

"When you arrive, safely disassemble your little device. Then put all your stuff back in their proper places."

I nod.

"You will be under close supervision to prevent you from doing anything stupid."

I nod again, perspiration coating my brow.

"After the disassembly. I want to have a little meeting in my office, just the two of us. While we're meeting, I'll have a special crew clean up the pieces of your little project."

I stand in front of him trying to keep from shivering, but my nerves are frayed.

"Now get out of my sight."

I don't need to be told twice. I adjust my pack and turn my back on Denning. I feel his bulbous alien eyes watching me from behind. It's not a pleasant feeling.

With effort. I progress towards the door. My brain tells me to bolt, but running shows weakness and I don't want the predator behind me to think any less than he already does.

My breathing quickens as my anxiety increases. Any moment, I expect Denning to change his mind. Any moment, I'm certain that I'll feel his claw wrap once more around the strap of my pack.

Then I find myself at the door. I put my hand on the handle and turn once more towards the beast at my desk. He casually leans against it, arms crossed, a stoic look on his fake face, but a sadistic smile on the real one.

"See you tomorrow," he says with a nod, his veil twittering minutely.

I say nothing in response, but turn away for the last time as I pull the handle and open the door. A rush of crisp air hits me, chilling and yet revitalizing. It reminds me that I've cheated death, and lived to tell the tale.

Sadly, there's no one to tell. Not yet at least. And honestly, it's not much of an accomplishment as I've cheated death only for the moment.

I step out of the Basic I Building, glancing back briefly. He's still there, unmoving.

My car's at the far end of the lot. I begin walking towards it, slowly at first, but with every step I quicken.

I don't know how much time I've spent with Denning and I dare not look at my watch. He may still be watching. He may take notice.

Before I realize it, I'm running. The lot isn't huge, yet suddenly my car feels miles away.

By the time I reach my vehicle, I'm sprinting. Fumbling with my keys, I unlock the door and plow into the driver's seat.

I don't remove my backpack and there's no time for seatbelts. I start her up and squeal away as quickly as the little four-banger will allow. I exit the lot, but only make it one block before slamming on the brakes. It's a red light. I would have run it, but there's another vehicle stopped in front of me.

I get ready to honk my horn, but before I can, something rocks my car from behind, the force pushing me against the steering wheel, the reverberations rattling my bones. My foot slips off the brake. My car lurches forward, smashing into the vehicle in front of me. Airbags deploy, knocking me back, forcing air from my lungs.

Dazed, I turn to see the display, but my rear window is so filled with cracks. I can't get a clear view through that spider-webbed glass. So, I open my door and lean out.

The Basic I building is nothing but a flaming ball, one that quickly deflates to the ground as the main support beam behind my desk loses integrity. I grin as I watch the building implode as sense of purpose rushes through me. It's the most beautiful thing I've ever experienced in my entire life.

The building is demolished. It seems clear everyone inside is dead. Hopefully, by ceasing Basic I's signal to the home planet the others will never arrive. Maybe they'll bypass Earth and invade some other rock in the cosmos.

I contemplate the worst-case scenario, the one where the others still show up. Even if they do it'll be at least a century before they arrive, and by then I'll be long dead. Still, I don't wish that future on my descendants. Or anyone else, for that matter. It's disgusting, really, how any one species could be so selfish as to consider a planet only for themselves.

The authorities will want to question me. They'll find evidence of the bomb with the fake on/off switch and locate remnants of my desk and place its proximity to the main support beam, but I'm not concerned. When the police hear this recording of Denning in my pocket… or any of the other recordings I've collected over the last few months, or see any of those experiments I never want to think of again, I think everything will work out. And I'll be okay, eventually. This was cathartic, to say the least.

But even more importantly is after all this time of confusion, I finally lifted the veil from my abusers, and for the first time in as long as I can remember, I am free.

About Shawn D. Brink

Shawn D. Brink hails from Eastern Nebraska and has been writing since he was old enough to hold a pencil. Shawn currently has four published novels to his name including his latest *My Gypsy War Diary*, a YA Mystery, plus many shorter works. In 2018, Shawn was included in *Nebraska's Emerging Writers: An Anthology* published by Z Publishing. Shawn is represented by Liverman Literary Agency.

For more info visit
https://shawnbrinkauthor.wordpress.com/

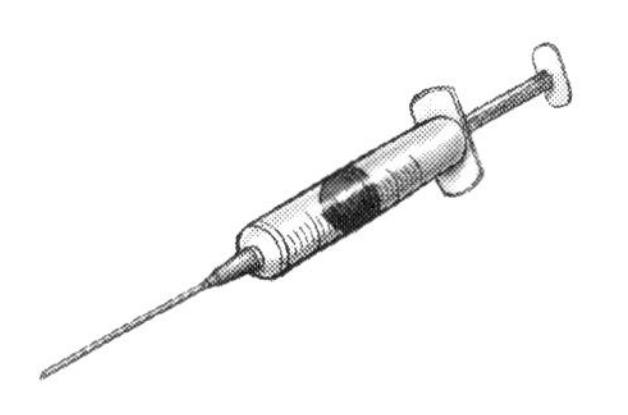

THE WIN

by Dori Ann Dupré

This fight is different than the ones before. The ones before were typical: he was selfish and aloof; she was bitchy and demanding. He was distant and did not appreciate her; she was too needy and never satisfied. The only time he kissed her was because he wanted sex; she was always too tired for sex and only had energy for the kids.

She moves the wheeled contraption holding plastic bags full of toxic solutions and see-through tubing wound around the pole and pulls it closer to his large high-backed chair. She adjusts her rolling stool alongside the table so she can be closer to him. The chair envelops his once muscle-rich, thick, healthy body, now desperately thin and getting thinner. He looks almost like a rag doll, that Raggedy Andy one with the red yarn hair, floppy limbs, and pale face. She wonders if that's what he feels like, a rag doll? A pin cushion? A misfit toy dropped into purgatory?

"I need some water," he utters, his voice parched from the fight's exhaustion and toll. She gets up from her chair beside him and walks down to the small break room at the end of the long hallway. The long hallway which is outlined by other people in a similar fight - the fight to stay alive.

But his battle is not the same kind as everyone else's in this place; this brightly illuminated yet dark place where everyone who is on the outskirts of the war tries – with a soft, concerning smile - to make it happier somehow, with its cheery volunteers, bright colors, Lorna Doone cookies, and toasty warm blankets. But it only ever makes it worse.

An elderly black lady with a smattering of freckles along her cheeks sits in her own big high-backed chair directly across from him. She is receiving her final infusion today. She only has Stage II. The surgeon got the tumor out seven months ago, and this course of treatment is being done "just to be sure." She is frail and tired from the fight, but damn it, she is going to win. She is going to wear her purple tee shirt that has "Survivor" written on the back in white letters. Her children and grandchildren have already walked in a parade in her honor last weekend where they wore their own tee shirts with her name on the back. They carried a torch, like on that TV show Survivor, and threw their fists in the air, and yelled fight-song worthy platitudes about "Kicking cancer's butt!" and "This walk is for Hattie Marks!" and "My Mamaw is a fighter!" It was a good show, no doubt.

The small, rail-thin prisoner who sits in Chair 15 near the break room wears his crumpled orange jumpsuit and a grey crew neck sweatshirt as the fuel for his waged war is pumped directly into his veins. An armed guard stands next to the curtain enclosure. He isn't allowed to sit down in the visitor's chair. Unlike the prisoner of war, he is plump with a tattoo of an anchor on his forearm. Like Popeye the Sailor Man. She wonders if he got that tattoo for the cartoon, or if he was once, in fact, a sailor. She doesn't care enough to ask.

The prisoner wears a skull cap on his razor-sharp bald head and looks up at the young, handsome oncologist as he steps into the small space and asks the prisoner if he caught the Laker's game the night before. The prisoner brightens. They talk about the surgery recovery progress, the prisoner's symptoms of dry mouth and tingling fingers and if he has any nausea. They discuss whether LeBron is better off in Cleveland or Los Angeles and if Seth Curry is more like Dr. J. or Isaiah Thomas circa 1983. The other prisoners have a pool going for what the Doc will say. The guard is the sworn witness to the Doc's answer. The oncologist thinks that Seth Curry plays like Isaiah Thomas but wishes he was more like Dr. J. Then he reminds the prisoner that his fight is far from over and that the odds for surviving this monster are certainly in his favor. Four, maybe five years, he could beat it for good. The prisoner forces a smile, but deep down he's unsure how much fight he has left.

The middle-aged woman in Chair 24 is always alone. The wife figures the middle-aged woman must not have any family or friends to speak of because who in the world would come to this horrible place by themselves? Even the prisoner has someone with him, for Christ's sake. The middle-aged woman sleeps under a grey hospital blanket, likely to combat the extra cold within her bones from the constant fight. She keeps her curtain closed each time, but the wife can see the middle-aged woman slumped over the side of the large puffy armrest through an opening. She is there every Thursday morning at 9 am, just like they are. Just like all these people are.

The middle-aged woman wears a white hooded sweatshirt with a penguin on the sleeve. The hood is pulled up over her blonde hair this week, a few stringy strands sticking out from the cloth. Her mouth is open as she sleeps, silently embarking on her fight alone. The pumping machine begins to beep, and a nurse in light blue scrubs walks past them both quickly. Time to change out the plastic bags. Time to wake her up and remind her to keep fighting.

The wife heads to the break room and grabs a pack of saltines and a Styrofoam cup. She fills it with Purified water. Not tap. Not Spring. But Purified. He is a water snob, after all, and his fight requires – and he deserves – only the best water she can get for him. She grabs an extra set of saltines, just in case he needs something in his stomach. He isn't eating much these days.

The only way that he can win an unwinnable war is by making small choices for himself each moment, each day. Choosing to eat, choosing his kind of water, choosing whether or not to get out of the bed. Or to shower. Or to pay his taxes.

She gets back to their spot and finds him with his hands spread out over his head, his bony knees up toward his chest, rocking back and forth. He looks like he is in pain. Acute pain. More than the pain he is used to living with every second of every day. She asks him if he is alright. He doesn't answer. Another choice. Not answering. Another small win for him. She puts his water on the small round table next to him and tells him that she's put it there for when he decides he wants it. He remains still. She tells him that she's brought him some crackers in case he wants them to help with the nausea.

Immediately, his hands fall from his head, his head jerks up, and his face turns to ash. She can tell he is going to vomit. Grabbing the small light pink tub resting nearby, she puts it underneath him and watches him as an acid stench-filled clear liquid explodes from his mouth into the tub. No choice there. Another check in the loss column.

He vomits a few more times and then settles down. He hands her the tub, a portion of it sloshes with the weak contents of his stomach. His legs go back down into seated position, and she can see the tears leaking out of the sides of his eyes. She walks over to him and puts her face next to his. His eyes are shut, his mouth in a grimace, as she wipes his tears with the pads of her fingers. She wipes them gently, along their natural pathway over his cheekbones. They are rough with dehydration. He has developed crow's feet that were never there before. No choice. Another loss in the fight.

As she continues gently rubbing where the tears have fallen, he pushes her hand away, telling her to stop. A choice. A win.

She reminds him that when he is ready for his water, it is sitting next to him. He glances over at it, picks it up and pulls it up to his lips. He drinks it all slowly. One more choice. Another win.

A cadenced beep begins to chirp from his wheeled contraption. A light blue scrubbed nurse walks in and checks over the digital numbers flashing on the machine. Another nurse comes in wearing a HAZMAT suit and the two nurses spout off dates and times and numbers to each other, reading off computer charts and plastic bags full of clear liquid. HAZMAT suit Nurse asks him his name and birthdate. He states it partially in a monotonous tone. No choice. Another loss. He knows that he needs to tell them this identifying information for the millionth time just so he can have their chemicals pumped into his body. To let him keep going. To fight a fight of small choices in an already lost war.

Bags are shifted, tubes are readjusted, buttons are pressed, and he shifts his weight to his right side. The nurses leave with the vomit pan, and he leans over and picks up the remote control to the TV mounted above their heads. He changes the channel to a cooking show. A choice. A win. He changes it again to a replay of the 1985 Chicago Bears versus the New England Patriots in the Super Bowl. A choice. Another win.

He sees Walter Payton, one of the best to ever play, dance around the Patriots' defense like a champion before remembering how that great player died when he was only forty-five years old. He sees William "The Fridge" Perry ram the football in for a touchdown, overrunning the defense with his massive girth. He winces at the brash sunglasses-and-white-headband-wearing quarterback and sees his beloved, hapless Patriots lose – badly – all over again. No choice. Another loss. But an old one. One he saw coming. One he had experienced before and grown past. Recovered from. Unlike this one. This impossibly slow loss of his own vibrant life.

An elderly couple walks into a room next to them and begins the process of getting comfortable. Whatever that even means in such a miserable place. The frail old man wears a red VFW ball cap and lies down in a bed, and she wonders who is his foe? Why is he bothering with this? More time with his wife? A chance? Or was he, too, relegated to a dismal war where only having small choices during the day was the definition of "winning," of "surviving," of "living a life."

She glances over at her young, mild-mannered, beautiful man, a man she has spent half of her life with, a man who ran the Boston Marathon and the New York City Marathon and the Mule Mountain Marathon in Arizona and has probably run more miles on his feet than some people have driven in their car. She watches his laden cobalt blue eyes as they gaze at the replay of an old storied football game from their childhood. She sees the evidence of his losing fight, the one with no choices of his own, through the gentle pacing of his labored breaths, the anguish surrounding the corners of his mouth, and from the sweat beads forming on his forehead. She sees his resignation to his torrid fate in his slumped shoulders, on his wrinkled shirt, and in his untied shoes. She sees it on his chewed fingernails and the chemically softened and graying stubble that brushes along his chin. More recently, he even wears it like a smack across his face.

She grabs a blanket from the warming oven and spreads it over his body as he sits back with his head resting to the left side. He doesn't move. He says nothing to her. He shuts his eyes to the sound of the old football game as his mind wrestles with the demons who've descended upon his soul. The fears, the suffering, the devastation, the realization that he's almost out of time. The regrets, the sadness, the unrealized dreams, the unknown. The anger, the frustration, the despair, the hopelessness. The understanding that "terminal" no longer means the long building where you catch your flight in an airport.

Watching his face twitch under the bright lights, she wonders if he has fallen asleep, or if, in his mind, he has picked up a katana sword and fights back the demons and all their polluted taunting. Is he fighting them back? Is he letting them choke him? Does he try at all? Are they winning right along with the monster inside of his body?

Are all fights worth fighting? She doesn't know. But she does know that as long as he chooses to fight, if only just to have a few choices each day he has left on Earth, she will fight as hard and as long as he'll let her…right along with him…until there are none left to be had.

She figures that this fight, an unwinnable game, will be their final act of love.

* * * * *

She brings him home after an eight-hour day sitting around in the torture chambers. The navy-blue fanny pack affixed to his hip gurgles every few minutes, announcing to them both that the death sentence is slow and steady and right on course. She carries a duffle bag into the house as he shuffles inside in front of her, his face grimacing, his clothing loosening, his agony dragging his feet like cement blocks directly toward their bed.

She can't remember the last time she made the bed. She can't remember the last time the bed smelled fresh and clean rather than like putrid sweat and strange chemicals. Like when she used to get a spray tan and couldn't wash it off until the next morning, only worse. He is starting to stumble a bit with his gait these days, the clotting in his left leg taking its bite out of him. He is tired and weak, growing weaker each day, and she cannot believe anyone with a fancy degree has the gall to tell him that he has some time left to live, whatever that even means, and something to fight for.

As he stops to bend over onto their bed from the crippling pain exerting itself from his mid-section, he puts his hands up on the top of his head and then slowly interlocks his fingers at the base of his neck. He looks like he was stuck in a standing sit-up, like the tens of thousands of those he's done over the years.

She decides to help him change his shirt. Maybe a fresh shirt will help. As if a fresh shirt will make this circumstance feel like anything better than the bowels of Hell. As if a fresh shirt is the answer. But it is all she has. The only dash of hope in this endless cavern of hopelessness.

She lifts the slightly damp cotton shirt up and over his head, revealing the puncture wounds along his small bulging gut, leaving their purple and blue marks, a rapid constellation of horror. The torture experts prescribed him needles to inject in there three times a day because he has so much clotting in his left leg. They want to give him a tad more torture so he can be tormented for a little while longer. After all…life…no matter how awful, no matter how dire and painful and enslaved it's become…is worth living. Life is the absolute, right? Got to keep hope alive. Got to keep up the good fight. Got to show that he's no quitter. That he's a "survivor."

Rah, rah, rah, rah, rah.

He's managing these needles, yet another fancy medicine she can't pronounce. She convinces him to do it, begs him. She offers to do it for him, but he doesn't want her to do any more than she's already been doing. Hers is a lengthy sentence of helping him "fight." Helping him head toward his early grave in the ugliest way possible.

He pushes her hand away from him as she tries to give him a new shirt. He doesn't want it. He kicks off his tan and black Merrell's, sturdy shoes that he's hiked with to the tops of several peaks around the country. They land next to his nightstand. Then he climbs into his bed, gingerly, not at all with the level of force he used to push her hand away. He gets to make another couple of choices today. No shoes? No shirt? No problem.

Stretching himself down into the folds of his bed, he pulls the tan-colored blankets up to his chin. She watches him slam his eyes shut as if he's hoping that if he shuts them hard enough, this nightmare will end, will cease, and he will at last evaporate into thin air.

The fanny pack moans another squirt of poison into his veins and their little white mutt treks into the bedroom and hops onto the bed. It licks his face happily, not realizing that he will never again be able to run with it down the street after work hours and early on Saturday mornings. Not realizing that he will never again be able to toss it into the pond out back and watch it doggy paddle back to shore. Not realizing that he doesn't have the strength to give it a Milk Bone.

He doesn't push the mutt away like he does to her, though. The mutt is his comfort of choice at the moment. The mutt is his refuge. The mutt is allowed into his fight. It hurts her, the rejection so real and irreversible. But it doesn't matter how she feels. She knows he needs something to let love him, and if it isn't her, then the mutt's love is better than nothing at all.

*   *   *   *   *

Later that evening, she comes into their bedroom to wake him. He's been sleeping for hours, and he needs to consume the symphony of pills to treat his sea of afflictions: anxiety, depression, nausea, acute and lingering pain, high blood pressure, and constipation. Oh, and he needs his Vitamin D pill. Can't forget that one. She sets his injection of blood thinner along with the small plate full of medicines on his nightstand and gently rubs his back. She whispers near his ear that he needs to get up so he can take his evening dose.

He stirs, grunts, and in perfect rhythmic pattern, the fanny pack churns again. He winces. He slowly sits up, and she hands him a cup of water. He deliberately proceeds to take pill after awful pill, until the last one is dissolved into his broken body. She hands him the syringe to stick into his swollen and marbled gut. He looks down and then over at the wall to speak. He will not look at her anymore. She can't recall the last time they shared eye contact of any sort. His beautiful God-given blue eyes. Why won't he look at her?

His parched voice commands her to go away; he doesn't want her to watch him inflict more pain upon himself. She tells him that she wants to take the used syringe and toss it into the plastic container for him so he doesn't have to get up. She also doesn't want it to fall on the floor and become a hazard because he has a habit of getting out of bed alone when he shouldn't. He makes a noise that sounds like half a laugh and responds, in that monotonous tone that's become his new voice, a voice of a fighter, that he does not want her to stay. Go back and watch her show in the living room.

She can check on him later. He wants to be left alone. Please pull the door closed on your way out. The mutt can stay.

Once again, he doesn't want her, his wife, in his hour of need. So, she does as he asks and brings herself to their couch. She buries herself under the old quilt that occupies the cushions and hopes he will be alright in the other room, whatever "alright" means. She is exhausted, mentally, physically and emotionally. The kind of long and drawn out exhaustion that accompanies subsisting on an adrenaline diet during repetitive traumatic occurrences. One wrong thing after another. One catastrophe, another emergency, this bad news, that negative diagnosis. She's read that end of life caretaking can become like war stress, living in constant fear and on fumes, a straight line of fight-or-flight, a highly primal numbing of sorts, where you go and go and go until one day, your body and your mind simply collapse. But she can't let that happen. He's counting on her.

And now, he is clearly toward the end, deteriorating and fast. How much longer can she go on like this? It doesn't matter. This is her fight, too.

She falls asleep at some point and meanders into a recently developed recurring dream. The dream where she keeps trying to dial a phone number but cannot seem to finish. Dial, dial, dial, and then she messes up the last number. Press, press, press, but she's pressing the wrong button. Hang up. Restart. Sometimes it's on a rotary phone, sitting on an awful brown panel wall, which looks like it's from the 1970s. Maybe someplace from her early childhood. Other times, it's a cell phone where she can't clear the wrong number properly from the small screen and needs to start all over again and again. Who is she trying to call? Her mother? The kids? The doctor? God? If it's God, it's clear that He'll never be reached. It's clear that He doesn't care. All the praying in the world by so many people has never helped him. All the positive thoughts and slaps on the back about fighting on… those sentiments are nothing but fuel for someone else's cause. Not his.

In the dream, the call never makes it through. She figures this is just another chapter in the story of their fight. Trying to call for help that never comes…but trying to call anyway. Because when you have nothing left, there's nothing more to lose.

In a start, she awakens to a thundering noise, a banging so loud the house shakes and the mutt barks. As she comes to, her eyes gradually focus and she sees him hopping toward her on one foot, his right foot. He jumps with all his might, slamming down onto the hardwood flooring, before leaping again in a mad dash across the room. The small figurines on the shelves against the wall rattle and move around. One falls and smashes onto the floor, breaking into tiny pieces. It was the one he gave her on their first wedding anniversary, long ago. Yet another sign from that cruel God who doesn't answer their prayers but seems to answer everyone else's?

Looking at him as he makes his way towards her, madly, furiously, she stands up, the quilt falling to her feet. The mutt stands off to the side, watching his master's early morning haphazard sprint. His eyes are closed. How can he see where he's going, she wants to know? As he makes it to her, he stops at her front and grabs her, pulling her to him, against his body tightly, like all the strength he had been using for the fight is now wrapped up in his arms in this one intense moment. He stands straight and tall, the tallest he has of late, his eyes slammed shut, a tear streaming down his right cheek. He holds her and rubs her back, up and down, with the tops of his fingers, strong but gentle and full of a passion that she never knew he had inside of him.

She pulls away to look up at his face, the teardrop having made its way down to his bottom lip. She asks him what is he doing, is he okay? He doesn't answer. His hands come up to her face, as he cups her chin and runs his fingers softly along her cheeks. He moves quickly and quietly but does not stop caressing her face, her back, her waist, all the loving and tender gestures from a man – who is still very much alive – who loves a woman. Who loves her.

When he finally stops, his eyes remain closed, his lips, dried and cracked, purse tightly together. She is overwhelmed with what has just occurred, with both the madness of his hopping and the genuine love and affection released upon her at once, all the intimacy, a lifetime of intimacy, given to her as a priceless and eternal gift. He is still, almost resigned, like he's finished what he wanted and needed to do. A choice. A win.

She helps him back to their bed. His gait is weak and stuttered, as if he's lost the ability to use one leg. When they get back to the bed she sits him down. His head hangs, his eyes remain closed, and she slides his legs back under the covers, pulling the blankets up over him and up to his chin, the way he likes it. She gets into the bed and moves next to him so she can hold him, make him feel that she is with him, her legs against his, her arm around his waist, the way they slept when they were young.

A few hours go by, and the early morning light flickers in through the closed blinds. It is one of those bright, early fall Carolina mornings, the kind where the birds chirp without a cloud in the sky. She looks over at the clock and sees that it is flashing 4:23, repeatedly. The power must have gone out again during the night. It's been happening more and more.

She looks over at him as he lays still, slumped on his right side, just as she left him, just as she held him through the remainder of the night. She puts her hand to his left hand, which rests along his side, and she feels his skin. Her heart jumps into her throat. It is ice. He is cold. He is gone.

How did she miss the moment that this beautiful man left this world, as he lay right next to her, within the clutches of her heart? She is sick to her stomach, but it quickly subsides. She looks at him, and with tears pushing through her lashes she whispers, "Goodbye."

* * * * *

The house is chilly for a seventy-degree set thermostat, and it's desperately quiet. Even the normal tap-tap-tap of the mutt's paws on the wood floor don't make a sound. She sits up on the end of their bed, the covers pulled tightly to the corners, tucked neatly as her mother taught her years ago in her youth. Four pillows sit angled at the top of the bed. The sun tries to peek through the blinds, still closed, still cut off from any joy that a new day has to offer. What joy is there in a world without him? How does the sunrise again when he is no longer here to see it?

The house feels as if the very heart of it had stopped beating. She understands losing a person; she understands how that would make her feel like her own heart stopped beating. But a house's heart?

The mutt stands by the doorway, staring at the wall next to their bed. He looks over at her once but keeps staring at the wall, at nothing. Is it him? Is he standing at the wall? She knows that dogs can sense and hear things that people can't. Can they see things too? Is he against the wall, his hands forged deep into the pockets of his favorite tan shorts? Is he wearing that red collared striped shirt that she dressed him in before the funeral home people carried his body away on a gurney as if he were a patient?

The air feels stale and devoid of movement and life. The room has no smell, not even of his sweat and chemicals, not even a trace of his real scent, the Old Spice Fiji bath wash, which still stands sentry next to their shower door. The carpet is even, his footsteps evaporated, just like the life that went out like a light in the dark and stillness of the night. And the last thing he did on this Earth was love her - the only man who has ever loved her.

The doctor said he suffered a massive stroke at some point in the night, the result of both his aggressive cancer and the extensive clotting he had in his leg. He said that he quickly faded into brain death and did not suffer. She laughed in the doctor's face at that one. He didn't suffer? What planet was this doctor living on? For the past nine months, every single second of every single day was nothing but suffering. Mental and emotional torment, physical degradation, and pain. Never-ending pain. Having to sit on a toilet for hours in a day trying to evacuate something that would never come out. Having to stick needles into his stomach three times a day. Having to swallow horse pills just to prolong it all.

All. The. Suffering.

For nothing but empty hope and a fight that he would ultimately lose.

And then all the outside suffering. The so-called friends that went away and never came to see him. The ones who made plans and never included him anymore. The whisperings of the neighbors when he tried to go for a walk outside. The ones who told him that God had his back. Being replaced at work by some moron who nobody liked.

She protested to the doctor that those shots were supposed to keep him from having a stroke. What kind of a doctor was he if he made him stuff those awful, bruising pricks into his gut three times a day just so he could end up having a stroke anyway? There are no absolutes in medicine, he told her. We can only do what we know should work. No guarantees. She knew that, he knew that, but it didn't make the knowledge that he chose the added torture, only to have it result in a stroke that killed him anyway.

Standing up from the end of the bed, she watches her mutt look back at her and then over at the empty wall. "Are you in here?" she asks out loud. To no one. Maybe. No matter what the preachers always say, they know nothing about the other side. And neither does she.

Her feet are bare on the carpet, her jeans hang low, her hair is unkempt and looks sadder in the magnitude of these last few days. The glaringly hot pit of despair grasps tightly onto her stomach like a scared toddler not wanting to sit on Santa's lap, and she finds herself clutching it, as if it will help quell the agony. Only, it doesn't. But at least she is trying.

All that she has yet to do. All the arrangements she has to make. All the things she has to gather. All the papers she has to find. And everyone…everyone says that they want to help…but no one does.

The part that no one tells her is that when the suffering is over for him at last, the one left behind is left to suffer alone. At least in his suffering he had her. She has no one. No one but the mutt.

She grazes her feet along the carpet, the bottoms of her jeans drag behind her. She opens one of the blinds next to the bed. His side. The light glares through like an angry stream of water as it's released from its dam, shining a sunspot onto the floor. In this moment, a flash of light screams at her from underneath the bed. Curious, she bends over, pushes her face to the soft carpeting and looks below the dust ruffle. And to her sheer horror, she sees them, all piled up like dead soldiers on a Civil War battlefield: several days worth of syringes.

She sticks her hand underneath and carefully pulls one out from the pile. The syringe is unused, its life-saving, stroke-preventing liquid contents still resting inside. She bends down again and pulls out another, sure not to stick herself. It, too, is full. One after another she pulls out fifteen total syringes, five days' worth of them, all unused, still waiting to be stuck into his gut.

She sits back onto the edge of the bed, holding all fifteen fully intact syringes in the palms of her hands as she suddenly realizes what really happened - what he has done.

He fought. He made the choice.

And he won.

About Dori Ann Dupré

Dori Ann Dupré is a fiction writer whose debut novel, *Scout's Honor,* went on to become a two-time award-winning bestseller. 2019 saw the release of her follow-up, *Good Buddy*, which won Honorable Mention in the Readers' Favorite International Book Awards. Dori is also a prolific short story and poetry writer, and has had her work published in several literary anthologies. She also served as a freelance writer for a local magazine and as a blogger on a bereavement website for widowed women. Dori is a veteran of the United States Army and resides in Raleigh, North Carolina with her two little dachshunds, Stretch and Slinky.

For more info visit DoriAnnDupre.com

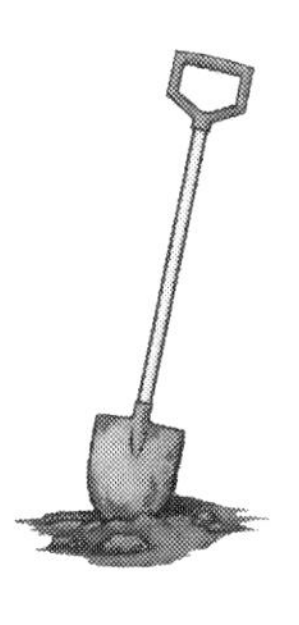

THE SCOOP

by Samuel W. Reed

He has the voice of an angel. When he croons, the hearts of both men and women melt alike. The birds stop to listen so they can copy his sweet soulful melodies. His lyrics pierce through you as they resonate from his vibrato lips as if he's intimately speaking to each and every one of us. He's a beautiful person, both inside and out. Both gorgeous to look at when he's all made-up on stage, but also on the inside, where he's a kind, thoughtful, and caring human being; a bright spot in an otherwise tarnished world. And that which is inside of him, his art, his craft, that which he expresses on stage, or in a recording studio, or into the spigot in the shower of the Plaza Suite, is equally, if not even more beguiling. But most seductive of all are the weeks, months, and years he's spent at the children's hospitals, veteran's homes, independent living centers, free concerts in the park, hometown fairs, personal engagements, private bookings, book signings, photoshoots, press events, and of course, his huge, sold-out arena tours around the nation, and now a dozen or more overseas, all for his adoring and numerable fans. The kid's going places, I'm telling you. A sure-fire investment, I'm certain.

That's what they say at least. That's what they've said. That's what's been written about me. That's what I'm told. 'Cause that's the image they created for me; the managers and agents, the producers and distributors, the studios and CEO's and their conglomerate boardrooms that make people like me out of Twinkies and pustules. I'm the image they want. But they don't know me, really. They could never know what's inside me, with this hunger I can't feed, and these cravings I can't stop, and the fears I have, not only of failure, but equally, and even more disdainfully, of success. What if this is it? What if this is all it amounts to? Is this what happiness feels like? Is this "making it?" Will it ever be enough?

I catch a glimpse of her from the corner of my eye, and we make contact. I don't know who looked at who first, she or me, but it doesn't matter anymore. I envision her, panties down, bent over a dryer in a laundry room of a twelve-thousand square foot home, and I know it's only a matter of time before it happens. It always does. It always starts with a look. And then there are words, and curious glances, and then things get sticky with feelings and emotions. But right now, it's only a look. Just like a thousand times before.

First, I have to make my way down this entire press line, acting like I give a shit, pretending to care about their stupid magazine, these stupid songs, and this entire ridiculous persona they cooked up for me so that I can fulfill my dream of being a star. Only I didn't sign up for this. I don't know what I signed up for anymore, but it wasn't this. The machinery behind the process of making dreams happen is a loathsome dirty grind. Artists are turned into products who are turned into brands in order to sell other brands, or products, or movies, all of which are owned by the same conglomerate owned conglomerates run by CEO's that donate earnings to politicians in order to pass legislation that will continue to concentrate the distribution of wealth and stifle their competition until there is a single ruling power and it's not us. But no individual voice can rise above it. Not mine or anyone else's. Large groups of voices cannot even overcome it. We've tried. We are slaves to a society we created, and only by appealing to that society can we and will we ever get ahead. We're willing slaves in our own nightmares. We're Winston Smith in a not too distant past. Or Jefferson Smith, on our futile trip to Washington. Both of these century-old examples just go to show how long this evolution has been going on. Will there ever be a time when these references no longer resonate? Or has it already happened? I can only hope that when it does, it's because we've overcome the issues, not succumbed to them.

I'm on the verge of setting forth on this entire diatribe when I self-consciously stop myself, take a deep breath, and smile.

"I'm sorry, what was your question again?"

I'm horrible at these things. If I could just get through one of them without making a fool of myself, I'd be stoked. All I have to do is nod and smile. Pose for the camera. Look like I know what I'm doing. And answer their stupid robotic questions with stupid robotic answers, downloaded onto me by my shrewd Agent and his overworked Assistant at the crack of dawn this morning. It's ridiculous how manufactured this entire process is. They send the questions beforehand. We give the answers beforehand. It's so anti-climactic. It's like we're making an Alfred Hitchcock movie, all the fun and creative stuff has already happened. All that's left now is to fake our way through it with a smile.

Finally, I get to her. She grins at me, eagerly. I've glanced at her no less than eight times since I walked into the room, and every time I caught her looking right at me, so either I'm crazy, or it's only a matter of time before this happens. She gives a long look before her wry smile turns hard and she places the microphone to her lips.

"The director of the film is quoted as saying that he wasn't interested in hiring a non-actor for the role, but that the studio pressured him due to their investment in your career." She pushes the microphone in front of me with a glint in her eye.

I stare at her bemused. That self-righteous bitch! How could she turn this into a publicity stunt for her own career advancement!

I pull myself out of my stupor just long enough to put words into sentences…

"I'm sorry, is there a question?"

Her glance washes over me like a sparring boxer who's ready to make the kill. She leans in for the KO.

"How do you respond?"

* * * * *

It takes three more interviews, four more hours, and several drinks at the hotel bar before her panties are tangled around her ankles, but it's not a washing machine she's bent over, but a beautiful leather couch in my suite at the hotel. I could just as easily have gone home, but there's nothing there for me but stale food and month-old messages on my answering machine, so I might as well be waited on, here, on the 23rd floor of this luxury palace where I have the type of view that makes L.A. look like a golden paradise shrouded in twinkling light instead of the rancid shit-hole it really is. A waiter brought a delicious-looking tray of smoked salmon and a charcuterie plate that Hannah picked out, but we've barely even touched it. We've been too busy chasing each other around the room, naked. Well, mostly naked. On the way to getting naked. She told me all about her teenage crush on me a few years ago, I've heard it all before, but something about her version seemed different. It rang more sincere, like she actually *did* have a teenage crush on me a few years ago and she's not just saying it because she thinks she needs to appeal to my ego to win me over or something, or for bragging rights to her friends. We strip down to nothing except her satin underpants and my one hundred and fifty-seven dollar designer socks and I corner her on that firm leather couch. She's already taken a couple toots off the rolled hundred on the end table, and as she leans over to take her third, or maybe her fourth line, I creep up behind her like a lion. She turns, giddy. Her heart is racing, as is mine, and we tear into each other like rabid beasts. She throws questions at me like knives, and I fire back answers, impetuously trying to defend myself. But she's persistent, and with my guard down she tears into my chest, baring the fathomless depths of my soul. I tell her everything. My desires to be an artist again. My need to be free of this burden. Free of these contractual obligations by corporate lawyers and businesses that are going to brand my face across soft drink cups from a national fast-food chain and make an action figure in my likeness if the movie hits a few base markers, which it's already projected well-beyond. And I'm only in it for ten minutes, if that. They needed someone who could sing, and guess what… that's what I do best. They also think my brand will help bring a certain identity to the film, which it will, and then they want to lock me into a series of Movie-of-the-Week style sing-alongs, and I'm sitting here complaining about it while they're paying me more than some single income families make in a year, per show, plus all the residual song rights, paid performances and promotions, et cetera, et cetera, et cetera. I go on and on. It feels great just to get it out.

She listens as I bang her from behind, and I think I've finally gotten her attention off the piece she's writing, but as soon as we stop I notice she grabs a hotel pen and pad and jots a couple things down. She clicks the pen, turns around and smiles. She looks incredible, like a posed photograph the way her long curly hair dangles over her smooth slender shoulders. Her eyes are piercing, even when she smiles, like she's looking right through me. She knows my heart's not in it. She knows everything about me now. Despite me just blurting everything out like that, she knew it already. I can only assume that's why she asked.

And then, she motions with her index finger for me to approach her, and she leans in, cheek to cheek, her hot breath against my ear and neck, sending chills down my spine as she whispers "Your secret's safe with me," and she kisses me. But then our lips separate and we each take a breath and we smile but the moment we had feels like it's suddenly gone, and a certain sadness washes over me.

I stand upright. I really like this girl. I can feel myself smirk. She's different. She's mysterious. She's a lost soul, like me. Someone I wouldn't mind getting even more lost with, but first—

I get up to go to the bathroom when she fires one more question at me, perhaps even more unexpected than all the rest.

"You got any weed?"

"Oh… No. Sorry."

She shrugs it off and hops on the bed, turning the TV on as I strut into the bathroom. She settles on some sort of reality show, a form of mental marijuana I suppose, as she hunkers down under the covers. I cross the cold tile floor, open the glass enclosure, and run the shower.

Raindrops splatter against the marble. Each pellet is as fine and soft as a gentle mist. Not one of those scalding, skin peelers like some hotels have. I could use a tad more pressure, honestly, but it's relaxing at least. I love a good shower. Fifteen minutes to escape. Twenty if I really don't give a shit. Just step inside my little glass and marble enclave here and let the mind wander.

I can't stand to do any more of those press events and I've got them booked all week. I'm really glad Hannah came over tonight. I wonder if she's found anything good on TV, and whether or not she's out there doing all my coke. I think about the story she told me about her father at the bar, and how he always loved Hollywood and everything about it, and how when she was little they came out here for a trip, and he met his idol, Jack Palance of all people, at some dive restaurant they just stopped in. And it took the whole meal for her dad to work up the nerve, but eventually he did, and he strode up to Jack for an autograph, and Jack was a complete jerk. Tore into him, told him he was eatin', and to leave him the fuck alone. Ever since then Hannah's known the city of angels was an ugly place, and that the business of entertaining was built around fake miracles and broken promises. Funny how when I was growing up, just some kid in the sticks who really liked to sing, I didn't see those nightmares. I never thought about the nuts and bolts of how things actually got done. How things were produced, and marketed, and distributed. I never thought about any of that. All I ever wanted was to sing. And, judging from what I can tell, all she ever wanted was to expose the façade, not just of this business, but of all businesses, I guess. And she's smart. She'll figure out a way to do it, too.

And with that thought, the thin rectangular piece of soap squeezes out of my hand, bangs against the glass enclosure and splats on the marble floor. I realize I've said too much.

Covered in lavender and cucumber scented foam, I rinse off as quickly as I can as thoughts equally rational and irrational storm my mind. She's going to write a story about me. She's going to expose me. She's going to let everyone know that I'm a brainless, no-talent, wannabe cokehead who overcompensates for my lack of artistry with brand-building and targeted networking for studio opportunities that repay me with inflated checks and a lot of ego stroking. And I loathe every minute of it because I just want to be me. And she knows everything. I'm a thinly layered veil, underneath which is all fragile emotion masked by unprotected sex, booze, and designer drugs.

But I do good for people, right? I uplift them. I entertain them. And I do good for the country. At least I try to. I support politicians. I mean, you know, like, the good ones. I give to charities. I host telethons and shit, when storms batter the poor people of the Southeast, or fires rage out here in California, or tsunami's terrorize people halfway around the planet. I try to be good. I do the best I can. I mean, I'm not George Clooney or anything, but who is?

And now *she*'s gonna ruin everything with some smear campaign against me because I can't see fit to keep it in my pants. So what, I'm a horny twenty-two year old? Who isn't? Who cares? Except my Agent, I mean. My Agent definitely cares. And the Studio. They care. It's in my contract. If something like this ever gets out, it's over. The whole kit and caboodle. I'm finished.

Fuck. And she's out there, probably typing all this into the notes section of her iPhone while I'm stuck in here rinsing the lavender off my feet. Christ! Who am I kidding? She's probably gone already. Gone to write her story before she forgets everything and has to come back for seconds to finish the scoop. But maybe, just maybe—

The glass door opens and water drips all over the tile floor. I yank a robe off the rod and quickly wrap myself up as I storm out of the bathroom into the room, and there she is.

I am immediately relieved, despite the inner quarrel I begin with myself, wondering if I should pre-empt any bad press with some sort of non-disclosure agreement, or just polite conversation, when I take a closer look. She hasn't moved since I entered.

"Hey, are you o—"

I step around the bed when I realize she's foaming at the mouth and her face is blue. A single stream of blood trickles from her white-rimmed nostril down her cyan cheek. My racing mind crashes to a screeching halt.

Oh... Fucking... No...

I flatten her on the bed and open her robe-- her bare chest in front of me-- I clamp my hands together like they do in the movies and I push down. She feels cold, like an old bath, when you start to get the chills.

Oh, Jesus. Not here. Not today.

God, you know I'm not a religious man, but if you know CPR now's as good a time as any to reveal yourself.

My prayers, such as they are, are fruitless. I stop beating on her chest and instead I grab her head in a futile effort to resuscitate her-- the slime from the oozing blood and vomit is slick against my mouth as I press my warm lips to her cool heavy body. She's infinitely still. No matter how much beating or breathing or pleading I do, she just lies there, eyes closed, limp. I gaze at her, examining her perfect body as she lies unmoving on the bed. She looks like a morbid doll-version of her former self.

I look away, over to her phone, and the notepad beside it on the bed. Across the top it reads...

CELEBRITY CRUSH-- total mama's boy-- a lot more to offer than meets the eye-- potential for real artistry-- Too good to be true?

Could it be? Hannah, the same girl I spilled my guts to thirty-five minutes ago, the girl I was afraid would run off and write some denigrating expose on my senseless misogyny, the girl I was afraid I might somehow actually be falling for, *actually* caught feelings for me, too? Real-life *feelings*?

And I killed her. Or she killed herself. Or either way, she's dead. I look down at her once more, and as my entire being begins to tremble and quake, hers lies ever more unmoving on the bed.

I fall to the ground, my hands upon my chest where I see for the first time, I'm covered in blood. Her blood. And her snot. And her death. The robe around me is spotted with her DNA, and as I finally wipe the sleeve across my mouth from our postmortem kiss it comes away looking as if my own flesh is rotting off of my face.

I'm finished. This is it. All I've ever worked for. All I've ever dreamed about… gone. In a single instant. I'll never recover. My image, my career… like the coagulating blood inside Hannah's cold veins, I can feel it hardening and drying up. And as the implications and consequences of my actions begin to take clearer shape in my mind, I am paralyzed by the certain fate that beholds me. I can see the headline now:

TEEN POP IDOL FOUND WITH COCAINE,
DEAD REPORTER IN HIS BED

Paralyzed, I panic, searching around the room, for what I am not sure, when I see it. The bag of coke, or what's left of it. I grab the baggie, race to the bathroom, and wash it down the sink, but it's a total disaster as the powder sticks, hardens, and clots the tiny hole they call a drain in this ultra-modern stupid piece of shit hotel. I use my hands to wipe it up and wash it down when I have the urge to suddenly stick a finger in my mouth for a quick gummie only I can't feel my index finger. I can barely feel my hands. I catch my hollow reflection in the mirror, but look away before I accidentally confront any real hard truths.

Back in the bedroom, I consider my options. I pull a sheet over Hannah to give her privacy, and begin to dry heave from the steadfast guilt that wafts through me. As quickly as I begin, it's over, and I throw my bag on the bed to start packing. Getting the fuck out of here is priority number one, until suddenly, it isn't. As I fetch assorted garments off the floor, my pants, a shirt, her underwear, a bit of clarity suddenly washes back over me and I realize I can't go anywhere.

I need help. Someone I can trust to get me out of this mess. Someone who will risk everything for me, just like I have for them. Only I'm quick to realize, there is no such person. No close friends keeping up with me 'til the wee hours of the night. My brother? Pshhh. Fuck him. I can't call my dad. Haven't said more than a few words to him since mom died. Besides, he hates it when people call after supper. There's no way I'm calling the cops, or an ambulance. If she wasn't already dead, I mean, of course, but given the circumstances. I sigh with a defeatist air until it strikes me, and I dig my phone from my pocket and call the one person in the whole world that I know I can call with something like this, who will help me to the best of their capabilities, and has probably even done it before, but for someone else, of course.

My Agent.

* * * * *

My Agent is out getting drinks with other Agents when I call. It's what they do. They sit around, wheeling and dealing, eating and drinking, jabbering along to whatever empty thoughts fill their heads, waiting for people to call them. And when they do, they don't answer. Someone else does. An assistant. Or voicemail. Or if you really suck and you're at the bottom of the food chain, the front desk clerk at the office. Lucky for me, I have his cell number, and he knows better.

"Alright, alright. I'll be there in a bit."

"Thank you. And please, come alone."

"Okay, I get it. But, you mind telling me why you didn't go home?"

"If anybody asks... I did."

And with that single line, he knows. We hang up. He promptly stands.

"Excuse me, gentlemen. Duty calls."

They nod to him, and he eagerly leaves.

I don't know how, but fifteen minutes later he's standing next to me in the hotel room. An impossible feat by any standards, as he claimed to have been in Santa Monica. But that's what Agents do. They make the impossible possible. That's why I called him. And yet suddenly, seeing him again up close and personal, outside of business, I'm immediately reminded how something about him always gives me the creeps.

Maybe it's his 'kill or be killed' attitude. Maybe it's his cool distance, a protective measure akin to a turtle in his shell, the less he reveals the less exposed he finds himself when true dangers do arise. He taught me well, actually. Until recently.

Recently, I've been slipping. I've been going out more. Staying out late. Staying in less. I've been working harder than ever, and when the work stops the party begins. Sometimes it's hard to tell when one starts and the other ends. It all rolls together; it happens so fast.

And the cocaine, I didn't even want it at first. I took a pill or two when I really needed the pep, and it was fine for a while. But I started dragging eventually. It was impossible to keep up at the rate we were going, waking up at the crack of dawn for the early shows, going to bed late after the après party. It's exhausting, but you feel like you have to do it all. They tell you that you should do it all.

'You're young,' they say. 'You can handle it!' And suddenly you're in situations you wouldn't normally be in. Staying out later than most kids your age on a weeknight. And you see things, of course. Things that shape you and normalize behavior that shouldn't be normalized. Not at that age at least. Maybe not ever.

It was my Agent, my one and only Agent, who insisted. It was after one of those club deals. You know, where they pay you a certain amount to show up and pretend you hang out there all the time, and then a red-eye to New York for a meeting the next morning, and a big show that night. I was doing press all day, local radio, a short segment on Today. I was ready to cave my assistants head in, or anyone else who demanded I show up anywhere but the hotel bedroom for a nap. And that's when my Agent introduced me to Larry. The White Horse. Bolivian Marching Powder. The big She. That was two and a half years ago. My career's been on fire ever since, and I've never looked back.

Until right this very second.

My Agent stands over her, appalled, limbs akimbo like he's never seen a dead body before. *Maybe he should be the actor*, I consider, *because he's convincing as hell.*

"How long ago did this happen?"

"I dunno, maybe an hour?" I ask like he might already have the answer.

"Does anyone know you're here? Family, friends?"

"No. Nobody. I booked the room in someone else's name—"

"Have you seen anyone since you've come in? You hang around the bar or anything?"

I immediately flash to the four dozen or so glances, glares, and flat out stares I've received since arriving, from the gaggle of underdressed women we encountered at the bar, to the teenager with her parents at the valet, to the lady in the elevator that insisted I autograph her forearm like it was some kind of cast or something.

"Yes, people have most certainly seen me here."

He takes a deep breath and tries again. The smell of 18-year-old Macallan and cigar smoke curiously fills the room, as if he's been carrying it around inside of him, just waiting for the right place to let it out.

"Did she ever leave the room for anything? Did anyone ever come to the room and physically see her here?"

He spots the cart of food with the charcuterie plate on top, mostly untouched, which answers his question. The salmon glistens, the fat turned to a gelatinous mass on the silver tray. My Agent walks over to the cart, inspects the decorative swirl of meats, cheeses, olives, and nuts upon the cutting board, and takes a piece of salumi.

I watch him in dismay.

"Okay, here's what we do..." He launches into a lecture that falls somewhere between a Boy Scouts of America safety preparedness speech and a dissertation by Ted Bundy on how to get away with murder. He bends over the body as he speaks, meticulously wiping the blood and the foam away from her face. His words are all a blur. My mind unspools like a deep sea fisherman's rod plunging headlong into the depths of the abyss. I look at Hannah, who appears so peaceful as she lies there in the bed, it's as if she's only asleep.

He walks back over to the linen-draped food cart where he admires the decorative display once more before taking the tray from the top and setting it on a table nearby. He nabs another piece of salumi and two Castelvetrano olives, popping the olives down his gullet like a handful of aspirin before ambling back over to Hannah. He peers at her like she's a puzzle waiting to be solved, and spits an olive pit on the ground. Then, he grabs her by the ankles and drags her across the bed. Her whole body's about to drop to the floor like a hundred-pound sack of potatoes when my instincts kick in and I barely snatch her head in time.

"Nice catch."

"Thanks."

"She's dead, stupid!"

"That doesn't mean we have to hurt her!"

My Agent rolls his eyes and quickens his step now that someone is holding the other end of her, and I almost fall over trying to hold on to this dear poor soul before he yanks a leg out of socket trying to zip her across the room. When he reaches the cart he lets go and her feet hit the floor with a single heavy thud. My Agent rips the floor-length linen tablecloth off the cart, and low and behold there's an empty shelf below.

"Perfect."

He takes Hannah by the shoulders and begins to fold her like a blue origami swan, intent on squeezing her beneath the cart to remove her from the room when he looks at me with an expression that I can only interpret as boldfaced irritation, and he huffs.

"You gonna help me or what?"

Together, much to my stupefaction, we are able to carefully fold her semi-malleable and precious body into an appropriate size to fit her inside the cart, and with the linen tablecloth and charcuterie tray replaced over top, you can't even tell she's there.

My Agent sends me down to the valet to get my car. Hopefully they won't remember I had a girl with me. My heart races as I ride in the elevator, guilt sweating from every gland, coating me in inescapable fear. I imagine him, twenty-some-odd floors above, rolling the cart down the hallway when her hand falls loose, dragging down the plush hall carpet beneath the white linen tablecloth as the Agent, a shadowy figure in his own right, nods to a passing maid, who sees the hand, jumps away in fear, and calls the authorities.

It's only a matter of time until they've got us.

A bunch of people stand around smoking. They spot me and want me to sign an autograph. The last bit of evidence that links me to the scene of the crime. And though I swore I would never do it no matter the circumstances, never were they more extenuating than now, and I refuse. The guy pins me to the valet stand with his glare.

"Seriously? Fuckin' jerk."

Great, now I look like an asshole. But what does it matter? In less than twenty-four hours the whole world will think that anyway. Or worse, they'll think I'm a killer. Unless we can get rid of her. Unless my Agent's plan works.

"Your vehicle, sir."

I turn around, half expecting a patrol vehicle with the back door open and the valet replaced by one of LA's finest, but it's not. It's my car, so I get in, as Sophie's choice suddenly creeps into my consciousness. What do I do? What do I do?

Do I drive? Go as far as I can go and run away forever? I could empty the accounts and disappear before anyone knows I'm gone, except my Agent. Or do I pull around back of this hotel and meet him at the cargo elevator like he suggested. How does he even know there's a cargo elevator back there? I knew he'd done this before. And if I flee I can be sure he pins the whole thing on me.

"*Shit.*"

I floor it and the tires leave the valet in a cloud of smoke as my former fan rolls his eyes and gets into his Uber. "What a loser," he snarls to anyone who'll listen.

I pull around back to see the Agent on his phone, checking his watch. Who's he calling at this hour? I feel my phone vibrate in my pocket and I ignore it. I don't have the time.

"Where you been?"

"Sorry, the valet took forever."

The Agent rolls the cart over.

"Pop the trunk."

I do, and the lid of the trunk swings open to greet him.

I watch from my rearview safely inside the car as he strips off the linen tablecloth revealing Hannah below. I search around the alley for anyone else in view. A guy smokes a cigarette on the corner up ahead, but he's the wrong direction to see anything, I hope. I hear a loud THUD and a CRASH and a CLATTER behind me and check the rearview again-- My Agent's glaring right at me, all hot and bothered.

"You gonna help me out or what?"

The car door slams shut as I get out and walk around the back. There she is, poor Hannah, half in the trunk, half out, with her legs snagged underneath the overturned cart. Delicatessen meats and cheeses lay splayed out across the concrete. The soft cheeses have begun to harden after hours of oxygenation.

"Get her feet."

The low rumbling and hissing brakes of a garbage truck entering the alley from behind charges us into high gear, as the damning truck slowly turns the corner and lumbers toward us. We leap into action before the truck makes the full turn, nimbly grabbing her ankles and kicking the cart free, we stuff her into the shallow trunk space with a heavy slam of the lid before the lights illuminate only us, and we hop in the car.

The door next to me pops open and my Agent jumps inside, fastening his seatbelt in a hurried, excited manner.

"So, where to?"
"Just drive."

* * * * *

We drive all night. At least it feels like all night. It hasn't been any more than a couple hours, but when you get as late a start as we did it feels like forever. Normally I'd be exhausted, but we're both wide awake, wired without coffee, without coke, without anything but the dangerous thoughts in our heads and each other. Just adrenaline and fear as we silently stare at the long lonely freeway as the dark expanse of the desert wasteland engulfs us.

I've never seen him like this, my Agent. He's in the zone, terrifically focused, or maybe he's just tired. Maybe we're both a little more tired than I thought. A little closer to a delirium that we both know is approaching, that we're just trying to stave off as long as possible before we go mad. How long we can keep the insanity at bay is anyone's guess. How close to it were we to begin with? Or has it been with us the whole time?

There's a shovel in the backseat. We picked it up on the way out of town. Still has the tags on it. I'm sure that wasn't curious: a handsome looking gentleman in a suit entering a big box store in the middle of the night, marching over to the home and garden section, picking out the sturdiest shovel they have, and carting it over to the lone cashier on duty. I'm sure he smiled at her with that winning "I love ya, babe" smile he sprouts whenever he wants something, before he paid in cash and walked out of the store, forever.

He's done this before, I can tell. Probably for some other shitbag client he represents. He's got a roster full. Just something about his demeanor, that put-out attitude, the way disgruntled parents get after having to pick up after their kids over and over, despite constant and repeated attempts to tell them to do it. Only this was an accident. It wasn't even my fault. Not that the press could ever understand that. Or the public. They crucify you on the first headline. But I know it. *We* know it. Or at least, I hope we do. Maybe we don't. Maybe that's why we're on our way out here. This is the end of the line for both of us. Maybe the shovel's for me, and this is how he gets rid of all his problems.

We're in the middle of fucking nowhere. Even the trees are too scared to live out this far, leaving only the occasional prickly pear and desert scrub brush to accompany each other. At long last we pull off on a deserted exit, take a right at the overpass, and almost immediately the road turns to dirt. I would have expected nothing less. I just spent $250 on a custom detail job on this car not 18 hours ago, and here we are off-roading in my cherry red Maserati. I hope the low-profile tires can handle the irregular gravel. I slow to a creep in order to watch out for any pits in the road, but before we get even half a mile around the bend he says "Stop."

I stop.

He looks at me, concerned, then peers out into the darkness of the desert valley beyond.

"Around that bush."

He points to a particularly overgrown scrub brush not twenty-five feet off the dirt road, and I pull off, not that there appears to be any difference between what is road and what is not road at this point. We slowly approach the bush as he waves his finger, indicating. I keep pulling around until we are hidden behind it from anyone else who might be along that road, which is most likely no one, just as he intended, until finally, I stop.

"We dig here."

The car doors pop open at the same time, and we emerge into our dark surroundings. A bitter wind whips around us, blowing my door against me, forcing me back against the car until I pry it open and shimmy out before it slams closed again.

My Agent grabs the shovel from the back, walks around to the front of the car, and tests the hard ground with the tip of the blade.

"I'll go first."

He pierces the soft sand with the sharp blade, and swiftly scoops it aside. The second scrape goes deeper, beside the first, and sprays off in the wind toward the road. The third clanks to the ground like he's hit concrete, and the Agent drops the shovel to the ground, shakes off his jacket, and carries it over to me.

"You mind?"

I take his jacket from him like his teenage girlfriend and he pushes up his sleeves, picking up the wooden handle once again. As my eyes adjust to the dark morning light, his silhouette begins to glisten as he heaves the blade into the dirt with all his might. I feel a rectangular box within his jacket pocket and open it to find a new pack of cigarettes. American Spirit. Unopened. My favorite kind. He must have picked them up for me when he got the shovel. His way of putting me at ease, or is he trying to link me to the body? It's too late now, I'm desperate and he knows it. Either way, he's an accessory. He wouldn't do anything to jeopardize his career. I pack the cigarettes against my wrist before stripping off the plastic wrap and flipping them open. Despite the wind, that intoxicating smell of fresh tobacco still wafts to my nostrils, firing up the memory banks of that smell and the last time I smelled it, with Hannah, mere hours ago as we played twenty questions and I chased her around the room like a feral cat in heat.

The sky begins to lighten as the sun nears the horizon, but to me, it's clear as day. Everything I've worked so hard for, for so long, is on the verge of extinction. I flash back to when I was little, before I met my Agent, when music meant more than anything to me, and all I wanted to do was sing. I sang in the shower, I sang in the car. I sang the theme song to every TV show I watched. And then my brother started filming me, and then other people started filming me, and I started singing everywhere I went, and life was fantastic. And then I started recording albums, and that was great, too, but the pressure started intensifying. And suddenly, singing became less and less spontaneous and fun, less and less something natural that I loved to do, but something more performed, more perfected, and more rote. And that's when I met my Agent. And he helped me become a star.

And it's everything I always dreamed of, only, it's not. Now, I dream of going back there, being back in that place, with those people who used to care about me before anyone else, and doing my own thing, whatever that is, I don't even know. That's what I dream of. Every single day. I think Hannah dreamed of that, too. A simpler time. Before our eyes were peeled open and everything that is wrong in the world could not be unseen.

"Your turn."

He admires his handy-work, which is roughly a two-foot by five-foot trench about two-feet deep, and he passes me the shovel. I dig and I dig, sweat dripping down my face, every fiber of every muscle burns, my joints ache, blisters form and pop like chewing gum on the soft palms of my hands. They're liable to bleed, eventually. I'll have calluses the likes of which haven't been seen since I used to work in my grandmother's garden as a prepubescent teenager. My mind immediately flashes to after her death when the garden grew over and dried up and withered just like this desert, and every known plant and vegetable was overtaken with rot, and bugs, and eventually death spread to its farthest tallest limb.

The sun rises higher over the valley, and the cool breeze is instantaneously replaced with a stifling heat. The work becomes more labored as fatigue quickly sets in.

"Stop."

My Agent glares at me with a stern brow. I never did like him. He always treated me like a second rate client, which, I dunno, maybe I am. Still, he's a dick. There's another body buried around here somewhere, I can feel it.

"Put that down and help me out."

He's short on words this morning. I can see why. I drop the shovel on the ground and climb out of the three to four-foot hole, dusting the sand from my body. I round the trunk to see Hannah, coiled in the back like a dead snake, and my Agent pulling her out by her ankle and wrist, elbows and neck, anything he can grab to force her out.

"Hold on!"

I race to her aid, carefully unfolding her appendages before they're snapped off like a chicken leg as my Agent grabs her head, and we hobble over to the hole where he wastes no time tossing her in. I scramble to hold on, but it's impossible under the gravitational pull of her dead weight, and she plunks the three and a half to four feet into the half-dug hole, head first.

I look down at her mournfully, painfully, grieving her loss, my loss, her truth, her profound power to bring out in me that which I was afraid to even tell myself, but before I can even put my thoughts together, he grabs a shovel and starts filling her in. Dirt sprays across her face, and I can't believe this is the end of it. This is the last time I'm going to see this horrible nightmare, staring me face to face. Now, I'll only visit it in my dreams, where it will haunt me for the rest of my life.

I watch the dirt as it covers her once lovely locks, and I suddenly realize, I loved her. Or, I could have loved her. She is the type I could love. She's the type I wanted to love. And still do. The first person I ever met that challenged every sense of who I am, and made me feel truly vulnerable, and comfortable, and bare naked after the persona was stripped away and only a person was left behind. There was a reason I unloaded all of my baggage onto her earlier, and it was because I trusted her. She wasn't like the others. I knew that instinctively. She wasn't part of the machine. I want to be with someone that challenges me like that, not with enablers who do nothing but help me ruin my life. And yet somewhere deep down I know that I'll never find anyone quite like her again.

"I think I loved her."

I can't believe I've blurted this out. My emotions are pouring from my chest and raining from the corners of my eyes.

"What'd you say?"

"Nothing."

He stares at me with the glare of a disgusted father.

"Jesus Christ. You're even more fucked up than I thought." He scoops the spade back in the sand and fills the blade with dirt. "Don't worry, once we get back, I'll check you into one of those places where you can rehab for a bit, you'll be out in a couple a weeks, and you'll be better than ever."

"What will you tell people?"

"We'll tell 'em you're exhausted."

He turns to toss the dirt on her when I yell.

"And what about her?" The guilt curdles in my throat and I choke up.

"What about her?" he yells. "She's dead, remember? You're not that fucked up, are you?"

Something boils inside me. A seething anger I haven't felt in a decade, since I was twelve years old and I made that first YouTube video that went totally viral and my mom drove me to the airport in Cleveland so I could meet my very first agent, Marcus Waddell, down in Atlanta, who told me to lose some weight and we'd talk.

And then, she stirs. At first, it's her leg, then an eye twitch, and then she's looking up at me from her grave, staring at me, and with a gasp of breath, she screams—

And in an instant, my Agent drops the shovel and draws his gun.

Fear flashes in her eyes as she senses the conclusion of this episode well before I.

"What are you doing?" I shriek.

"It's time to end this."

"But she's alive!"

"I'm sorry… Did you want her to write a story about this? About you, coking her up, killing her off, and driving her out to the desert to bury her alive? Sounds like a great first date, Michael. She'll blow your whole career!"

I stare at him, pistol in his hand, aimed into the shallow grave and the poisoned girl inside.

"I can't allow that to happen," he continues. "I won't allow that to happen. I've got too much invested in this."

He cocks the hammer—

"No!" I reach toward him, and he swings the gun at me—

"What are you doing, kid? If this gets out your career's over! You hear me? End of story. And you know that! That's why you called me. You knew I could take care of this. Just like I always do. I take care of you, Michael."

I stare at him, deflated. He's right. But still, is this what we've devolved into? Is this what we've become? I slowly bend over and pick up the shovel in admission and he trains the gun back on her.

Hannah's scared eyes look deep into mine, stabbing through me with their agony and distress, quivering and pleading with me to do something, but I can't. Despite my love. Despite my resurrection of spirit and driving passion to live a renewed life, I am paralyzed. My legs are sewn into the ground like I'm watching the episode play out on a 3D TV screen right in front of me, and the only thing I can control is the angle.

My Agent glances at the gun in his hand as he puts his sights on my latest screen crush. He draws his tongue into the corner of his mouth in slow motion as a wicked display of delight flashes across his brows. And without second thought or fear or even knowledge, I suddenly find myself instinctively mid-motion, swinging the shovel around full-force like I'm batting for the outfield, and I catch the unprepared target squarely in the nose. My Agent drops to the ground, writhing in the dirt, blood squirting from his face. He cries out a horrible, gnarly moan through his shattered skull like a half-slaughtered bear flailing in agony.

I reach down into the grave, and with fearful eyes she gives me her hand, and I pull, yanking my zombie princess from the dirt as the writhing pig squeals its way in circles in the sand before he catches the edge of the desert grave and falls in with a shallow thud. His neck cracks and his body drops limply overtop, and there, on the dusty floor of a distant valley, he lies eternally.

I look at the shovel and grow squeamish; a Rorschach of blood across it looks like the face of the devil. The sandy desert floor is drenched in the pig's fresh blood. I scoop the sharp metal blade under it, into the hard rocky soil, and turn toward the lifeless body in the hole, and drop it in. With every grain of dirt I shovel, another regret is shed until every insurmountable problem of my past is dead and buried. It only takes a half-hour to fill up the hole, and the time goes by pretty quickly with the sweet smell of Hannah's tobacco smoke wafting around me. When I finish, the mid-morning sun beats down around us and I look off across the valley. She saddles up next to me and rests her head against my shoulder.

The Agent won't be missed. I mean he will be, for a while, from his wife and kids. But he's a dime a dozen at the office. Most can't tell one from another. They're interchangeable. Nobody knows who they're dealing with half the time. And he was a shit husband and even worse father to begin with. Once his wife gets the life insurance policy, she'll be thanking her lucky stars. Maybe she already is. She always knew her prospects as his starter wife would be limited, and with a vanishing husband it's much cleaner than a California divorce.

I touch her crusty hair with my callused, bloody hand and we watch the distant sun as it crosses the wide open sky. Dark-colored birds begin to gather and we get the hint. When there's fresh blood it never takes long for the vultures to circle. I toss the shovel into the bush, we get back in the Maserati, and I'm careful not to scratch it as I pull around the scraggly bush. I creep back on the dirt road toward the highway. Within a couple minutes the tires hit the asphalt and it's smooth sailing from here on out.

As I shift into third gear and plow down the highway I feel a cool hand in mine, and I squeeze. The fire burning inside of me catches on, and it isn't long before her blue scales begin to warm into an omnipresent pink glow. And finally, she speaks.

"Thanks for saving my life."

I glance at her soft appreciative smile and offer my own.

"Thanks for saving mine."

She squeezes my hand tightly and settles in for the ride. Who knows how long before we find where we're going? It doesn't matter anymore. We're not in any hurry. All that matters now is the future we create for ourselves from this moment onwards. We can write our own future now. We can create whatever version of life we want, as long as we're together.

About Samuel W. Reed

Samuel W. Reed is a novelist, film producer, director, and screenwriter from the riverfront town of Paducah, Kentucky. After spending his formative years wandering between the banks of the Tennessee River and the shores of the Carolinas, Sam moved west where he has written and produced numerous projects for film, TV, and the web. Sam was instrumental in the decade-long production of the groundbreaking disability-rights documentary *CinemAbility: The Art of Inclusion*, he has ghostwritten screenplays distributed by Sony Pictures Entertainment, and he wrote the narration for the SXSW award-winning film *Take Me To The River*. Sam currently lives in Los Angeles, California with his wife and two children, where he works as a writer, director, and film producer.

For more information, please visit samuelwreed.com

TADA!

by Dane G. Kroll

The sun never quite rises in New Century City. We're always in a moody twilight. Sure, the suburbs and the oceanside residents get to enjoy the dawn with the rest of the world, but the heart of the city is almost like its own realm. Skyscrapers reach as high as the clouds and surround the uptown and business districts. The towers of steel form a barrier that some might think protects the city from the rest of the world. But in reality, all it does is keep the danger and the madness of New Century City bottled up and contained. I wouldn't say it's a prison, exactly. More like a theater, and this show is only for us.

New Century City is our stage. The greatest city in the world. Nobody will deny that. Even the citizens in Mercury City across the country couldn't. Their crime rate might be lower, but what we lack in mortality rate we make up for in pizzazz. All we want is to be entertained. If that means somebody has to die, then so be it. If you're still alive then you're still a part of the show.

That's the key, right there. Unlike the rest of the world, New Century City figured it out. Death has been pushed to the backs of our minds. We don't care anymore. Capes flying around saving lives left and right. Ghosts attacking us every week. How many times has the universe been restarted? Books of conspiracy theories saying you might have actually only existed for minutes. You might not have been alive in the last version of our universe, but you remember it anyway. It's enough to drive a man crazy. That's why New Century City exists. It's our distraction. It's our second chance.

Nobody is born in New Century City. Talk to anybody, you'll discover they grew up in some no-name town or a smaller city but wound up here at some point in their life. Maybe it was a crisis that destroyed their home and they had nowhere left to go, except to a city that would welcome them with open arms. Maybe a job pulled them in; after all, there is always an opening somewhere; people go missing, die, or simply finally have their fill and leave. There's an even simpler reason: they wanted to live where the action was. And right there is my audience.

We're home to some of the greatest superheroes the world has ever seen. Hundreds of men and women are running through alleys and over buildings in the name of justice. It's extraordinary to witness. Their flashy colors and dazzling capes are hard to miss. Look up at any time and you'll probably see somebody flying overhead. I even find myself getting caught in the spectacle every now and then.

The superheroes aren't important though. They are merely role players. They foolishly believe in a calling. They believe that the city cried out for help and they were the only ones that could see the path to safety. They put their lives at risk because nobody else has the ability to do so.

That's silly.

Coincidence and circumstance gave them great powers. That doesn't make them special. That makes them lucky. They were in the right place at the right time. And instead of helping the world with their newfound powers, they put on a costume to maintain the status quo. Sure, they've saved some lives, but our mortality rate is still sky-high. People miss the point. This isn't divine intervention. A superhero wasn't created because we needed him. A superhero was created because we were bored.

And boredom is the mother of creativity. My audience never really pays attention to the seconds that go by in which anything can happen. The universe is old, and it is large. There is plenty of room for manipulation.

A lot of time goes into creating a city as grand as this place. Days, weeks, years are forgotten, and along with those, millions of lives have come and gone. That's where the true power is. The power of misdirection. People never stop to turn and look at the failures that the city created: scientists and test subjects dying to create the perfect formula, pilots in fiery crashes of new awesome technology, and professors getting lost in undiscovered worlds looking for the ultimate knowledge.

While the world watches the "stars" play their roles, it is really the people behind-the-scenes directing where the heroes go and where to watch the action. that hold the true power. Why rely on divine intervention when all this world needs is a little push in the right direction?

Take my current production, for example. I call this show, "The Illusionist's Assistant." I am standing on the sidewalk outside of The New Century City Bank and Trust. It looks inconspicuous from the outside. It's just another building along the street with the rest of the cityscape. There's a plaque at the side of the entryway dedicating the building to Paragon, New Century City's greatest son.

Paragon comes from a dynasty of superheroes. His grandfather upheld the mantle, then his father, even his brother wore the cape for a bit. While one of a handful to carry the name of

Paragon, this one was surely setting the bar for those that came before him and those that will follow in his legacy.

When we first met I was foolish enough to challenge Paragon one on one. I was still getting my feet wet, trying out new gadgets, and seeing what worked. Some people denigrated me for what I did, but it was all in the name of research. I spent fifty thousand dollars in an attempt to steal a diamond that was only worth thirty thousand. My colleagues laughed at me. I had to lay low for several months until another disaster emerged and Paragon passed my case down to the NCPD, who in turn gave it to a detective that was easily bought off. Finally, all the attention was off of me.

I could get gadgets and guns from dealers any time. I could use holograms and build trap houses that looked like alternate worlds all day, but in the end, Paragon would figure it out. He would use his brute strength and stubborn tenacity to overcome the odds and put an end to my schemes. The Illusionist was nothing more than a laughing stock. Nobody believed I was capable of anything.

You see, I was performing all wrong. The only person I was fooling with those gadgets was myself.

That was when it dawned on me. I wasn't starring in my own show. I was merely playing a minor role in Paragon's story. He was the protagonist and I was the antagonist. I had become more focused on defeating Paragon than I was on stealing. I needed to change my act. I needed to recast my show. So, I changed the script.

I put myself behind the scenes and turned myself from the antagonist into the producer. I've heard it a lot in the past. "Be the star of your life story." That's not accurate though. At least, not if you want true wealth. Success isn't about beating my opponent to a pulp. No, success for an illusionist is to fool the audience into believing that they saw something that didn't actually happen. Paragon is no longer my enemy. He is my accomplice. And I am nothing more than a director of my own narrative, creating an illusion in which I have little more than a cameo role.

I can see through the entryway that the bank is already crowded. Even though the sun won't break through the steel buildings for three more hours, people are already starting their morning. Even though it's early, the line already journeys back and forth between the ropes in the lobby. It's Friday. Payday. Just as I had planned.

The city runs like clockwork. It has to or nothing would ever get done. With all the super-powered fighting and end-of-the-world scenarios every week, if city workers weren't efficient the world would have ended not by the hands of a crazed supervillain, but by the simple act of businesses not being opened the next day.

You can shrug off the end of the world once you get used to the dozen or so that happen every few days. For the general populace, you're completely impotent, so you might as well go about your life. But not having your coffee in the morning, that will really mess up your day.

The front entrance of the bank is congested. Several people are waiting to join the line for one of the tellers. A dolly with several packages has been left unattended, taking up precious room in the entryway that another desperate soul could be occupying.

I humbly join the line for the teller. There's a quick glance from the woman in front of me. She doesn't recognize me. It's been several years since I was on any of the news channels. Not that it would matter anyway. I've altered my look. I have a dazzling mustache now, and I dyed my hair to a slick black. It's changing the eyebrows that really does the trick. I nod my head at the lady and she goes back to staring at the tellers ahead of us. Her glare may have the superpower to make the line go faster. That would be unfortunate. Timing is everything in my work. Faster or slower, it costs me money.

There are twenty-three people in the line before me. Most of them are looking to cash their checks and be on their way. I know this. The banks know this. That's why the vault is near capacity at the moment. I can see it from where I'm standing at the back of the line. Two guards stand watch outside of the bank cage. They keep their eyes on a few customers that look suspicious.

The guards have only offered me a fleeting glance. My suit gives off a professional flair that makes me look more like an employee than a customer. That isn't by chance. Gone are the days of the dreadful colors and silly masks. Those costumes are a dime a dozen. All the good outfits are taken, and nobody cares who is new on the block. If you want to be remembered then you have to give them something fun, something for them to go home and tell their friends about.

The familiar rumble of the bullet train comes barreling over the streets. The 'C' Rail is the fastest way around the city. Unless you want to go north near the coast. Then it's a wash. Despite that, the transit system is an amazing piece of work and a true testament to the work people put into this city.

Three hundred sixty-three days of the year the train is on time for every stop. Even I'm impressed. I know the difficulty in keeping a schedule.

People gather on the platform in front of the glass doors waiting for the green light to enter the train only after the passengers inside have already left through the exit on the opposite side.

By now though, those poor passengers are discovering that this is one of those two days that the train is not going to stop on time. In fact, it isn't going to stop at all. The conductor has already abandoned his train and left the passengers to their fate. That's what union wages will get you. And they say crime doesn't pay.

The bullet train charges through the stop without a hint of slowing down. If only I could see the faces on the people desperate to catch the train as they watch their chance to get to work on time disappear down the rails.

The bullet train typically travels at a velocity of one hundred miles per hour. You could push it to one-twenty if you wanted to. I want to, of course.

The thundering sound that follows is nearly right on time. Two seconds early, unfortunately. That'll cost me a couple thousand dollars. I can take the loss. These missions don't cost much anymore. Just a little bit of planning time.

Paragon flies through the clouds like a cannonball. He's on his way to save the bullet train. He's got three minutes and twenty seconds before the train hits the bend. If it isn't slowed down in time, then the train will lean off its hinges and then we'll have an even greater disaster on our hands. While a pleasant thought for my overall plan, it isn't necessary.

The next turn of my trick is about to come into play. My lovely volunteer is about to present herself. She is currently perched at the top of the New Century City Bank and Trust, dozens of stories in the air. She'll be joining us shortly.

I found her just last week. She was perfect. She put out an ad looking for a friend, a job, anything to keep her distracted. Her cheating, abusive boyfriend was neglecting her. She just wanted somebody to pay attention to her. I reached out. We chatted for days. I finally proposed to her a way to get everybody's attention, even Paragon's. When even he took notice of her then she could do whatever she wanted. Her boyfriend would come running back to her or she could leave him for somebody better. Me perhaps, I coyly told her. But I needed her to do something for me first. To prove she was worthy of my attention.

Paragon's appearance in the sky is her signal. She takes a deep breath of hope. Then she steps off the ledge of the New Century City Bank and Trust.

I don't need to watch her fall. She'll hit the ground in thirty-four seconds. That'll get me further inside the building near the register counter.

Paragon is too busy to notice the poor girl. Her last thought is that she has failed me.

Then a parked car's alarm begins to blare from the street. The sound of crunched metal doesn't quite register with the people in the surrounding area. Not at first. Their eyes were closed. It's instinct. Sudden movements scare the mind. Ignorance is their protection. Their weakness.

Finally, the truth begins to settle in. The young girl's body is awkwardly sprawled out across the destroyed frame of the car. Blood is splattered everywhere. It is a wonderful performance.

The screams begin to drown out the car alarms. Heads turn to see what all the commotion is about. The story begins to spread. She had just fallen out of the sky. Like a dam bursting, the crowd of people in the lobby all force their way toward the bank's exit. They all want to catch a glimpse of what just happened. Their paychecks can wait. It's the cost of the show.

And they aren't the only ones. The bank employees, some with the same curiosity as their customers, others with the sense of duty that it is their responsibility to get to the bottom of the matter, join the crowd outside.

I take my moment.

While the crowd is rushing for the exit, I maneuver the opposite direction into the bank. Nobody is looking my way when I jump the counter. Why should they be? I'm just a guy in a suit and tie. I look a lot like every other civilian in here.

It's a smooth transition from one end of the counter to the other. A part of me actually wishes that somebody had seen me. I move spectacularly. But that's the curse of being good at what I do. Nobody is supposed to notice.

The sleeves on my jacket tear away, allowing the back and collar to drop to the floor, uncovering a more unflattering brown that resembles the jackets worn by the employees at the bank. It hardly goes with my complexion. You'd need to have pale skin and dead eyes to really make the jacket work.

To add the finishing touch, I reach into my breast pocket and pull out the one item that ties the whole look together: my name tag. I quickly pin it onto my jacket and adjust my collar so it's neat. The nametag reads Todd Dawes. Sometimes I can't help myself.

Time is ticking. My watch says forty seconds have passed since the lady jumped. The next cue is late. That'll cost another thousand. And it's coming out of their cut.

Across the city, Paragon has caught up to the bullet train. His super-senses will prove quick enough to figure out how to save the day in swift fashion. He can't necessarily stand in front of the train and bring it to a standstill. The momentum would kill everybody on board the train. Though it would save in overall destruction costs. Something the mayor has been riding the superheroes about lately.

No, he'll get in front of the train and slowly bring it to a stop against his own momentum and flight. That'll take a little bit of time though. That's my window.

A van comes screeching to a halt in front of the bank. Finally.

Four men in ski masks charge out of the van while one waits in the driver's seat. They don't notice the commotion outside of the main entrance. It doesn't matter why the lobby is clear, just that it is. Their target is the bank itself. The fewer people inside the better.

"Hands up!" shouts one of the men in a ski mask. He points his gun directly at me.

I immediately put my hands in the air, just as ordered. He doesn't know I'm the one that hired him. He isn't supposed to. The four thieves rush the counter. The man giving orders keeps his gun trained on me while the other three jump the counter, with less style than me, if I do say so myself, and join me on the other side.

"Open the registers!" shouts the robber with the gun pointed in my direction. He's the leader. His name is Ross. I hired him through a friend. He did some work with The Mind Melder recently. It wasn't an impressive job. Two of his fellow bank robbers ended up melded into one person during the fiasco. Their names were Pat and Rick. They just call him Patrick now. So, I guess that part worked out.

"Now!" Ross yells at me.

"I don't want any trouble," I say. "Please, don't hurt me."

"Then open up the vault, too!"

I've studied the bank fairly well over the last few weeks. I know how to open the vault. Opening a register is even easier. They have similar models in other banks. You rob from one bank, you rob from them all. I also know where the silent alarm is. I point the men toward the vault. I push a button that unlocks the door. As their eyes are turned and their mind is on their greed they don't notice me push the silent alarm, alerting the authorities to the robbery in progress.

It'll take the cops nine minutes and eleven seconds to arrive at the bank. Pitiful results on their part. They blame it on the crime rate, and outdated equipment and cars. Personally, I think they've just gotten lazy over the years. They could have the fastest tank in the world and it still won't compete against a man in a cape with super-speed. That kind of perpetual shame has an effect on even the best of us.

The thieves get to work quickly. They begin to stuff their bags with loose bills and fill their duffles with packs of thousands of dollars. I watch helplessly as the three robbers snicker and celebrate their good fortunes.

"You've got three more minutes, then we have to go!" shouts Ross.

At this point, the train has been stopped. Paragon is reliable like that. He'll take a moment to check on the passengers to make sure they are all okay. Meanwhile, the police are taking their sweet time meandering through the streets on a bloodthirsty prowl. Finally, Paragon has a chance to hear the call of the silent alarm.

That's my cue.

"Do you even know what you are doing?" I ask Ross, with the gun still pointed at my face. He was instructed not to kill anybody. Mainly because that would probably be me. He hasn't killed anybody so far in his career. That's a bit comforting. There's still danger in working with amateurs. But they come on the cheap.

"Shut up," says Ross. He cocks his gun to try to further intimidate me.

"This is the New Century City Bank and Trust," I say. "People are counting on this money. You can't take it."

"You have insurance," scoffed Ross.

That was all that was needed. Paragon surely heard my words loud and clear. Of course, he could have found the place on his own. But that would have taken seventeen more seconds, and I need to get this show moving. It already takes five seconds for him to listen to me say the location of the robbery. That's the one drawback for people with super-speed. They have to wait for the rest of the world.

"Wrap it up!" shouts Ross. "Let's go!"

The four bank robbers hustle out of the vault with their heavy bags of money. The weight slows them down by ten seconds.

Unfortunately, their escape is cut short. The sound of tires deflating also deflates the excitement in their hearts. The four burglars look outside. The wheels on their getaway van are melted to the pavement. Added to that the doors to the van have been welded shut with heat vision. Their fifth comrade, the getaway driver, isn't going anywhere.

Paragon hovers above the street, peering into the bank. He has his arms resting at the hip, making sure his symbol is clear for all to see. Even superheroes aren't afraid of showmanship. Frankly, they are worse about it than most villains. When was the last time you had a proper supervillain display a symbol on his chest?

That's okay. You can't have a proper illusion without a little eye candy.

Paragon's hair sways in the wind. I swear it's perfection. His tranquil pose harkens back to the days when my father caught me returning home after sneaking out of the house. It's a mix of patience and inevitability. We're not getting out of the bank without going through Paragon.

"What do we do?" one of the robbers asks in a panic. He began to pace around the lobby of the bank. His fear only helps to raise the tension with the others.

"There's gotta be a back door!" shouts another.

"There's no back door, you stupid idiot," says the third thief. "It's all on lockdown! We're screwed!"

Ross, always with the cooler temperament, has another plan. He looks back at Paragon. The two meet eye to eye. It was a test of wills. Paragon was looking to save as many lives as possible. That was his promise to the city. Ross just wants to escape. There is a middle ground somewhere in there.

With a forceful grip, Ross wraps his fingers around the back of my neck. He squeezes, sending my muscles into a spasm. I tense up from the pressure as he forces me forward. He's going to use me as a human shield.

Together the five of us begin to walk slowly toward the front entrance of the bank. Toward the inevitable confrontation with Paragon.

Ross is whispering in my ear. It's not necessarily to me. He knows Paragon has super-hearing. He's talking to him but making sure I hear every word.

"Nobody has to get hurt," whispers Ross. "We can all get out of this situation in one piece. Just don't do anything rash. If I see you even flinch this guy gets a bullet in the skull. Bam!"

Ross's breath is warm against my ear. He talks a big game, but I can feel the shake in his grip. He's not as confident as he wants the others to think. Remember, Ross has never killed before. But there's a first time for everything. I hate working with amateurs. They always try to improvise.

Their getaway van has already been disabled by Paragon. The only other option for escape is to run.

"Get the door," Ross orders the others. Two of his men step forward. Cautiously, they open the double doors of the entryway, giving Ross and myself a clear path to the outside. We carefully tread around the abandoned dolly of packages inconveniently parked by the front door.

As soon as Ross and I hit the sidewalk the other thieves file in line behind us. I am their one bargaining chip and the other four are going to use it to their best advantage, even if that means looking like a conga line of criminals.

"Let him go," announces Paragon. "Nobody has to get hurt today."

"I'll let him go when you fly away," shouts Ross. He digs the barrel of the gun into the side of my head. It sends a throbbing pain through my temple.

"I can't do that," says Paragon. "You have a lot of other people's money."

"It's mine now!" Ross yells. "Possession is nine-tenths of the law!" He laughs at his own joke. Even in this dire situation I can't help but roll my eyes. I instruct my assistants strictly not to improvise during a show. This is a prime example of why.

Paragon is unamused. You can always count on him to drain the laughter out of the room. Sure, he could shine a smile and light up the crowd, but when it comes to situations like this he's all business. That's the kind of attitude I expect out of my heroes.

Ross treats this like a game. He's already veered from the initial plan I laid out for him. When Paragon came around he was supposed to surrender, not take a hostage. There are contingency plans, of course, but the path of least resistance is always best.

I see Paragon's concern for my life. He doesn't want to lose any hostages. I wonder why though? The odds tell me if I die I have a pretty good chance of coming back when another demi-god tries to recreate the universe.

Why then was Paragon always so concerned about the loss of life? It's another question that always made me wonder about him. What was he trying to prevent? What does he think he is saving us from? So many of us are driven to a life of crime because when we look around ourselves we find the world is nothing more than a joke. And we're the only ones that are in on it.

Or are we?

I can't get existential right now. I'm in the middle of a show. I have to focus.

"Do you really think you can beat a bullet at point-blank range?!" Ross threatens Paragon, and vicariously, me. He gently brings down the hammer of the gun just so he can cock it again and give his threat that much more meaning.

"One last warning," says Paragon. "Let the gentleman go, drop the bags, and surrender."

Ross shakes his head. I can already predict the plan forming in his head. He thinks he can escape in the chaos after shooting me. He's not holding any money. The four thieves will try to run. The other three will be slower. They'll be Paragon's first targets since they have the money. That'll give Ross the precious seconds to escape down an alley. If he's lucky he can sneak into a building nearby and use their network of basements to disappear into the city. He won't have escaped with any of his prize, but he'll be a free man. Runaway and live to fight another day. That's Ross's way of life.

BANG!

There's an explosion of wind and then… quiet.

You see, here's the thing: Paragon actually *is* faster than a bullet at point-blank range.

That's why he's my real assistant for this particular illusion.

Paragon stands triumphantly between myself and Ross. The barrel of the gun is bent in Paragon's hand. The bullet exploded inside the chamber. Ross's hand will be needing medical attention. Frankly, he brought that on himself. He shouldn't have improvised. But I had accounted for that. That's the mark of a good illusionist.

You never know when you'll have an unpredictable volunteer try to ruin your show. You have to be ready for when somebody goes wild. You have to be prepared for anything.

Ross stares at Paragon in horror and awe. I think this is the first time they've ever met. In fact, I know it is. It's one thing to hear about his power, and another to see it in action. Ross drops to his knees. He begs for mercy, like they always do.

"Please," begins Ross. "Please, I was just hired to do a job. That's it. This wasn't my plan. I'm not the mastermind. Please, I'll tell you everything."

With Ross's forfeit, the other robbers surrender as well. They drop their bags of cash onto the pavement. I remain standing. I let my knees shake a bit. Acting was always one of my favorite hobbies. I could have been a star. But it doesn't pay nearly as well.

Paragon makes quick work of the four would-be robbers. He quickly cracks open the van and places the four men inside with their fifth compatriot. Then Paragon seals up the van with his heat ray vision and wipes his hands clean of the situation. Just another day in the life for Paragon.

As soon as the threat is neutralized, the crowd that has been watching the hostage situation unfold from the streets charges in. They are anxious to greet their hero and celebrate yet another victory.

Paragon puts out his arms. He holds off the crowd for a moment. He walks over to the bags of money that are on the ground behind me. He lifts three bags per hand with ease. The crowd cheers his feat of strength. Then he walks over to me.

"Are you alright, sir?" Paragon asks. He doesn't recognize me. My disguise is perfect. Next time, I'll add a pair of glasses.

"Yes, yes," I said with a deeper voice than usual. "Thank you so much. I didn't know what to do. The guy had a gun."

"You did what you were supposed to do," assures Paragon. "You were very brave."

Then he hands me the money with a smile. I take the six bags as best I can. They are all heavy. I find a way to manage. I try to hit the gym every day. Strength is not my forte, I'll admit, but I won't have people calling me weak.

"There's $782,234 in those bags. You can double-check it if you like," offers Paragon.

"Thank you, Paragon! Thank you!" I cry with glee. I sort of wish I didn't have to do this part, but the irony of it all makes a little groveling worthwhile.

Once the money is out of Paragon's hands the crowd once again sees their window to rush forward and demand their attention of New Century City's Greatest Son. He puts his hands up modestly and says his greetings to his fans.

I slip through the crowd toward the bank entrance. Nobody is paying me any attention anymore. I can just fade into the background for all they care.

I open the door to the bank. The dolly with the stack of packages is still sitting there, right out in front. Without anybody looking, I walk directly for it.

I pull the lid off the top package to reveal a hollow interior. With everybody distracted by Paragon on the street, I slip the bags of money into the container disguised as a series of packages. It's just the right size.

And at long last, it's time for the finishing touch! The second tear away jacket and pants. Gone is my brown suit and tie and what is left is a bright blue delivery shirt and tight shorts. There is a hat tucked away in the pocket of my business suit. I pull it out and put it on, completing the look.

All of this is done in a matter of seconds.

I roll the dolly out of the bank, making sure to keep my head down, not that it matters. All eyes are on Paragon. It's kind of him to provide the misdirect. He has been an exceptional Illusionist Assistant.

There's a bit of pride in what I do. The other villains, they'll ask how I do it. They'll want to know the secret to my success, how I keep fooling the police, the capes, and all the other villains. But it's simple, really. I changed the game. Capes aren't a part of my audience anymore. They're my partners. My volunteers. All I have to do is raise the curtain and invite them in. And this particular show, my dear friends, is just the opening act.

About Dane G. Kroll

Dane G. Kroll writes what he loves, and he loves giant monsters and horror. Tired of watching reruns and remakes, Dane took his film degree and started writing his own books to entertain himself. In his novels *Black Friday* and *Psalm Springs,* Dane brings to life the classic 70's and 80's vibes of the slasher horror movies he grew up on. In the fantasy epic *Eluan Falls,* a society is on the brink of collapse as the empire crumbles under new regimes and crazed magic. Adventure and exploration is the name of the game in the sci-fi opera *Lariat Rhodes and the Perils of the Fantasy Stars.* Plus, his on-going series *Realm of Goryo* ushers in a world on the brink of annihilation from giant monsters, aliens, amphibious beings, and more. His world-building books are imaginative and action packed, causing readers to have a hard time putting them down.

For more info visit danegkroll.com

About The Illustrator

Jared Sloger is a freelance artist living in Papillion, Nebraska who specializes in sci-fi, fantasy, and wildlife art. He has been trained in various traditional and digital media, and is a graduate from Metropolitan Community College and Bellevue University with an associates in Graphic Design and a bachelors in Art Management.

In the past he worked for *Arts for All* as their Beginning Drawing, Character Design, Cartooning, and Graphic Novels instructor and currently divides his time creating art, teaching private art lessons, and chilling with his cat Mia.

His prior work can be found in the groundbreaking social rights film *CinemAbility*, in various branding redesigns for local companies, and illustration work for independent authors Bryan Davis, Eric Reinhold, Patrick M. Green and Scott Appleton.

You can find more at The Art of Jared Sloger on Facebook.

THANK YOU

Thank you for supporting independent authors by reading *Miscreants, Murderers, & Thieves*. If you enjoyed it, please consider telling your friends or posting a quick review on Amazon. Word of mouth and positive reviews are the absolute best ways for readers like you to help independent writers reach a wider audience. I encourage you to seek out the work of all of the talented contributors who participated in this anthology, and sincerely appreciate your continued support.

For more information about Samuel W. Reed and Reed Press, visit www.samuelwreed.com where you can sign up to be eligible for free book giveaways, sneak peeks, promotions, and updates on all of Samuel W. Reed's latest work. Plus, you'll be one of the first to get a glimpse of the next book in the *Miscreants, Murderers, & Thieves* series! Sign up today!

Thank You For
Supporting Independent Artists!

Samuel W. Reed
Reed Press

www.samuelwreed.com

twitter/instagram
@samuelwreed

facebook
@samuelwrite

Made in the USA
Monee, IL
31 January 2020

21092856R00155